THE
CANVAS

THE
CANVAS

A Big Picture Mystery

Lane Stone

LEVEL
BEST BOOKS

First published by Level Best Books 2023

Author Photo Credit: Lane Stone

First edition

ISBN: 978-1-68512-540-0

Cover art by Level Best Designs

This book was professionally typeset on Reedsy.
Find out more at reedsy.com

Cordy and Emma

"Dogs are the best personal trainers."

—MARY B.

Praise for The Big Picture Trilogy

The Canvas:

"*The Canvas* takes us on a thrill ride with twists at every turn as Emma Kelly maneuvers intrigue and murder behind the glamorous world of high-end art sales. Loved it!"—M. A. Monnin, author of the Intrepid Traveler Mystery series

"When a famous artist is gunned down in public, art recovery expert Emma Kelly (*aka* Emmaline Abbot) sets off in pursuit of an art forgery ring that threatens more than pocketbooks and reputations. From Washington, DC, and New York City to Cologne, Germany, and the Vatican, Lane Stone's *The Canvas* sweeps you into the shadowy world of international crime with its roots in Nazi Germany and its sights on the seats of unimaginable power. This fast-paced, action-packed sequel to *The Collector* will grab you from page one. A must-read thriller!"—Connie Berry, *USA Today* bestselling author of the Kate Hamilton Mysteries

"Fun and illuminating, with a few threads left dangling for the next installment."—*Kirkus Reviews*

The Collector:

"Lane Stone knows her art world of fraud, deception, and shifting alliances but she wears her knowledge lightly. The reader is privileged to follow along as her protagonist explores whodunnit and, most of all, why. A fun, engrossing read that teaches you what you don't know about a world in

i

which value is after all just a matter of perception."—G.M. Malliet, Agatha Award-winning author of the St. Just, Max Tudor, and Augusta Hawke mysteries

"An intoxicating blend of murder, intrigue, and culture with a dollop of romance. Lane Stone displays her knowledge of art while teasing us with a thriller that spans continents and keeps readers thoroughly engaged. A page turner with a saucy heroine who defies conventions."—Arlene Kay, Cosmetic Crimes Mysteries

Chapter One

My world, the art world, was full of happy people, but I was a lone and lonely outlier. Since January, sleepers, lost or previously misattributed art works, found to be masterpieces, had washed up in prestigious auction houses, like Christie's, Sotheby's, and Sutton House. There were too many of these newly identified paintings. Once brilliant collectors, curators, and advisors were now stupid. Their knowledge morphed into longing. This reverse alchemy was all for art. They went to the ocean and, as each wave crashed to shore, declared, "We don't know what that sound is." Those were my thoughts that day as I waited with my husband in the outer lobby of the National Museum for Women in the Arts, blocks from the White House, beloved monuments, and that odd uncle everyone is nice to because he's rich—the Smithsonian.

Julia Belvedere Jones was statuesque and, at over six feet in height, would have been tall without the stilettos. She was one of the most famous living artists in the world. Now, she strode toward Elliott and me, and we stepped away from our post by the security guard's desk to greet her.

"Dr. Kelly, thank you for coming to Wash...Oh." She faltered but recovered quickly. We shook hands, and her braids fell forward over her shoulders when she dipped her head to take in my face, using her eyes as a camera. Click, click, click.

"Please call me Emma." I introduced her to Elliott, and he said it was nice to meet her. He stifled a grin when she studied his face next. She was as subtle as her paintings.

The early warning system in my brain booted up the way it did when someone I didn't know was a little too curious. Yet her interest seemed benign, almost to the point of amusement.

"We were happy to come," I said with a smile, inhaling information the way I do. *What was behind her reaction when she saw our faces?* "This isn't really my specialty, but I've known Linda for years." Linda Ensign was the museum's head, the Alice West Director. Her call surprised me since neither my art recovery agency, nor my side hustle as an adjunct professor in art history at New York University, qualified me for what the two women said they wanted, which was to act as mediator in their dispute.

In my peripheral vision, I saw the security guard's shoulders bob as she chuckled at something. I turned and read the young woman's name badge. *Georgia O'Keeffe.* She was about a hundred years too young to be the mother of American modernism, so maybe the museum had assigned all their employees the name of a woman artist.

I turned my attention back to the artist. "I was surprised when she asked me to come in for a consult on this, uh, whatever it is." I stopped talking and gave her time to hint at whose idea it had been to ask for me.

"Linda suggested asking you to act as the mediator, and I agreed." Ah, there it was. "She's an admirer of yours because of your scholarship on women in the Bible who have been misrepresented by artists, so she knew you were quite familiar with similarly themed paintings. I Googled you, and when I read you had *declined to authenticate* that *newly found* painting by Tamara de Lempicka and how you handled the forgery, I was impressed." The way she emphasized the specific phrasing I used told me she knew just how this game was played. Hard to believe that was last month. My world spun so fast that it seemed like a day ago.

That was all high praise, and I thanked her. "She knew about the Lempicka misattribution?" Forgery was a slippery word. "So much for keeping it confidential so no one would be publicly embarrassed." That would be my excuse if Julia didn't let the subject drop. A woman in Texas claimed she found the painting in her Mexican grandmother's attic. Lempicka had supposedly copied her own iconic, *Self-Portrait in a Green Bugatti*, but this time with her daughter behind the wheel. *Kizette in a Green Bugatti* was the new painting's name. It wasn't inconceivable since she had, in fact, painted *Kizette in Pink*, 1926; *Kizette Sleeping*, 1934; and *Baroness Kizette*, 1954. And she spent the last years of her life in Mexico. A labor union, UAW, planned to buy the painting as an investment and loan it to an unnamed museum. Had the sale gone through, the museum, the union, and the dealer brokering the transaction would have learned how much embarrassment three million dollars could buy.

"I swear I think some people work in art just for the gossip," she said with a low chuckle.

I nodded because I knew people like that. "That job was a one-off for me." I don't do modesty, so I didn't make some comment about luck. I worked hard, long hours.

"Still, it couldn't have made you any friends."

"I don't care," I said.

She laughed, and when she twirled to speak to Elliott, the full skirt on her yellow, black, and red dress fanned. "Is she for real?"

"The most real person I have ever known."

Julia Belvedere Jones had made a name for herself, portraying classic feminine themes in a contemporary setting. She splashed onto the art scene with *Not Female Rage*, of Judith holding the head of Holofernes. She took the account from the biblical apocrypha, as had Caravaggio, Botticelli, Artemisia Gentileschi, and Klimt, and her work was compared to the best Renaissance and Baroque painters, but she painted with the clarity—the realism—of a photograph. A gallerist, or maybe it was her agent, coined the term *representational modern* to describe her work.

She led us along the marble floor of the Great Hall to the heart of the museum. The room glowed from three crystal chandeliers. This former Masonic Temple was built in 1903 and had been in this museum incarnation since the late eighties.

"Goodbye, Georgia," I said to the security guard. She could take a break from surreptitiously looking at us and listening in on our conversation. We hadn't said anything even mildly salacious.

"Are you still on sabbatical?" I asked Julia as we walked. Elliott followed in our wake. As Assistant Director in Charge of the FBI's New York field office, trailing behind wasn't something he did very often. It was good for him.

"Yes, but I'm beginning to have ideas again," she said. "You know, I painted the first Righting Women piece twelve years ago. I needed a break."

"I read you've been sailing for the last year."

"Island hopping! It's been delicious." She smiled at the very thought and then shook her head. "I would have known about this holy mess sooner if I hadn't been off the grid."

In the United States, a visual artist had certain rights over her creation, no matter who had physical ownership of the work, under the Visual Artists Rights Act, or VARA. She could prevent the use of her name on any work she did not create. Julia Belvedere Jones was exercising that right. *This holy mess* was a world-class museum buying a painting that the artist, once she saw it in the museum's online catalog, said was not her work.

Add to this the fact that the museum had just re-opened after being closed for a two-year, $80 million renovation. I didn't know how much they'd paid for the painting. Seven figures? Eight? Whatever the amount, it was going to be a fiscal and reputational hit at the worst possible time for the institution. None of that told me why I had been called in. She was within her rights to deny she was the artist.

"I understand this was a primary sale. Your dealer knows nothing about it?"

"My dealer died six months ago." She stumbled over the words.

No gatekeeper. An inaccessible artist. The stage was set.

We kept walking, headed to the elevator at the end of the room, which would take us to a staff-only area. Marble staircases with cream-painted architectural banisters added by the museum, flanked the hall and led to a mezzanine. To my surprise, she turned left. Ninety degrees. Sharp. I was anxious to see the controversial painting, and there was only one painting I wanted to see even more. The only Frida Kahlo painting in Washington,

DC, was at the NMWA, and that's where we were being led.

"Thank you! I wanted to see *Self-Portrait Dedicated to Leon Trotsky* again," I said. "I think Kahlo is the only artist who comes close to Rembrandt with self-portraits that are—"

Julia raised an eyebrow. "You're kidding me, right?"

"If I was, I didn't know it," I answered with a laugh.

She stooped to look me in the eye and from that position, pointed to the wall. My eyes followed her muscular arm, then the length of the hand that created masterpieces. Not to the Kahlo painting, but to its neighbor.

"Bathsheba?" I said as I walked over to the large oil painting. "Wait, this is it?"

"Ye-e-es," she said. The painting was signed *JuBeJo,* as all hers were.

"But not yours?" I asked slowly.

"No! Definitely not."

I studied the three faces arranged in a triangle. "Mmm–." Then I squeezed my lips together to keep from screaming. I pressed the back of one hand over my mouth and reached for Elliott's with the other. It wasn't there. He stood behind me, and both of his hands rested on my shoulders. I forced myself to exhale. "Elliott, are you seeing what I'm seeing?"

Julia put her hand on her hip. "You look hot—both of you. What's the problem?" She spat out a laugh. "I mean, except for the fact that this is a forgery!"

"This is why you were staring at my face, and his, at the entrance?"

"Uh-h-h, yeah."

Elliott hovered over my shoulder and studied the painting. "Bathsheba's face…. it looks like you, Babe." I waited for him to track the rest. He dropped his arms and walked in front of me for a better look. King David was my husband's very own movie-star handsome self. Saving the worst for last, Uriah the Hittite was painted as my former husband, Jason. He had been a Special Agent in the FBI before being brutally murdered, tortured to death, in the line of duty. He was assigned the case that got him killed by his boss, Elliott.

"God, goddamn it," he said when he realized what he was looking at.

Julia's expression hadn't changed. "Sorry to spring this on you, but when I saw what you two looked like, for a second, I thought...."

I pointed to the painting. "You wondered if we were in on this?"

"Sorry, I just had to be sure."

"Let me ask you a similar question. Did you ask for me because Bathsheba looks like me?"

"Hell, no. I didn't know what you looked like five minutes ago." She gave a huff.

"I wonder if that was what Linda was thinking?" I asked.

"We will most certainly ask her," Julia said. She looked at Elliott, who was still studying the painting. "You have every right to be mad. Whoever painted this should have asked you." *Yeah, let's go with that. An invasion of our privacy was what this was.* Did she know who the third figure was and our story?

Jason's horrific murder three years ago had shattered me into a million pieces. When I put myself back together, I left out all the rules. I was free to search the world for my one beautiful thing, even if it meant living two lives and lying my way through each and every day.

Chapter Two

"Why is it still on display? Didn't you ask for it to be taken down?" I took my phone from my handbag and held it up for her permission to take a few photographs. "May I?" She wasn't the owner of the painting, and if she hadn't created it, she never had been, but it seemed like good manners to ask. The image would come in handy as I worked to get to the bottom of who painted me, my husband, who had stepped aside, and my former husband in this tableau.

"It's nothing to me. Go ahead." Julia looked all around us as she spoke. "I appreciate what this museum does." Until the last century, there were no women in the canon of the most famous artists in history. It was the National Museum for Women in the Arts' mission to right that wrong.

"What is it they say? Anonymous was a woman." Except the woman I stood talking to was now in that canon.

Wilhelmina Cole Holladay founded the museum in 1983. She and her husband, Wallace, were art collectors specializing in works by women because, as she said, "You can't collect everything." They soon discovered that women artists were not even mentioned in college art history textbooks, and she made it her life's work to establish an institution that would collect, exhibit, and research women artists of all nationalities and eras. The doors opened, figuratively and literally, four years later. NMWA changed the art world, and not just for women. There was far to go, but there was no going back. Women artists were finally seen. Their mission *was* noble, and the museum thrived, but I felt certain a curator, or maybe Linda, had made a mistake with this acquisition.

"I'd like this handled as quietly as possible, but I want it dealt with, and soon!" Julia went on. Neither party had gone public with the dispute. No one did discreet the way old money and new museums did. "We were afraid talk would start if it was moved for no reason." She exhaled like someone who needed a drink or a cigarette or sex. "I'm in a good place right now. For the first time in forever. Or at least in a long, long time. I don't want anything to mess that up."

I knew what she wanted me to do, but since I'd only been in the building a few minutes, it was unreasonable for her to expect me to reassure her. I waited a beat to see if she would say more. When she didn't, I walked closer to the painting and sniffed it. It was there. The faint smell of oil paint.

Two women visitors to the museum walked up to see the Frida Kahlo painting, and I moved back. While they read the signage, my list of questions grew. I shifted my weight from one hip to the other. That's what I did when my brain galloped. I thought of it as my mooring.

When the guests moved away, I pulled a small magnifying glass out of my Louis Vuitton. "Stand behind me," I said to Julia and Elliott. They made a wall and hid me as I studied the painting's brush strokes.

"Can I ask you something?" She asked from about a foot behind me. I nodded but kept examining the painting. And thinking. "How come you chose the nuclear option with the Lempicka?" Words like, *declined to authenticate* disrupted the art market. If I said it wasn't a Lempicka, collectors would know what to do. They wouldn't buy the painting. The verbiage I used meant gallerists and auctioneers didn't know how to value it. The union's investment committee planned to pay $3 million. Considering the market for the artist's work, that was too high. Art is a safe and smart investment, but only with the right number of digits in the price. And, if it wasn't by Lempicka, what was it worth? A hundred dollars? How much would a collector pay for a work that may or may not be by the famous author? I hoped that would force someone's hand, but so far it hadn't.

"I wanted to send a message. I figured the right people would know what I meant. Why didn't you?" I asked.

"What? You don't think I'm sending a message? I believe I'm being very clear."

I turned to face her. "No, I meant, why didn't you choose the nuclear option? Why didn't you withhold comment rather than disavow?"

"Dunno." She chuckled. "I guess because of what this taco stand is trying to do. Sure, it'd be a slap at the forger, but the museum would be hurt, too."

I backed up and pocketed the magnifier. "I need a few more minutes out here. Is there someplace we can meet with Linda to talk later?"

"Linda's waiting for us in her office," Julia said.

"*Linda* hoped we could begin this discussion together." The museum director stood as stiff as one of the marble columns and glared at Julia. Her silver hair was close-cropped, and she wore dangling ruby and platinum chandelier earrings. Statement jewelry. Glamour.

"Good to see you again," I said. She was so angry she trembled, so I pulled back my extended hand. "This is my husband, Elliott Baldwin."

"Nice to meet you," she grumbled.

I looked at one woman, then the other. Had the artist met us in the vestibule to tell me her side of the story first? Probably. It wouldn't help her. Any more than my friendship with Linda Ensign would help the museum. "We've only been talking for a few minutes," I assured her.

She took a deep breath in and blew it out. Her earrings swung back and forth. "The woman from the Macquarie Gallery hasn't called me back."

In spite of myself, I gasped. "You bought this from the Macquarie?" I stretched out the pronunciation of one of the most prominent galleries in the world like there could be two with that name. Its mothership was in Chelsea on West 24th, the main drag for gallery hopping, but it was part of a global network of twenty spaces. Macquarie was highly respected. Though admittedly, in the art world, the standards were low, so that didn't mean perfect.

"I've reserved a meeting room for us so we can speak privately." Not an answer.

"Linda, did that Certificate of Authenticity show up?" Julia asked. Not sarcastic, just asking.

"I was assured it's on the way. I'll see you on the second floor." The museum director twirled on her heel and was gone.

"See you in a few minutes," I said to Linda's retreating figure. Julia nodded but stayed, waiting for me to do something, anything, interesting. "Thank you," I said, which was code for, *and you can leave now, too.* Too bad cryptography was not her gift.

Elliott, however, was a brilliant decoder. "I need to catch up with some people at the Hoover Building." He leaned over to kiss my forehead. His lips lingered an extra beat. "And you don't need me leaning over your shoulder." His fingers pressed into my bicep. "Call me when you're done here." He ran his eyes over the painting one last time. Dread and worry lines creased his forehead, and his jaw tightened. I wanted to throw myself at him and yell that I loved him and we were okay. No, we were better than okay. That I didn't care what anyone said or thought. My reassuring words would have to wait. His meetings wouldn't start for another two hours, but he was leaving. He was either giving me space to work, or he was getting the hell away from me and the painting that threatened to blow our lives up.

I turned and faced the painting, my back to the artist. "Would you please excuse me?"

"Oh, sure thing. I'll hang out over here." Her talent, her greatness, her name was such that I actually felt it when she moved away.

A brush stroke on the right side, mid-way up, bothered me, and I took my time examining it. Then, I stood back and looked at the composition again. The painting was exquisite. And it had been given pride of place next to the Kahlo, though the subject matter of the two could not be more different. That spoke volumes. It was like being given the best table at a restaurant.

I looked again at the triangle of faces. Then, I left it and walked to the elevator at the far end of the floor.

Julia met me there. "So?"

I laughed. "You know you didn't paint it. Why do you care what I think?"

The door opened, and we stepped in. "I do not want to go to court to prove I didn't paint that goddamn thing." She stabbed the button, harder than necessary, with a manicured nail painted with black polish.

"Are you thinking about what Peter Doig went through?" I asked. She'd be crazy not to.

A Canadian man, Pete Doige, with an *e*, sold a painting, *Riviere Grand*, to his corrections officer for one hundred dollars after he was released from jail. Peter Doig, no *e*, a Scottish figurative artist who was compared to Gauguin and whose paintings sold for north of ten million dollars, had to go to court to prove he did not paint the painting. In 2011, a friend saw it at the corrections officer's home and told him that it was a Doig—no E. They mailed a photo of it to Sotheby's. Someone there, who never saw the actual painting, responded, "Your work has the trademark eeriness of the empty landscape and a stratified composition which recalls his later work." The owner took the painting and that letter to the gallery owner, Peter Bartlow. Doige was dead by then, but Doig had his dealer, Gordon Veneklasen at Michael Werner Gallery, threaten a lawsuit if Bartlow continued to claim the painting was by the famous artist. The corrections officer and Bartlow sued the artist for tortious interference, for a cool $7.9 million, and a court declaration of *Riviere Grand*'s authenticity. Doig used VARA to prevent his name from being used on a painting he didn't create. The case lasted four years. Four years. Though he was victorious, it cost him over two million dollars in legal fees and maybe his marriage. Julia Belvedere Jones had to be thinking that could happen to her.

"I know you didn't paint it," I said.

"Other than me telling you I didn't, how do you know?" she asked.

"You don't paint white faces—or at least not that white."

"Connoisseurship, nice. Is that how you made your decision on the Lempicka?"

I shook my head. "Well, science had the final say. I asked for an analysis of the paint. The lab found traces of resin and lead in it. She never used either. Of course, that was to make it dry faster. I was just the human in the loop."

"But what alerted you to ask for the tests?"

"First, the price. It was just too high. I haven't told anyone the next reason. The steering wheel in *Kizette in a Green Bugatti* was on the right, which is the correct side for that car."

"Huh? So what?"

"In *Self-Portrait in a Green Bugatti*, the steering wheel is on the left, which is wrong. It was on the right in the Bugatti type 43. If Lempicka had a reason to paint her self-portrait that way, why would she switch when she painted her daughter?"

She whooped a deep, throaty laugh. "Brilliant."

"In that Bathsheba painting, I saw a mistake that I don't think you would make." I waited to see if she noticed it, too.

She laughed again. "You noticed King David's shadow?" In a painting in light colors, the light source washed out the scene, and there were few, if any, dark-colored shadows. A black streak on the floor tracked the line of the king's robe.

I nodded and laughed. "And what about the floor! You've never painted a floor like that, have you?"

"I *never* paint floors! Critics say I cut my subjects off at the knees. I want viewers to have a dialogue with my work, not stand outside looking in." That was exactly what a tiled floor on a grid did. It was designed to let the viewer know how *far* outside the painting he was.

I was enjoying the conversation. "If I give you my number, will you call us when you're in Manhattan again?"

"Sure," she said. "Don't know when that'll be. I'm heading back to the high seas as soon as...."

The elevator doors opened, maybe not in slow motion, but that's the way I would always remember it. The gunman wore a knitted ski mask, and his mouth was open. The semi-automatic was pointed at the artist, but he hadn't expected her to be so tall, and he had to raise the barrel five, maybe six inches higher before he fired. Once. Twice. Three times. When he looked at me, he had already lowered his gun. I wasn't the target. One of the most talented artists that ever lived was.

I dropped to my knees with a thud because my hands still covered my ringing ears after the deafening noise of the gunfire in that small space. I cradled the artist's head, which was up against the back wall of the elevator. My right hand hovered over her torso, looking for some wound to press to stop the bleeding, but the three bullets had ripped her open. She stared straight ahead, and I turned to see what was in her line of sight. The gunman was still standing there. He was not muscular; he needed the gun to feel like a real man. His running shoes were cheap. His clothes were cheap. He was cheap.

"See you in hell," she whispered to him. I was proud of her strength, and I was proud of her hatred of him. Her eyes found mine. "I didn't paint it." Then she was gone. I felt the whoosh like the world had contracted just a little. Was that what it had been like the moment Rembrandt or Mozart died? The gunman turned and ran.

Hormones mixed with adrenaline were flammable. Rage was a brand new cigarette lighter from the 7-11 on the corner. I pulled my arm from around Julia's head and propelled myself up from the floor. Time sped up as I chased him along the far wall and then up the hallway on the New York Avenue side of the building. The building was large. I didn't care. I could run forever. At some point, the elevator door closed behind me. Where was the shooter going? There had to be stairs. Of course. Laws or building codes or something, right? There was a door helpfully marked Stairway, and he vaulted in. Keep running? Why not? But there was something more important to do. How had he known where in the elevator the artist stood? Had he seen us get in? Or had someone told him?

Before I got to the stairwell, I yelled to anyone who could hear me, "Lock the building down." I ran into the stairwell just as he ran out one floor down, at the mezzanine level. When I came out, I yelled, "Georgia!"

The elevator doors opened on the first level. People screamed when they saw the body of the dead woman on the floor. I heard crashing glass and dropped cutlery and looked to the right, through the tables in the café. Jeweled hands that had rested on petal pink tablecloths now made reflex self-defense gestures. The shooter yanked his mask off and threw it down as he ran. I took my phone out of my pocket, because that's what normal people did, and videoed him plowing through the ladies who lunch.

"Georgia!" I yelled again over the half-wall to the floor below.

With one hand on the banister, he swung himself onto that beautiful stairway. Then he loped down a few steps at a time. He was halfway down, then almost at the bottom, when suddenly he flew back like a rag doll. Georgia had body-blocked the guy so hard his head hit a marble step and bounced up and down. The gun took on a life of its own when it hit the floor. It spun like a Coke bottle. When it finally stopped, it pointed at its owner, the artist's killer. He was out cold.

Chapter Three

Georgia O'Keeffe was on her cell phone talking and, at the same time, directing the other guards to take positions at the entrances. I was still up in the Mezzanine Café looking through the balustrades at the scene below. Some of the restaurant patrons ran to the stairs in sheer panic and bottlenecked there.

The heroine guard walked around the shooter's body, holding her hands palms out. "Ladies, ladies. I need you to wait there, where you are. Please."

The man on the floor twitched, or at least one shoulder had.

"The police will be here any min—" She continued to reassure them.

"Georgia!" I screamed. "He's getting up."

I plowed through the twos and threes of women, ran to the stairway, and loped down; I skipped more steps than I touched. He was on his feet and had her in a headlock.

"Let. Her. Go." My voice was low and slow as I walked around to stand in front of them. I hadn't decided on the next move to take, but in seconds I would. In the last year, I had been up against some men who made this punk look like a tricycle-riding, bedwetting thumb-sucker.

In one move, his hand went into his pocket and came out with a switchblade. He flicked it open with his thumb, and then it was against Georgia's neck.

"Hey, it's okay," I lied. "Just leave." I held up my index finger. "Just do one thing." *See how easy this would be.* Except it wouldn't.

In my peripheral vision, I saw Elliott in the outer lobby. I kept talking. "Let her go." I made eye contact with Georgia, then dropped my eyes to my finger, still pointed up. She slowly closed her eyes and then opened them. She knew the strategy.

Three. Now Elliott crouched and moved toward us. *Two.* He was almost close enough to jump the guy. *One.* I grabbed his arm and pulled it away from Georgia's neck. At the same time, she kicked out her legs and let her weight and gravity take her out of the neck hold and away from her assailant's grasp. I grabbed her shoulders and pulled so we were both prone on the floor.

"FBI!" Elliott yelled. "Drop your weapon!" He held his gun with both hands.

He had to be bluffing, I thought. *He wouldn't fire a gun with art on the walls.* Though later, I would self-edit that to claim, I thought, *with people around.* That played better in most circles.

From the floor, I twisted and looked at Julia Belvedere Jones's murderer. Without Georgia's body shielding him, he was different. Weak. Surprised. Had he really thought he would be walking out of here? His eyes darted side to side. Whoever he was looking for wasn't there, and it bothered him. He scanned the Great Hall again. I heard him make a huffing noise that was a combination of a growl and hyperventilating. He had honestly expected someone to save him. Suddenly, he gnashed his teeth and twirled the knife in his hand. Still snorting, but faster. No longer positioned to slit a throat, now converted for stabbing. He made eye contact with me, still on the floor, then lunged. Before he moved an inch, Elliott took his shot and saved my life. Though his enemies would later call it "discharging his firearm in a public place."

Chapter Four

Around marble-top table dominated the upstairs conference room where the police officer had parked me. I was alone and had my pick of any of the six dove grey leather chairs. That was one decision too many, and I wanted to break down. All the way down. I jumped when the glass door to the soundproof room opened. My collapse would have to wait.

Elliott reached for me before the door closed behind him. Bits of what sounded like a hundred conversations from the police activity below us in the lobby came in with him. He swore when he saw the blood on my dark green dress, but not being a squeamish man or fussy about his FBI-appropriate wool suit, he still pulled me into him. The door closed, and there was just us in the room. There it was again. In my head, I heard that grunt the killer made.

Within seconds, Linda Ensign opened the door, and the cacophony from downstairs was back, and I welcomed it in. "Emma!" she yelled.

The adrenaline was wearing off, but enough of the drug was left in my system for the there-then-gone noises to threaten to push me into giddy hysterics.

A Washington, DC, police officer was on her heel. "Ma'am, you will need to go back to your office and wait. I'm not going to tell you again."

"Why?" Linda asked her.

"Witnesses have to be separated until they are questioned."

"But I wasn't a witness; she was." She turned and pointed at me. "And why is he in here?"

Elliott moved around her and held the door open. Subtle.

"Alright, alright," she said.

"Linda, the painting needs to be examined," I said before the door closed again. The officer rolled her eyes.

They stopped, and Linda held the door open. "What good would that do?" she asked. "It was painted by a living artist, or at least she *was*, so dating it doesn't mean anything. And since this was a primary sale, why should we have it X-rayed?"

"Let's go," the officer said.

I wasn't done. "At least, move the painting out of respect for her. Put it in a safe spot. Cover another work with black draping and hang it there."

"Well, well, so you think she *did* paint it?" I hadn't said anything like that, but if she thought I had, there should be relief in her voice. Rather, the short question was filled with incredulity. Where had her certainty that she had a Julia Belvedere Jones in the museum gone? That meant I had to reframe the world that surrounded the murder. The head of the museum that acquired the painting had doubts.

"She didn't paint it," I said, shaking my head. If she had, she wouldn't have been surprised when she saw what Elliott and I looked like.

"Ladies!" the officer yelled. We had gone too far. I knew a little something about doing that. No, it wasn't the officer who came to drag Linda away. Another woman stood at the open door. "I'm Detective Angela Sanchez." The uniformed officer was dismissed, and the museum director left, and the three of us remaining sat around the table.

"You are ADC Elliott Baldwin?"

He nodded, and they exchanged pleasantries and shook hands. She turned to me. "Did you ask Ms. Ensign, or is it Dr. Ensign, to remove the painting because your faces are on it?"

I didn't like small talk, but after that degree of bluntness, I might rethink my position. It was an odd opener from a homicide detective. For now, I would sidestep her question.

"It's Ms. Ensign," I said. "The painting should be removed so it can be examined. I don't know if they have the equipment here for that or not. The

National Gallery of Art does."

She nodded and touched her tablet to wake it up. "The way I understand the situation is this museum bought the painting named...I don't know what it's called, so for now, let's just call it *Eathsheba*, which may or may not have been painted by the victim for fifteen million dollars. And then Julia Belvedere Jones said she didn't paint it."

The exact figure was news to me, and I blinked. The human brain didn't have a sense of what fifteen million of anything was since we haven't experienced it the way we did small numbers every day, like a dozen eggs. Our brains were helpless at accurately thinking about very large sums, so we skimmed the surface of their enormity. At the same time, I wasn't surprised since I lived and breathed in the art world. I nodded at her summary.

"Do you think she was murdered to shut her up making that claim?" she asked.

"I think it's too early to make that connection, but maybe." I let my sentence trail off.

Elliott touched my arm, gently reassuring. He was there. Was he thinking we should let her go off in any direction she wanted, as long as she wasn't asking about our faces on the painting?

"Do you think it's a forgery?" Detective Sanchez asked.

Forgery? I answered the question I wanted. "I think it's misattributed. Julia Belvedere Jones did not paint it."

"No doubt at all?" I saw the beginning of a smile of victory. She was leading me into a trap. If you didn't count the elevator's security cameras, I was the only witness to a famous artist's murder. Wouldn't it make more sense to ask me what I saw? Or did they not care, since they had the murderer. He was lying on the floor of the lobby. "Nothing on the *she painted it* side of the ledger?" she asked, almost smirking.

"The gallery the museum acquired it from is quite prestigious. One of the oldest and most famous in the world. That surprised me." The detective nodded. "Even with that, I know Julia Belvedere Jones didn't paint it because she told me with her dying breath that she didn't. Detective Sanchez, you're not concerned with the murder. You're interested in the $15 million, aren't you?"

"I'm interested in everything that happened here today."

Knock, knock, knock. Linda Ensign was back. She banged on the door frantically. She, along with the din from below, were with us in the conference room before Detective Sanchez motioned her okay.

"Bettina Vogt committed suicide!" she yelled, waving her arms, palms up. *What next?*

The detective swiped at her phone. "I'm sorry, but who is that?" I was curious, too.

"She's the gallerist we bought the painting from. Well, she brokered the transaction." She paused and gave a half-shrug, like the distinction was at the tomato slash *tomahto* level. It wasn't. "Emma, you know her!"

I shook my head. "Sorry, I don't know that name."

"But she recommended that you be brought in because of your success stopping the acquisition of *Kizette in a Green Bugatti.* I remember those were her exact words."

"I don't know her," I repeated. *If she was selling a fake Belvedere Jones to the museum, why would she recommend someone with a recent, high-profile success?*

"Just as well," Linda added.

"What do you mean by that?" Elliott asked her.

"Nothing," she lied, and not very well.

"Where did you hear that Ms. Vogt committed suicide?" Detective Sanchez asked her.

"A friend at the Macquarie Gallery just told me she's dead." Then, for emphasis, she added, "Too!"

Elliott was listening to something in his earbud and shaking his head. He put up his hand to say *whoa.* "Ms. Ensign, we don't know that yet. Would you excuse us?"

She huffed and was about to protest when Elliott once again opened the door for her to leave. "Emma, the painting has been moved," she said over her shoulder. "Thank you. Excellent compromise. Wouldn't want to look insensitive." Finally, she left.

"Her landlord let NYPD in for a wellness check, which had been requested by her employer when she didn't show up for work this morning. They found a suicide note but no body. They're looking to see if she took her life someplace else."

"She's the missing puzzle piece, isn't she?" Detective Sanchez stared into the middle distance as she thought aloud.

"Whoever was paid the fifteen million dollars is who you're looking for," I said.

"Good point. Didn't the money go to that gallery?"

"They may have been selling it for someone," I answered.

She opened the door but, in a Colombo move, turned and said, "I forgot, what was the name of that painting? I mean, its real name."

"*Shame*," I answered.

"Oh, yeah, that's right." She smiled. "You're free to go, Ms. Kelly."

Chapter Five

That night, Elliott and I stood in a steaming shower in our hotel room and held one another tight. The shooter had been identified as Vince Tucker. He had a New York driver's license in his wallet. The ski mask was out for DNA testing. Surprisingly, he wasn't in the system. It was unusual for a criminal's first arrest to be for murder. The DC police, officially the Metropolitan Police Department of the District of Columbia, combed through his background and social media posts, with each thread ending with a white supremacist tirade or association. The fact that he didn't have a phone on him slowed the process down, but not by much.

"I don't like it." I rested my head on his hairy chest.

Elliott chuckled. "No one likes a racist murderer."

I tilted my head up to look at him. "It's too pat. The museum now has an undisputed, except by me, Julia Belvedere Jones painting in its collection. The grantor, the National Endowment for the Humanities, *didn't* make an embarrassingly unwise grant award."

"Babe, for you, it's always about the art. Maybe this time it isn't."

"Then who was the killer looking for in the museum?"

He dropped his hand from my back and picked up the hotel shampoo. "Is this about me shooting him?"

"No—" The question took me by surprise. The FBI didn't do non sequiturs.

"We would have *all* our questions answered if I hadn't killed him. Is that what you're thinking?" If he scrubbed his scalp with any more force, he'd lose the rest of his close-cropped hair.

"That's not—"

"I didn't exactly have a choice, did I?" He rinsed the suds off his head and looked at me as I stood with my arms folded over my breasts. "Nothing to say to that?"

"Oh, I can speak now?"

He exhaled. "Yeah."

"I don't have anything to say." I climbed out of the tub put the hotel bathrobe on, and wrapped a towel around my hair. I was a few steps out of the bathroom when I heard him growl in frustration. A couple more steps, and he picked me up and dropped me on the bed.

"Don't rip this bathrobe. We'll have to pay fifty dollars."

"I hate it when you figure things out, and you're right."

"There's a card here that says so." I reached into the pocket and held it up.

He rolled over onto his side, his head propped on an elbow. "I want us to have a relaxing weekend in Georgia with your parents. That's all."

"Can't we still go? The local police didn't tell you to stay in town, did they?" The last I'd heard, he was being treated with professional courtesy. He offered to surrender his gun and was politely told that would not be necessary. Georgia O'Keeffe or I, or probably both of us, had been in imminent danger.

I rolled over and put one hand on his cheek. "You're not a killer," I whispered. He turned his head and pressed his face into my palm. "You're not a killer," I repeated. He covered my hand with his and pressed it to his lips. I told him what he needed to hear again and again. "You're not a killer."

Chapter Six

TUESDAY

We ate matching room service breakfasts and twinned in the heavy white hotel bathrobes.

The Marriott's address was Pennsylvania Avenue, but the entrance was on 14th Street. That may have been the least confusing part of Washington, D.C., for me. Elliott and I read sections of the *Washington Post* and the *New York Times,* and in between bites of poached eggs and fried potatoes, we talked.

"You didn't really sleep, did you?" he asked. Long vowels were all he had of a southern accent, having been raised as an Army brat. My light Atlanta accent was similar.

I shook my head no. Then, he held up a page of the Times for him to see. "Here's her obituary. There will be a longer piece on her this afternoon."

"That's the one you were interviewed for?"

I nodded. "I gave them a statement in exchange for their agreement to not use the image of *Shame* in the article. I don't want people to think they're experiencing her work when they see it." I read more in the art section of the *New York Times,* looking for any accounts of more sleepers. "Why is art crime always covered in the golden ghetto section of the newspaper?" I pinched the bridge of my nose. "A crime connected to anything other than art involving this amount of money and a murder would be on the front page, above the fold." Having heard this grievance from me many times before, he uh-huh'd

24

on cue. He folded his section of the paper and reached over the table for my arm. "Babe, that's not what's really bothering you, is it?"

"We knew Julia Belvedere Jones for, what, half an hour, but I feel like I'm grieving."

"She seemed like a nice person. We'll be sure we do right by her memory." Still holding on and looking into my eyes. "Is that all? What you saw and went through yesterday would mess with anyone. You might need to see someone. Most people would."

I smiled at him. "Neither of us wants to repeat that year of crazy I had after Jason died. I promise I'll think about it." It wasn't triggered by his death, though. The sight of his tortured body broke my world. My quest to find my one beautiful thing—a missing painting—righted it again. I was closer every month. Nice empty lanes ahead.

"Deal," he said. Before he picked up his newspaper, he motioned with two fingers to his eyes, then mine. "I'm watching you." I returned the sign to him. I knew he wouldn't let me spin out again.

Occasionally, we checked our phones for emails. About Julia Belvedere Jones's murder. About Bettina Vogt's disappearance. "How can they not be connected?" I asked. "And if they are, it wasn't a racially motivated attack, right?"

He pointed to his phone with his fork. "Too early to know if there's a link. Let's not worry about that right now. Okay, Babe?"

"No word on Bettina Vogt's whereabouts yet?" I asked, anyway.

"Nada. Without her, it's going to be hard to find out who the Bathsheba forger is. Right?" Its real name, *Shame*, sounded knowing and targeted.

It felt natural to bat questions and answers back and forth. I didn't answer, and he looked up from his section of the newspaper. "What?"

"Does the artist—"

"Forger," he corrected.

"He or she is also an artist. The painting is good. Anyway, whatever you want to call him, does he know us?" My voice was low to keep from waking up any ghosts. "It could have been painted from a photograph."

"If it wasn't, then the person would have known Jason, too." Right eye squinted, nostrils flared. "That means it would be someone who knew us from a few years ago, not someone we recently met." We were quiet for a minute. Wheels turned in our brains but without traction. I had no idea who painted *Shame*.

"It's so odd. I mean, why would someone do that? And give it that name," I said.

"Let's say it was painted from photographs of us. Any idea who it might be in that case?" he asked.

"If it was by one of the more prolific people working now, someone on the Art Crime Team might be able to help."

"Since you know more than any of them, got any ideas?" he asked.

"I think he or she is right-handed. That's all I have."

He squeezed my kneecap under the table and laughed. "That doesn't give me much."

"If I didn't already know Julia Belvedere Jones didn't paint it, this would be more proof, that's not subjective, that it was created by someone else. She's left-handed."

He raised an eyebrow and sat back. "Tell me more."

"You can't see brushstrokes in Belvedere Jones's work. That was part of the genius of her technique. In a small area in this painting, they were there, and the paint was layered like something was being corrected or covered up. I think it was part of the side of a hand, like where a right-handed person would rest it—"

"When he's painting with his left hand?" He tried out the motion, using a spoon for a paintbrush. "Hmm. Why didn't the museum curator notice that?"

"They thought it was a primary art market sale, that they were buying it from the artist. It didn't go through the scrutiny that a purchase from the secondary art market would have." I tapped away on my phone. "I'll ask Linda if she plans to have tests performed now, but I doubt she will."

"Why not? Isn't she at least curious?"

"She doesn't want to know," I explained.

"That painting should have been named *Schrödinger's Cat*. For now, it's both by Julia Belvedere Jones, a famous artist, and not painted by her." He yawned, stood up, and stretched. One hand was behind his head, and he twisted his torso in one direction, then the other.

I smiled at the astuteness of his comment. "It's a conspiracy of the willing."

Several car horns blew at the same time, and I looked out the window. Commuters were unhappy with a double-parked UPS truck that blocked a traffic lane. With the cacophony, I almost felt like I was back in New York City.

"I don't know how much more proof is needed to make a definite statement that she didn't paint that Bathsheba painting. Remember how surprised she was when she saw us? That wasn't the reaction of someone who painted us."

"Babe, I agree with you that Julia Belvedere Jones didn't paint it, but now that she's dead and can't use that law—"

"The Visual Artist Rights Act. Yeah, the act was written for living artists, so lawyers will have to work that one out."

"Does the museum get to say it was by her?"

"Art authenticators, scholars, the art media will weigh in. Her estate…. I wonder who that is? Has whoever she was in 'a good place' with been informed?"

"DC police are handling all that," he answered.

"She said her dealer died six months ago. Can you find out how?"

"Sure." He thumb-typed a text to someone.

My own phone pinged, and I picked it up and read the latest bad news. I leaned back in the armchair and willed my shoulders to relax. "This is Linda Ensign's answer. She's not going to have the painting X-rayed. That's disappointing. It was asking too much of her, I guess. I don't see how she can keep her job when the truth comes out about that painting, even if she raises the money to return the grant proceeds to the grantor."

Elliott looked over my shoulder out the window, thinking. "I wonder if *we* can force the issue and have it examined. I'll talk to the Art Crime Team. The problem is as long as the museum says the painting is real, they haven't suffered a loss. That means there wasn't a financial crime. Let's give this a little time and see how it plays out."

I went back to eating, and after a few bites, asked him if the museum employees had been questioned.

"Just those that were working yesterday. Maybe the DC police should look at all the employees."

"I think her murderer was working with someone. And that someone there told him where she was standing in the elevator." I remembered his name, Vince Tucker, but couldn't bring myself to say it.

Elliott was typing again. "I'd like to know if anyone had a recent windfall."

"Has the Art Crime Team interviewed anyone at the Macquarie?"

"They tried, but they've lawyered up. Said this Bettina Vogt wasn't in a position to broker a sale." He rolled his eyes when he said, *in a position.* "Well, that's what she did because *Shame* was on the wall of that museum. What does that even mean anyway? Like she worked in a clerical position? Maybe the receptionist?"

I laughed. "Trust me, Macquarie is sales-obsessed. Every employee knows that and has some connection to the numbers. They're holding out."

"Before their legal counsel told them to shut up, they told us they weren't paid for the painting, which is the opposite of what Linda Ensign said in her statement."

Twelve million dollars from the National Endowment for the Humanities was transferred to the museum. That much had been verified. According to Linda, the grant money, along with some of the museum's own funds, was transferred to the Macquarie Gallery. "With today's banking regulations, shouldn't that be a simple transaction and a straightforward trace?"

"Hope so," Elliott answered. "The FBI has used accountants since 1908 and forensic accountants since 2009."

"Is that so, J. Edgar?" He squeezed my hand and laughed at himself. "They wouldn't have turned this over to their attorney if they didn't know something about the transaction or something we don't know about Bettina Vogt."

"Do you think someone at the gallery knows who really painted *Shame*?" he asked.

"If they were involved with the sale, they would never, ever admit it even if they did. They would want the painting to have been painted by Julia Belvedere Jones."

"To keep their commission?"

"And reputation." I added as my phone rang, "It's Bobbi." He smiled and shook his head. Bobbi Stokes was my best friend, or at least the closest I would ever have to one. Her escort service employed impossibly handsome male actors and models. The business brought in money and intel, which she used to punish sex-traffickers and turn their victims into survivors. People in jobs like my husband's overlooked the nature of her business because of her success. Her coven included pimps and directors of women's shelters and a lot in between that moral spectrum, like restaurateurs. With these networks, she scaled up, again and again, as globalism, the internet, and cryptocurrency demanded her to do. I was honored to be her friend.

"Emma, I have Valerie on the call with me." *What?*

I slumped in my chair, and Elliott looked up. I mouthed, "I'm going into shock." Then to them, "Good morning, Bobbi and Valerie."

His eyes widened. *Are you joking?* All these two had in common was their Manhattan DNA. Valerie Patterson, my former sister-in-law and ex-boss at SIRA, a fine arts insurance agency where I once did fine art title underwriting, was a mess. Her hyper-efficient assistant kept the world from seeing the truth by managing her hyper-perfect Instagram grid, with the single requirement of making it jealousy-inducing. Valerie's bespoke reality, created by the metaverse, alcohol, and prescription drugs, would not be possible in any other time or any other place than today in New York City. Bobbi Stokes was the opposite. Her ability to judge a person's character was what legends were made of. She made truth and reality a partner, not an aggravation.

"Emma, where are you now?" Valerie's words rushed together.

"We are still in D.C., and we're flying to Georgia tomorrow to spend a few days with my parents."

"No, no, no." *Nononono...*

I shook my head, breathed, and addressed the other woman. "Bobbi, what's going on?" It had to be important for her to cooperate or collude or whatever this was with Valerie.

"Julia Belvedere Jones's murder is on the news," Bobbi said, getting only slightly closer to the reason for the call.

"Of course. It would be," I said.

"Bobbi and I each received a call this morning asking about Bettina Vogt."

"Wait, Elliott is here with me. I'll put you on speaker."

"Uh…." Bobbi would have asked me not to do that, had I given her half a chance, but he needed to be in on this.

"Where did you hear that name?" I asked.

"Taylor Tyndale called both of us," Bobbi said. "This Bettina Vogt is helping them with a new acquisition."

"Is this Taylor and Stephan Tyndale we're talking about?" The husband-and-wife money managers owned an extensive art collection.

"The very ones. She and her husband plan to bid on a painting tonight," Bobbi said. The top pieces were auctioned in the evening, not in the afternoon.

"Bid? If they're working with the Macquarie Gallery, why is the painting being auctioned?" I asked.

"What does Macquarie have to do with this?" Valerie sounded annoyed by having to get me back on track.

"Bettina Vogt works at Macquarie Gallery." I was told that, but did I *know* it? Hadn't it been someone at the gallery who had requested the police do a well check?

"No." She drew out the word. *Look what I have to put up with.* "She works at Sutton House." I made eye contact with Elliott. He walked away to call someone. Would the auction house be next to obtain the services of a lawyer or five? Of course. It wasn't just any auction house. It was founded in 1744 and last year sold $7 billion of art, jewelry, clothes, and cars in six hundred auctions. It existed in the same rarefied loftiness as Macquarie Gallery.

I picked up a few words of Elliott's conversation. Strategy meetings and positioning would happen today, and someone from the FBI Art Crime team would be at the auction house and back to the gallery before the day was over. Tomorrow at the latest. Talks would begin. Lawyer-o y lawyer-o.

"Did Bettina leave the gallery to work at Sutton House?" I asked. Neither of them knew the answer to that.

"Who knows, and who cares? After I hung up with Taylor, I called a friend at Sutton House and told him that *Ms.* Vogt had better take *my* goddamn phone call. Guess what he said?" If anything, Valerie spoke faster than before, but I heard something more in it. Pleasure. "He wanted to know if this had to do with Julia Belvedere Jones's murder!" She was titillated and planning how to leverage her imagined involvement for her social advantage. I added it to my mental to-do list. How did someone at Sutton House know to make that connection between the artist's murder and their employee?

Bobbi cleared her throat. Subtle. "Like I was saying, they'll be at the auction tonight, checkbook in hand."

"He intends to place the *winning* bid," Valerie said.

I laughed at that. "They sound confident. What are they bidding on?"

"The recently discovered Rembrandt," Bobbi said, cutting Valerie off, her tone measured. The painting would be the star of Sutton House's marquee Old Masters Week sale. Art industry journalists knew next to nothing about the painting. The *New York Times* was reduced to publishing what was little more than a courtroom drawing of it. Not a single photograph. "And they have six hundred and fifty million reasons to think they will be the new owners. They've been working with this Bettina Vogt person. Now she's not taking Taylor's calls."

"Or mine!" Valerie whined, in case we forgot. Got it.

I let my head fall back again and looked at the ceiling. Exhale. Too late. My brain gathered data, analyzed possible outcomes, discarded illogic, and then waited for me to catch up. I stood and immediately began rocking from one bare foot to the other. Left. Right. The motion wasn't to self-soothe. Rather, it was to order the facts as they flooded in. The famed auction house had the Rembrandt, but Macquarie Gallery's name and reputation were now connected to *Shame.* A collector was about to bid on another sleeper with a connection to the missing Bettina Vogt. And there were so many ways forgeries got into the market. The US market, the GB market, the EU market. None were immune. "No way the bidding will go as high as $650 million.

The most expensive painting ever sold was *Salvator Mundi* by da Vinci for $450 million. The second was when $300 million was paid for *Interchange* by Willem de Kooning. Who is it that thinks this painting will bring in so much more?"

"Uh, well, about that," Valerie started. "Her husband wants to negotiate a private sale before it goes to auction."

"So you're telling me the Tyndales intend to pay $200 million more than the most expensive painting ever sold without at least trying to get it for less at auction? I don't understand."

"I just assumed it was to pay less than the hammer price, but Emma, you're saying they may have to pay more if it doesn't go to auction?" Bobbi asked.

"I don't see how the painting can realize even half a billion dollars," I said.

Valerie said, "Maybe he's seen bidding from the chandelier." That was a fake bid by the auctioneer to spur real buyers on. Not illegal, but not done at Sutton House.

"A chandelier bid on a Rembrandt? Ridiculous." Ordinarily, a work like that would be on display during the auction house's preview before touring its facilities in Los Angeles, Hong Kong, Dubai, and London. This one hadn't, though.

"What if theirs *isn't* the winning bid?" Valerie asked. "That's not a chance they want to take."

"I'm sure the bidding will be intense," I said. Surely, they were wrong about that price. Like by an extra digit. "It's going up for sale so soon?" The eight, almost nine-inch by seven-inch work was painted with oil on copper. It was another self-portrait of Rembrandt Harmenszoon van Rijn. The only name it had was *Self-Portrait, 1650*. The use of copper as the substrate and the subject being typical for the artist gave many people in the art world a warm, fuzzy feeling, but I wasn't one of them. Copper was more durable than wood or canvas, and lucky for later generations, it didn't rot, mildew, and wasn't eaten by insects. That also meant it was the easiest *canvas* on which to imitate the effects of time. *Check*. Rembrandt painted forty self-portraits, so genre, *check*. Two were on copper, both in a museum collection. One, in J. Paul Getty Museum in Los Angeles and one at the Nationalmuseum in Stockholm. One art critic's answer was that this painting had been in a private collection and incorrectly described. It was convenient and led in a straight line to the answer everyone, but me, wanted. Once again.

"It appears so," Bobbi said.

"I've tried to follow the testing, but I haven't heard a word. I'm surprised they've authenticated it." It wasn't possible for a painting like that to be attributed quickly.

If the painting was, in fact, by Rembrandt, it would revise a segment of his biography. The artist took a break from painting self-portraits for seven years, beginning in 1645, and returned to etching. If rumors were true, this wasn't just any Rembrandt, if it was by him. Some experts said Rembrandt's self-portraits showed introspection and how he felt about his life and work through the years. Others said he painted them because they were popular sellers at the time. If the answer was the former, he may have out-Rembrandted himself with this painting. But was that enough to jack the price up that high?

"This Bettina Vogt was their contact, and so it's understandable they would be concerned at not being able to reach her," Bobbi said.

I agreed. "You said she was the Tyndale's contact at Sutton House. What does that mean? They are legacy art collectors. I doubt they would need any hand-holding with the bidding process, but if they did, only the most senior members of staff would work with them, or with their art advisor." Neither answered. "You're sure she *is* employed there?" I pressed.

"Yes, uh, part-time in the accounting department." Bobbi's tone was almost apologetic. "The more I hear, the more unlikely this sounds."

It was obvious neither woman knew that Bettina Vogt was missing. How long would that stay out of the news?

"How did you get mixed up in this?" I asked.

"I was wondering that, too, Bobbi," Valerie whined. "You called me before Taylor did."

"She, uh, had concerns."

A beep-beep told me I had a text, and I picked up my phone. It was from Bobbi. **Later.**

"I still don't know what this has to do with me," I said.

"Tell her, Valerie," Bobbi said.

I cringed at her little girl giggle. "I may have mentioned your doubts about the painting. She wants to know more. Emma, I never, ever meant for that to discourage them from adding a Rembrandt to their collection. The painting's provenance is impeccable. I was thinking that if you called her, you could reassure her."

I snorted a laugh. My doubts about the painting grew to suspicions at the mention of Bettina Vogt's name, and now Valerie wanted me to say it was authentic. "Sutton House has all the resources needed to put her mind at ease." They didn't authenticate in-house for private sales, but they could use their equipment for a scientific analysis. Or was that the real reason to go the sale route instead of an auction? "Here's another suggestion. Private firms use AI to compare artwork to works by the same artist. They may be able to get a preliminary opinion by this afternoon. It'll take a few weeks to get the heat map that highlights the areas of primary concern for human connoisseurs to investigate further. Do you think they would consider that? Bobbi, do you want to propose that option?"

"I could try."

"Where has the painting been for the rest of its life?" I asked.

"Like I said, the provenance is unassailable. It has been in the private collection of Sir Graham and Emmaline Abbott from 1909 until about two years ago," Valerie said.

"I'll be there this afternoon." At some point, I stopped breathing. I am Emmaline, and I'm married to Graham Abbott.

Chapter Seven

Elliott opened the door to the taxi that would take me to Reagan National Airport, and the Marriott attendant stood down. When I kissed him, he whispered, "How many art forgers do you know?"

Our plan was for me to fly to New York to learn what I could to identify the *Shame* forger, and he would stay in DC coordinating the FBI's assistance to the local police in case this became a financial crime because of the NEH funds. The first question was important to us personally, and the latter was central to a possible art fraud charge.

"Just the few I've interviewed for research. I'll start with them. I can only think of one forger good enough to paint like that, but Shaun Greenhalgh went clean when he got out of prison." I shook my head. The taxi driver cleared his throat. "Good luck following the money."

"We're on it. Come back tonight so we can make our morning flight to Georgia."

I thought about other forgers during the short drive. Elmyr de Hory was long dead. Tony Tetro was not active. No, *Shame* hadn't been painted by a big-name forger. This was personal.

* * *

My real reason for returning to Manhattan was to see the provenance package of a painting purportedly by Rembrandt. The papers had to be fraudulent, using our names as former owners to give the work the patina it needed. Choreographing value in the art market was just that easy. If it had been ours, I would know it. Of course, I would.

I would use the downtime in the short flight to think about *Shame*. I relaxed into the first-class seat and enlarged the photo of the Bathsheba painting on my tablet. Did someone who knew us, or thought they did, paint or commission the painting? Or was it painted from photographs? What it implied hurt me. Who would go to this much trouble to cause me pain? *Shame* was created with the intention of wounding.

The work was representational, as Julia Belvedere Jones's paintings were. The focal points, our three faces, were arranged in a triangle, the structure of many paintings. Though in the Hebrew narrative, the two men would not have been in the same room, here they were. The king with cards he wasn't showing. The soldier, annoyingly devout, refusing to come home to be with his beautiful wife, which would conceal the paternity of the child she carried. His virtue would not allow him to have sexual relations with her while their people were at war, just as the king's lack of it couldn't stop him from taking what he had no right to. There were no pillars of light from above, lighting each countenance the way an old master would have painted it. Instead, the faces had an inner glow—like a photograph with perfect studio lighting. David had the highest wattage. He was king, after all. Fair play. Uriah glowed less than his king but still enough to attract the viewer's eye. David, the King, and Uriah, the Hittite, locked eyes, and Bathsheba looked away. Wait, Uriah's gaze was lowered. He would have seen his wife in the corner of his eye.

I studied the expression painted on Jason as Uriah's face. Both he and his sister, Valerie, inherited the wealth-or-die gene. It made Jason self-absorbed. It made Valerie crazy. She had the idea that Elliott was somehow responsible for her brother's death. If she saw this painting, all hell would break loose.

Then there was Bathsheba's face, whose luminosity was even more subdued. The paint color was creamy and rosy. Beautiful. Had she had agency? When David instructed her to come to him? Obviously not when artists and biblical scholars suggested she was a seductress. Always the default position when so little was written about a woman. Whore, harlot, and loose were words men called women they couldn't have, and women

36

called other women when they felt insecure; and how I might be labeled when the world learned I was married to two men. Since karma might be real, I'd never used those terms, and I never would.

I relaxed now that I had my answer. Whoever painted this had never met me. Nor Elliott, and certainly not Jason. So, why had he used our faces to model his subjects?

Chapter Eight

F. Scott Fitzgerald famously said, "Let me tell you about the very rich. They are different from you and me." One way was that they made you sign a Non-Disclosure Agreement at their door. The leisure class was made up of families with over $30 million in investible assets. Counting Stephan and Taylor Tyndale, there were presently 167,699 of them.

Taylor greeted me with the opposite of the Full Manhattan, which was two air kisses plus a squeal. In this case, it would have been: "You know Valerie Patterson? I love Val! I can't believe this."

Individually and as a married couple, their art world pedigree was sterling. The wife-husband duo had received honors and accolades at home and around the world for their patronage of the arts and culture. She was created a Chevalier de l'ordre des Arts et des Lettres by the French government. The British Prime Minister appointed her the first American trustee (without dual citizenship in the UK) of the Victoria & Albert Museum. He was a Trustee of the Metropolitan Museum of Art. The accolades were deserved.

Mrs. Tyndale and a middle-aged man in a regulation-attire expensive suit, who she introduced as her attorney, faced off against me at the threshold of the apartment. According to Wikipedia, she was fifty-two years old. She wore a multi-color wrap skirt with a sleeveless black silk blouse. Bare arms in a New York winter was the equivalent of a pointless staring contest with the elements. Was she reckless? Of course, she was. All Bobbi's clients were. Or maybe it had been ages since she'd felt the cold. And Taylor Tyndale was tense. One of the most tightly wound people I had ever seen. It wasn't the manufactured drama, which was Valerie's specialty. This was something else. I didn't know what—yet.

With one hand, the man held out a leather portfolio upon which rested the NDA, corners tucked into little triangles, and with the other, he handed me a Montblanc pen. I took the form and pad and pretended to read. Sure, I'd sign it. That didn't mean I took it seriously. If I learned of criminal activity, my signature would not help them. A glance told me the document was standard boilerplate language. Nor did I pretend to be offended. I was always cooperative on the outside.

The pen interested me more than the words on the document. Last year, Stephan was awarded the Montblanc Arts Patronage Award for his support of the arts and culture. Was this the pen they gave him? No, the barrel was the standard black resin. Too bad.

I signed, and she uncoiled a little. Had she doubted I would? She had asked for *my* help and might have thought that I could and would walk away at this bit of inconvenience. What she didn't know was that I *had* to see proof of the impeccable provenance Valerie claimed the painting had. Any painting could have a story. Like, *I can't say it's a Picasso for sure, but my great-granny had an affair with old Pablo.* That's a story and a sentence phrased to keep the speaker out of jail. Documentation was needed for it to be a provenance. Taylor Tyndale either had material proof, or she didn't. Were Graham and I listed as previous owners? The only instances I knew where the provenance was fabricated, but the painting was correctly attributed, was with stolen or looted art. But had we owned the painting? His family certainly could have had a Rembrandt. No. Not this painting, I argued with myself.

Once I returned the $500 pen to the lawyer, I was allowed inside the Tyndale home. Central Park Tower called itself the "tallest residential tower in the world." Being part of Manhattan's *billionaire's row* should have been good enough, but the building was an overachiever. Or maybe it was a bullshitter. There were three floors below ground and ninety-eight stories above—but the top floor was the labeled 136th. Now, *that* was suspicious.

The Tyndale's had a north-facing view, and I saw Central Park over her shoulder, through floor-to-ceiling windows about forty feet away. Maybe the couple, like their building, always wanted more more-ness.

"My husband is at his office," she cooed. "He said to call him when you arrived." She held up her phone to show me how that would be accomplished. Her hand was less than steady, and I wondered why.

I saw a generous hallway-cum-gallery, to my left. "Let's walk and talk." Audacious, but she might be more likely to talk away from her attorney.

Her *so-do-something* look hit the unprepared man on the side of his head so hard he swayed. What did she expect him to do? Throw the Montblanc pen at me?

"Diana Al-Hadid." I stopped in front of a seemingly weightless panel. I pointed to the next work. "Miya Ando." One of her hypothetical horizons, painted on aluminum. "Mark Hagen." A large white acrylic on burlap painting. We turned to the opposite wall. "Rita Ackermann." I stopped showing off when I reached two photographs framed together. We were almost back to the foyer. "Who is this?"

"It's Barbara Bloom." Her voice was silvery, with a boarding school level of control. Speaking like that, while clearly stressed out, had to take a herculean effort.

"All works by contemporary artists, and now you're investing in a Rembrandt. Why?" I asked.

"The one criticism we hear of our collection is that it's too tough. Not soft enough. It seems it has too much of an edge. We intend to rectify that." They were probably told by an art advisor that works in their collection should be 'in dialogue' with one another. That it would enhance the works and strengthen their collection.

She smiled at me and placed a call to someone she had on speed dial. "I'll get Stephan on the line now. Look, the short and real answer is because it's a Rembrandt." By definition, collections can't be complete, but these two were certainly going to try. *Self-Portrait 1650* would either be a strange bedfellow to their other works, or its acquisition would make their collection wider-ranging. After a quick check of the phone screen, she whispered, "Or do you not think it is?" There it was. Doubt.

"I haven't seen it, and authentication isn't my area of expertise, but the auction house can arrange for a material analysis. It's going to be more difficult to date the painting since the substrate is copper. Still, it could be dated the same way copper and bronze archaeological objects are—"

"It does not need to be tested! I've had thirteen experts weigh in on it." The call to her husband had gone through, and the bellow from the phone echoed, wall to wall. She put us on speaker, as if that was necessary. "Taylor, I thought you were going to tell her she did not need to come after all." The way his voice softened when he said his wife's name made me dislike him a little less. So, he did know his wife had asked me to come. He wasn't under the impression I'd been in the neighborhood and stopped by uninvited and unannounced. I didn't know what she had told him about how she contacted me, but I was sure the only name checking was Valerie Patterson's, executive with SIRA Fine Arts Insurance. She wouldn't mention Bobbi Stokes.

"Uhm," she said. I shrugged off her apologetic look. I was thinking about those thirteen authorities he boasted of. He didn't say they all agreed the painting was by Rembrandt. What did he mean by "weigh in on" it? And had they seen it? Had he shopped for the opinion he wanted? You could always pay someone to tell you your work was valuable. But why would collectors like the Tyndales want to do that?

"Did you consult the firm that specializes in Rembrandt authentication?" I asked.

"No, they wanted three or four weeks to tell me anything." That was a more reassuring answer than saying he didn't know such an organization existed. These experts, with their deep nerdery on individual artists, played an important role in attribution.

Like with Monet's *Lily Pads, 1882*. An authenticator of Monet's work pointed out that the artist moved to Giverny the *next* year, so the water lily garden hadn't been built in 1882. It was that degree of specialization you needed for the authentication of a multi-million-dollar work of art.

"Look, Rembrandt's paintings are discovered all the time. Like *Head of a Bearded Man* just a couple of years ago," Mr. Tyndale said.

The gross exaggeration was served up with a side dish of annoyance. "The painting can't be a sleeper *and* have this great provenance." And he had not chosen a good example to support his point. The postcard-size image of melancholy was donated to Oxford's Ashmolean Museum in 1951, but thirty years later, specialists said it was a copy. That finding was recently overturned in an interesting, objective examination. "Yes, that painting was attributed *to his workshop* because some of it was by an unknown hand. A dendrochronologist, Peter Klein, matched the wood panel it was painted on to Rembrandt's *Andromeda Chained to the Rocks,* which was created around 1630. His childhood friend, Jan Lieven's *Portrait of Rembrandt's Mother,* was painted on a piece of it, too. The wood panels used for all three paintings were from a Baltic region oak tree felled between 1618 and 1628. Factoring in two years for the wood to season, the time frame made sense," I explained. Science said it was so. Why wouldn't these collectors take advantage of that level of technology? From what I'd seen in the apartment so far, money was no object. Quality without ostentation at every turn. He hadn't spoken again, so I forged ahead. "You may have heard stories about some authenticating bodies, including a few with links to the artists' estates, others with hidden ties to galleries, colluding to keep supply down." It also kept outsiders out and insiders rich. I didn't mention that it was the Rembrandt Research Project that had mistakenly labeled it a copy because, in this case, they were wrong, not double-dealers. "I can assure you the bad actors are the exception, and I'm happy to refer you and your wife to reputable experts and labs." Surprisingly, he hadn't tried to interrupt me. "Mr. Tyndale, are you still there?"

"I am," he snapped.

"What I'm saying is we no longer have to rely solely on subjective expertise for forensic analysis." In some circles and in other decades, I could be shot for that heretical comment. Mr. Tyndale's reaction would expose his level of knowledge about the art market. And, hopefully, along with it, the real reason for his resistance to having the work analyzed.

"The painting's not a forgery." He let my comment pass. The guy was hell-bent on parting with his money. Maybe it made sense from where he stood. As money managers, mastering risk had led Stephan and Taylor to staggering wealth and prestige on a global scale. They were the opposite of risk-averse. Elliott said wealth managers were nothing more than money launderers because of the role they played in hiding and moving money to offshore tax havens. Risk didn't bother them.

I would try another approach. "A painting can't be a forgery. Only documents that come with it, like a COA, a certificate of authenticity, or an import export permit, or bill of sale, or art catalog, can be called that."

"Your point being?"

"In a case like this, we should move away from blaming the thing and point the finger at people and their actions. That's why the police don't investigate the fake; they investigate the object's creator." I hoped that had lowered the temperature in the room. I wasn't judging him for falling in love with the painting. He could still buy it. He could look at it twenty-four-seven for all I cared. It was too soon for it to be considered part of Rembrandt's oeuvre, even as 'by his workshop.' After I saw the documents Valerie said listed Graham and me as previous owners of the painting, they could all go to hell.

"May I see the provenance package?" I pressed. Works of art depict stories, but they also *have* stories of their own. Its provenance was a *documented* account of where it traveled every time it was bought and sold. Not rumors or legends passed down from ancestors or assumptions. It wasn't always possible with family items. How would an owner know that decades later, he would need to prove his grandmama owned a certain painting that had hung in her dining room when he was a boy? Not so in this case. They claimed to have the type of recorded history of ownership I was looking for.

"Taylor, darling, show her your copy. It's just the one page." Left. Right. Independent proof of a 17th-century painting's existence was condensed to fit on *one* page? A list of previous owners wasn't provenance. Verification of those owners was. I expected a dossier, with images of historical records, reports from scientific findings, along with other supporting documents. I wasn't saying it would be easy to track how the painting had moved through time and space—it wasn't with paintings even a hundred years old, and this they claimed was created almost four centuries ago—but I expected more than a single page.

Her attorney was where she left him by the entrance door, like a handbag.

"It's in my desk. Would you get it, please?" She held the phone face up in her palm, and with the other, she pointed in the direction of the living room. Both slender arms looked like ads for haute joaillerie.

"Stephan, should I go to Sutton House?" When the phone didn't respond, she held it up to her ear, where it clanked against a large canary yellow diamond earring. "Stephan?" There was no Stephan because while she gave the attorney his instructions, I had gently tapped the red circle on the screen. It hadn't been easy to do, considering how her hand trembled. "I guess he had to take another call," she explained, thinking she was covering for another time when he was rude to someone.

It was better for everyone involved, the Tyndales, me, even Rembrandt, if we left our options open on going to Sutton House. What we didn't need was a veto from Stephan. Would the venerated house pull the piece from the Old Masters auction if I presented my case? My reputation in the art world started with my scholarship on the intersection of art and religion, mostly on how artists inaccurately portrayed women in the Bible. I opened my art recovery agency a year ago. My work in peripheral areas—like when I was hired as a consultant with the Lempicka—had been lucrative. Most of my art recovery successes were not publicized, and that was fine by me. But would they give up their fee and commission on $650 million for me, especially since I couldn't tell them the reason for my doubts?

For now, I needed more information. "Mrs. Tyndale, you asked to meet with me. Was it because you saw a red flag?"

"You see, it was Bettina Vogt who warned us about the other bidder."

"Ah, is having competition for the painting the reason for the brain-freeze price?" I asked.

She grinned, enjoying being such a bad girl. "Of course, she couldn't give us a name, only that he's in India. She found out how high he planned to go and told us. But you know anything can happen at an auction. That's why we're pursuing a private sale. When I heard that Bettina was also involved with *Shame* and there was some scandal attached to it, I wondered if we were doing our due diligence. As you probably surmised, my husband wants to go ahead." They were the embodiment of the way the art business worked. It was based on handshake transactions, closed social circles, limited questions asked, and, most important of all, extreme confidentiality. She was wise to make it apparent they had done their due diligence. Was that the real reason I was here? So they could say Emma Kelly *weighed in on it* if they made a forgery claim later? Good luck. Treading carefully was as natural as breathing to me. "Luckily, now everything is, well, settled with the Julia Belvedere Jones painting. Bettina's name has been cleared. Everything's changed."

"Settled?" I asked.

"When it was authenticated this morning—" She stopped and corrected herself. "It was X-rayed this morning."

"An x-ray isn't authentication. And that's not how attribution works." Left. Right. "Broadly, there are three ways to authenticate works of art: forensic scientific analysis, connoisseurship, which is a stylistic analysis, and provenance research. You need all three. Usually, scientific analyses play a permissive role. Those findings take obstacles out of the way of authentication. Other methods of getting to an artwork's story take up where it leaves off." I shook my head. "I'm not telling you anything you don't already know. I've read your CV."

"All I know is what I read in the *New York Times*, and you said yourself this isn't your area of expertise." Just when I thought I couldn't listen to that high-pitched, sing-song cadence for another sentence, she made me want to hear more.

"I didn't see anything in the *Times* this morning." I had an urge to open the *NYT* app on my phone, which I resisted. *Shame* could have been X-rayed this morning, though Linda's response to my text said she had no intention of doing so, but that would have been just a piece of raw data. There was also material analysis of the pigment, the paint used. It should take three or four weeks for the deliverable. Writing up the Report of Finding took time. It had to be written in a legal but accessible way in case the document's author later had to go to court as an expert witness. There was no way a reputable firm had an opinion ready for the public this quickly.

"The online edition. It said the Belvedere Jones painting at the NMWA most certainly was by her and that she was paid $15 million for it."

I wanted to scream 'no' as loud as I could. It was conceivable, but doubtful, that I was mistaken about a right-handed artist painting *Shame*, but I wasn't wrong believing the artist. As for the proceeds of the sale, Linda Ensign told us the money was transferred to Macquarie Gallery. Elliott wanted proof of that, but the gallery's lawyers stood in the way. Had the money stopped there? The FBI could find that out, too.

Taylor's phone pinged, and she read a new text message. Suddenly, her head jerked back, and she blinked wildly. She wobbled, and I reached out to steady her. "Are you alright?" Something had truly scared her.

She pointed to her phone. "This is from Valerie. Bettina Vogt committed suicide."

I corrected her. "Unless they've found her body, she's only missing."

She nodded like she was thanking me for the good news. I saw terror in her eyes and didn't see how my few words could have pushed it far enough away for safety. For balance. For the restoration of her world.

She rubbed the base of her neck and took a few deep breaths to steady herself. "Can I ask why you care so much? After all, it is our money." She was frightened, but that didn't stop her from doubling down. We went into the living room, and the attorney stepped back from the desk.

"I care about scholarship." I cared about the art. "When an object moves between collections, it changes meaning. In addition to major museums, there are a few private collections around the world that practically *certify* the works in it. If misattributed artwork gets into a museum or in the collection of prestigious and established collectors like you and your husband, incorrect information is used by scholars and researchers in the future. For example, an absolute catalog raissoné of Modigliani cannot be written because of one forger–."

She interrupted, though I doubted she'd been listening anyway. "Would you include collectors like Sir Graham and Emmaline Abbott?" She picked up the paper on the desk and handed it to me.

I took it from her and gave myself a little internal pep talk before reading it. Incomplete provenances were the norm with centuries-old artworks, but here, I expected to see a forged or false record. These were sometimes due to collusion. Occasionally, by ignorance. It was time to see which this was. I read:

sale, Amsterdam, May 23, 1798, no. 156, for 450 florins to Roos; marchese d'Vrea, Genoa; cavaliere Domenico Odone, Genoa and Vienna (by 1857–before 1875; sold through Miethke to Lippmann-Lissingen); Joseph Ritter von Lippmann-Lissingen, Vienna (by 1875–76; his sale, Hôtel Drouot, Paris, March 16, 1876, no. 35, for Fr 175,000 to Wilson); John Waterloo Wilson, Brussels (1876–at least 1886; his sale, Paris, March 14–16, 1881, no. 91, for Fr 200,000, bought in); Wilbrenninck, The Hague; [Boussod, Valadon & Cie, Paris]; Maurice Kann, Paris (by 1901–d. 1906; his estate, 1906–9; sold to Duveen); [Duveen, Paris, 1909; sold for $262,980 to Altman]; Benjamin Altman, New York (1909–d) sold to Bernard Abbott; Bernard Abbott, Bath; Gregory Abbott, Bath; Sir Graham Abbott and Emmaline Abbott, Bath, (2022; sold to?)

The format followed the American Alliance of Museums format, using semi-colons when the work was passed directly from one owner to the next. A period indicated a gap between owners. I saw none. Auction houses, dealers (like Duveen), and agents were written in parenthesis or brackets to set them apart from private owners. Benjamin Altman, founder of the B. Altman and Company department store, was the prestigious art collector who donated the Met its first Vermeer along with twenty paintings either by or attributed to Rembrandt, along with other works. Maybe the provenance was correct through the Altman purchase? I went over the dates again. According to this, the painting was in Altman's collection when he died in 1913. His entire collection was bequeathed to the Met. It had to be displayed together forever. It wasn't possible for it to be sold to Graham's grandfather. Did I have to share that with her? Not now.

Bernard Abbott. Gregory Abbott. Graham's paternal grandfather and father. To me, they were words engraved on bronze plates on the frames of their portraits, hanging on walls over fireplaces in large rooms. Not flesh and blood art-collecting people. Who had asked Wikipedia and Google to cough up these names?

My eyes flitted back to the other familiar name on the page, Duveen. The infamous dealer's career was dotted with misattribution. Some led to his financial gain. I'd revisit that angle later if I needed it. If Graham wasn't a previous owner, none of the rest could be trusted.

"Who is the seller?" I asked.

"Anonymous." She smiled and looked around like she was about to share a state secret. "Bettina told us it's them," she whispered and pointed to the paper, still in my hand.

"Who?" *Keep the dread out of your voice.*

She tapped our names and whispered, "Sir Graham Abbott and Emmaline Abbott. Through intermediaries, of course. It's like an extra benefit. To own a Rembrandt and one *they* owned." That sounded like more than her being an anglophile. She was star-struck.

I shook my head. "Sutton House will not auction the painting without confirming the identity of the seller."

"Remember, they may not need to auction it if we negotiate a private sale." If anything, her voice was chirpier, the pitch higher.

"Who initiated the sale?" I asked.

"Huh?"

"They're initiated either by a client wishing to sell artwork with Sutton House as an exclusive agent or by a prospective buyer who is interested in purchasing a work of art discreetly. Which was it?"

"Sort of both, I guess."

"I give up." I illustrated with raised hands, the backs facing her. I wasn't surrendering. I was going to let them blow that $650 million. I had come to see the names on the painting's documents. I had stayed to do my bit to protect the scholarship around Rembrandt's work. I hadn't signed up to keep these fools and their money from parting. Had even I fallen for her 'Oh, I'm so rich and helpless' act? I had enough contacts in Manhattan to find out for myself if this was a case of art laundering, or money laundering, or some other felony.

"What do you mean?" She sounded shocked, but not.

"Maybe the seller lets the buyers think it was all their idea, or maybe the other way around." She looked me in the eye, suddenly an adult, so I went on. "It's always a little more of one than the other, isn't it?"

She grinned again. "Are we still talking about art?" she whispered.

I relaxed a little and gave her one last freebie. "I would advise you against buying art without knowing the seller." Money laundering. Ever heard of it? Drugs, sex trafficking, and arms dealing were larger, but the art market was the largest legal, unregulated market in the world. The only remaining industry of its size and risk that was not. Did she really want to swim in that ocean? She wasn't tough enough. Nor was Stephan. I could already tell.

"Did Bettina tell you anything else at all about who the other interested party was? Other than he was in India?" I asked. Someone with a financial interest gave her secret information designed to increase the amount they were willing to pay. Not by rounding up, either. They wanted to own a Rembrandt, so they would ignore even that?

"No, she said, or really she implied, her mother told her about them." She exhaled. "I appreciate what you are trying to do, but if Sir Graham Abbott and his American wife, Emmaline, want to keep their business private, they should be *allowed* to do that. They have that right." She *was* determined.

"Can we go to Sutton House now?" I asked.

"Why?" she asked, tapping the pointed toe of her loud but feminine, Miu Miu heels. She was in a hurry for something.

"To see the painting. That's where it is, right?" To see the complete provenance package, I thought. To talk to an adult. Where was the documentation showing it was acquired by the Abbott family, and who they sold it to?

"No, it isn't." I had forgotten about the attorney until he spoke. The sound startled me, as if the Regency period desk had all of a sudden said something.

"It's not?" Taylor's question sounded like a challenge. "Then where is it?"

He stammered. Seconds ticked by without him uttering one intelligible word.

"Of course, it is." Taylor put him out of his misery. Did he not want us to go to the auction house? Or did he not want me to see the painting? She leaned over the desk and scribbled something on a cream-colored notecard. "Going out for an hour or so," she called to someone in another room. I

49

almost smiled, thinking how Graham did that, too. He assumed someone who worked for us heard him, and he or she always had. "Call the car." She turned to me and said, "Can you come with me?"

"Sure."

Taylor walked through the living room, and as she reached the foyer, a young woman opened a closet door and held up a scarlet wool coat for her to twirl into. I still wore my coat since no one had offered to take it when I came in. The NDA was more important. And if I hadn't signed that, I would need my coat because I would have to go right back outside. I quickly buckled the belt and followed her out. Finally, I would see the painting.

"Thank you," I said to the lawyer. It seemed someone should.

Chapter Nine

Taylor pressed the button to call the elevator, then turned and watched the entry door to her apartment close behind us. After the lock clicked, she looked up at the four corners of the ceiling. There was a security camera mounted on the elegant wood trim of each one, and she intended for me to take note of that. The elevator came, and as I stepped inside, I felt the pressure of her hand wrapping around my wrist. She palmed me the note card. I took it and held it by my side.

"Do you need to go to Sutton House?" she whispered.

"Make me a better offer." It would have to be mind-blowing to surpass seeing that painting.

"I have somewhere else to be. That's the address of Bettina Vogt's mother. Would you speak with her? Find out where Bettina is. Surely, she's heard from her. She isn't answering my phone calls all of a sudden, either." She took a breath. "That's why I panicked this morning and got Valerie and Bobbi involved."

"Call and make the introduction," I said.

She tapped out a text with a manicured index finger. I would have snooped from over her shoulder, but I was a member of the thumb tribe, which made her slo-mo painful to watch. Torture for someone who lived at my speed.

"Do you have a photograph of the painting?" I asked.

"Sure." She finished the text and opened a file of photos on her phone. "Bettina's mother and I were in school together at LeRosey." The Swiss boarding school was the most expensive in the world. There it was. I had a doctorate in Art History and years of experience, and we were in Manhattan with access to cutting-edge technology to analyze the painting—electron emission radiography was just one example—but she chose to put a whisper in her ear from a schoolmate above all that. Someone in her social milieu. She and Stephan would probably buy the painting they hoped was a Rembrandt before this evening's auction. At least she had the sense to be nervous about it. Then what? Rembrandt specialists would not leave this alone. Now, that was an expensive education.

The missing woman was connected to paintings that touched each of my lives. I wanted to find her. The Tyndale's money wasn't my responsibility.

"Here it is." She smiled and tilted her head, like a proud mom, before holding the phone out for me. There was a lot of glare, and the painting sat at an angle.

I took the phone from her for a better look. "The people at Sutton House didn't know you were taking this, did they?"

She giggled and put her fingertips to her lips. I expanded the image with two fingers and stared at it. "So what do you think?" she asked.

"It's hard to tell much with a photo." No way I was going to be a fourteenth expert for them. I was saved by the opening of the elevator door.

A silver Mercedes S 580 sedan waited at the curb, and the doorman opened its back door. Taylor leaned in and spoke to the driver. "Alfred, she'll give you the address for where she needs to go."

"I don't need a car. I'll walk," I said.

"But you can't." She glanced at the notecard in my hand and raised an eyebrow. "I mean, are you sure? It's too cold to walk."

I pretended to give the address a quick look. "It's not that far."

"It's, like, ten blocks from here." Her gaze flew from me to the doorman to Alfred.

"That's nothing." It was a half-mile walk I could use to make phone calls her driver shouldn't hear. She wasn't being driven to this somewhere else she needed to be? Now, she would have the car to herself. What was so stress-inducing about that?

"Uh, uh," She looked up West 57th Street. "Good idea, I'll walk, too. Sorry for the trouble, Alfred." Her tone was fake-courteous, but at least she'd spoken to him.

The doorman smiled, closed the car door with an almost inaudible push, and walked back to his post by the entrance. Taylor and I turned and watched the Mercedes pull into traffic, like it was sailing away to Ellis Island, leaving us on a foreign dock, bearing up as well as we could under the circumstances. What just happened here? Was it too cold to walk, or not? Or was she going without me to Sutton House, which, at 20 Rockefeller Plaza, was about a mile away, twice the distance?

Once her car turned the corner, she sprinted away without another word. She ran to the crosswalk at the other end of the block and raised her hand before she was at the opposite sidewalk. A taxi pulled up in seconds, and she was gone. Uptown. To a destination, she didn't want Alfred to know about. Where she was headed was none of my business, but with that smile on her face, it wasn't the dentist. She was overdressed, suffocating in signifiers of wealth, and I hoped he was worth it.

Of course, the temps were low. It was New York City in the winter, but the sun was bright, as high energy as the city. I couldn't see the Met on the other side of the park, in the UES or Upper East Side, but knowing it was there was enough for me.

I walked away in the opposite direction but turned at the end of the block to place my first call, which would be on the phone secreted in the lining of my makeup bag.

"Emmaline, I didn't expect to hear from you yet, and I am delighted. Did you sleep well, darling?" *Dah-ling*.

"I did. What are you having for dinner?" That was the way Graham and I spoke to one another. Tenderly. Solicitous. The blare of the car horns around me be damned. It was early evening in Bath, England.

He listed what the cook would prepare, and I pretended to be reassured by the healthy meal. "I'm following up on a rumor about a Rembrandt for a friend. Hope this doesn't sound like a crazy question, but does the Abbott collection include a Rembrandt? Or did it?"

"Why is everyone on the planet interested in that little painting all of a sudden?" He chuckled. I stopped breathing somewhere in the middle of his question. "We have something probably from Rembrandt's workshop. It's at Emrick Hall."

We live in Bath, not in the family home, in Northamptonshire, which was in that muscular Gothic style. His mother did, and his two sisters, forty-seven-year-old twins, and their families spent most weekends there. The arrangement allowed Graham to keep them at a two-hour car ride distance away. Bath was in the other direction from London, so there were no drop-in visits.

So, it was still in the collection. The ownership record Taylor showed me had it sold two years ago, but Bettina thought we still owned it and were selling it now.

"I'd like to get your reasoned opinion to see if it's even that." Graham thought I was an art advisor in the States.

"Has anyone asked about it recently?" Who were these interested people?

"A granddaughter of an old friend said she was an art student, telephoned Mother asking to see it. She's American and was coming over to visit her grandmother. Her last name is Vogt, which I only remember because she telephoned on our way to *vote*."

Relax your voice. Relax your fists. "The election was last month, right? Did she visit?"

"Mother put her off." I could imagine that equation. Family member of a friend versus she's an American. "To my knowledge, she hasn't heard from her again."

Careful. If his mother was asked to verify the young woman's story with her friend, her antennae would go straight up. His mother was no fool. "Graham, I don't want to alarm anyone, but would you check on the painting, please?" Had it been stolen? That would stop the sale in its tracks.

"Already have. It bothered me that she knew *Self-Portrait, 1650* existed and to contact us. Our holdings, if referenced at all, are supposed to be described as *in a private collection*." When he said the painting's name, I held my breath again. "And before you ask, no one has substituted a forgery for it like in the movies." I smiled. Graham was several steps ahead of most people when it came to security. He was a retired Royal Navy pilot and had never lost that sense of vigilance. He liked to say, "Only the paranoid survive."

"What's the size of the painting?"

"Twenty-five centimeters by about eighteen." Close enough to the Tyndale coveted Rembrandt. "The canvas has been well cared for. It's in a temperature and humidity-controlled space."

Time started up again. "Canvas?" Not copper. Of course, Rembrandt could have painted more than one self-portrait that year, but that didn't matter. There was no copper painting in the Abbott collection, proving the provenance was falsified for the Tyndale version. This was enough to delay or, maybe, cancel the sale. I was so relieved my feet hardly touched the ground.

"Canvas, of course. Darling, I'm sending you the photograph I took while I was there since my secret has been disclosed. Who told you? Mother? Or one of my sisters?"

"Told me what?" My phone pinged, and I put him on speaker to check the message. It was a text from him with a photograph of a painting in an ornate frame. The second photo was of the back. I spread my thumb and index finger over the image, enlarging it. There it was. Collectors' marks played a central role in reconstructing the provenance of a work of art. The stamp for a prestigious art collection like ours was well-known, so it could be duplicated. Had someone gone to that trouble with the copper version?

"Happy anniversary, Emmaline. I had your name added to the painting's title. I love you."

"Graham, I don't know what to say. That's too generous." I had never taken anything from him or his family. The jewelry I wore when I was in England would stay with them. Both the family heirlooms and the price upon request expensive pieces from Graham. All I wanted was his help finding and returning to Poland Raphael's *Portrait of a Young Man,* the most famous piece of Nazi-looted art, still missing. That was all. Graham and I had a copy of *Portrait of a Young Man* running round the clock on a facial recognition app. It searched Facebook posts, Google photos, newspaper articles of interviewees in their living rooms. Hoping to see a painting over a shoulder, in a foyer, or in a reflection in a mirror. The computing speed needed was costly. That was just one example of what we did. We continually scanned the dark web, deep web, and open-source intelligence platforms for certain keywords. We weren't getting any hits. Some day we would.

"Come home soon. We have that event at the V&A on Friday night."

I chose to marry Graham. I made that choice. When he proposed, I was so far outside of the rules constructed by gender or history or safety that decisions were easy; they came quick. His question. My answer. Would my life today be so very different if we had simply kept dating? Not really. I wouldn't be breaking the law, but that was about it. Besides, half-measures showed a lack of commitment to the Raphael. I didn't waste much time thinking about it. I made my beds.

Chapter Ten

My second call was to Elliott, on a different phone. I told him about the *New York Times* online article while I retraced my steps back to West 57th Street. "Do you know anything about this so-called authentication of *Shame* that happened this morning?" I asked.

"I haven't read that article. I'm toiling away in a guest office at FBI headquarters in northwest DC. And, yeah, Linda Ensign changed her mind, but I don't know why. She called in a favor from a friend at the Smithsonian. I just hung up with him. It didn't sound to me like what he found proved the painting was by Julia Belvedere Jones. You're telling me that's what the Times article says?"

"I haven't read it either, but that's what Taylor Tyndale told me."

"He told me his report was not going to be made public until it went up the chain there. I should have gotten my own expert." I heard papers being shuffled. "Here's what the Smithsonian did," then he slowly read, *"a macro X-ray fluorescence scan* to penetrate the layer of paint."

"Do you think she agreed to have it analyzed because she had someone who would give the answer she wanted?" I asked. Though that wasn't like the Smithsonian to agree to do that.

"Maybe. Who knows? She's *your* friend. Does it sound like her?" His words were clipped and mounting in irritation. He had me on speaker, and I heard him typing. "I'm looking for that article now. Let's play 'guess the leaker.' Hm, would he have done that? I didn't peg him for the type. Here it is. Shit. What's this business about Julia Belvedere Jones being paid for the painting? Why would the Times print that? It's true we verified the money went to the gallery." I didn't like the sound of that. The FBI couldn't find out, but reporters could? "I've got two agents from the Art Crime Team flying in, and I'll have someone interview Linda Ensign to ask if she was the leak, since she has a lot to gain by the painting being legit."

"Or at least by everyone believing it is," I reminded him.

A few seconds later, I heard a low growl, dotted with profanity. "Babe, you're mentioned. They start out describing you as a bigger-than-life figure in the vibrant state of feminist scholarship in contemporary culture. He says, "Her cool girl look implies the art world isn't something to overthink and that her success in it is accidental. It's anything but." In the next paragraph, he writes the tests you want aren't needed for a primary sale of a work, only in the secondary market." I hadn't expected a smoking gun, like when Titanium Dioxide from the 20th century was detected in Zinc White on a painting supposedly from the 19th century, which had been painted by renowned forger Wolfgang Beltracchi.

"That's exactly what Linda said yesterday. She has to be the source of the leak." I tightened my chignon. "Elliott, can you get DNA from where I think there's a bit of a palm print?"

"I could try, but I doubt it would do any good since the painting was out in public, where anyone could touch it. I don't like the way this writer is questioning your expertise."

"That's sweet. Linda's in a bad spot because the technical analysis of *Shame* should have been done by the Macquarie Gallery in preparation of the sale."

"How do we know they didn't?"

"If they had, they would make the findings available instead of lawyering up. She'll have to admit she accepted the painting without insisting on those reports," I said.

"We learned more about that painting. Thank goodness this part isn't in the article, which makes me think the guy at the Smithsonian lab isn't the leaker. If he wanted to talk to the media, it would be to share what he found. Anyway, they X-rayed it, and there's a painting under the painting."

"An underpainting?" Technology, not the same, but at that level, which did no damage to the work of art, was what was available for the Tyndales if they would only use it.

"Well, it's really a drawing. A weird little sketch. Does that mean anything?"

"That would be an under-drawing instead of an under-painting. Might be an abandoned composition beneath the paint. Just the fact that it's there doesn't prove Julia Belvedere Jones isn't *Shame*'s artist. How weird? What was the drawing of?" I was standing in the shadow of a building and moved into a column of sunlight to warm up.

"The infrared image he sent me shows a vase with a few flowers in it and bones."

"Bones?" I stopped in my tracks at the craziness of what he described. "A drawing of flowers and bones?"

"Yeah, in the container, like a jar or vase," he answered.

"Human?"

"I think so. I'll have someone verify that. To me, they look like a femur, tibia, and fibula. All the larger leg bones."

"Elliott, if there are other instances of Julia Belvedere Jones using that motif, it could be used as proof that she did paint *Shame*."

He chuckled. "Too bad I don't know an art expert who can tell me if she knows of any examples."

"Very funny. I can't think of anything, but I'll look through some catalogs later. And I can contact someone on her catalog raisonné committee." If anyone would know, the authors who literally wrote the book, or critical catalog, listing all the authentic works by Julia Belvedere Jones would. "Anyway, I still know she didn't paint it."

"To save time, I'll have someone run it through an art app, too." There were phone apps for people who saw a painting and wanted to know the name of the artist. Like Shazam for cultural objects and art.

"On the other topic, have you found Bettina Vogt?" I asked. "Valerie found out she's missing and told Taylor Tyndale. Of course, she phrased it the way Linda did—that she had committed suicide."

"Still no word on her whereabouts. No Jane Does in a hospital or morgue. No nothing. It's starting to look like she wrote the suicide note and then changed her mind. Hopefully, she'll turn herself in. If she doesn't, NYPD will find her, or we will."

I told him about my strange meeting with Taylor Tyndale, stopping before I got to the part about her arranging a meeting for me with Bettina Vogt's mother. "They refuse to have the painting analyzed. They want to buy it so much they are ignoring red flags."

"No cure for stupid. Are you going to Sutton House now?" he asked.

"I don't think it would do any good. The Tyndale's are trying to negotiate a private sale, so it may not be included in tonight's Old Masters auction."

"Hold on." He closed the door to the office they gave him to use. "The article is wrong about where the 15 million dollar payment went. We're getting closer to having it frozen. It went to the Macquarie Gallery, then it bounced out of there and seemed to disappear into the ether. That is, until we found it in Italy. That's a country the US has an MLAT with–."

"What is that?"

"A Mutual Legal Assistance Treaty."

"Thanks, you saved me a Google," I said.

"The money went from the gallery to a newly opened business account, in an Italian bank, but their government is going to place a hold on it."

"Elliott, that's such good news."

"I don't know how long the hold is good for, though. We have to get them something solid."

"Does Linda know all that?" I asked. "She'll be able to repay NEH, so she should be relieved."

"Nope, if she cooperates with the agents that go to question her, I'll let them tell her. Now, about this Rembrandt, what made you suspicious?"

I had a handful of reasons now, but he was asking what made me suspicious enough to drop everything and take the next flight to New York this morning when Valerie and Bobbi called. He knew I would do that for Bobbi, but not Valerie. "Rembrandts don't just show up like this one did. And then there was Bettina Vogt's involvement," I lied. "Then, when I saw they were hellbent on buying it quickly—that's out of the ordinary for serious collectors—that made me even more curious." Some people, maybe the Tyndales, collect art as a way to buy a life, to accumulate cultural capital. Like Taylor said,

"Because it's a Rembrandt." Why would such giants in the collecting world be that reckless?

"A fool and his money, right? Look at the comments section if you get a chance. Lot of people are coming to your defense. I'll read you one. *She is a strong voice against the ideologies of violence and patriarchy.*" What did that have to do with art?

"Very nice. Probably my mom, though."

"Will you be back in DC tonight?"

"Of course."

* * *

I climbed the steps to the entrance of a residential building. The doorman opened the door, but I turned and walked back down to the sidewalk. I had one more call to make.

"Bobbi, I'm in New York. Why were you on that call with Valerie this morning?"

"To help Taylor, like I told you."

"The real reason, please."

She exhaled. "When seismic sums of money move around, I hear about it. And then I make it my business to see what's behind it. It may be innocent as an Eagle Scout or not."

"They're innocent?" I asked.

"It's all relative. Anyway, it bothers me that two large transfers have an intersection, Bettina Vogt."

"Me, too." I rubbed my forehead. "The *New York Times* said Julia Belvedere Jones received the $15 million. She didn't. I knew that yesterday. Plus, to pretend to be that indignant would take *some* balls."

"So where did the money go?"

"A corporation in Italy, which means nothing." I told her the money was going to be frozen by the Italian government, at least for now.

"I need to find out who the principles are in that company. I'll let you know what I find out," she said.

"The FBI is looking for it, too."

"Cute." She laughed and hung up.

I went back to the steps. Did I want to go in? There would be a trial. Probably several. The NMWA would sue Macquarie if they didn't get the money back. The Macquarie would go after Bettina. I might be called on to testify, which would bring publicity. Was it worth taking that chance? No telling what the Tyndales would do. Keep their mouths shut and pretend to have a Rembrandt? Or maybe they and the Sutton House would use something called the doctrine of mutual mistake.

This mysterious Bettina Vogt was involved with two counterfeit paintings that I knew about. One had to do with my life in New York, and the other touched on my UK life. I didn't understand either, but I knew I had to get there before the FBI. I climbed the stairs again. This time, I let the doorman do his job. "Third time's a charm," he joked.

Chapter Eleven

I introduced myself to a maid wearing a black dress, white frilled apron, thick tights, and sensible shoes from some distant era and asked to see Vanessa-Maria Boscolo. If the demure young woman bowed, I would leave. She gave me an unconvincing and uncertain smile, then nodded at a woman and man standing together in the middle of the living room.

The apartment was much smaller than the Tyndales', but had a strange charm. It was closer in size and solace to our 1928 building than theirs, too. Elliott and I had a two-bedroom apartment in the Village with a view of Washington Square. This building pre-dated ours.

A late-thirty-something guy was holding both shoulders of a rigid, petite woman. She turned away from him and locked eyes with me. Her scarlet lips were pressed together in a tight line. She held onto a pendant on her necklace, either for the comfort of it, or to keep him an arm width back. I knew an SOS when I saw one.

The man said, "Suicide's not the end of the world. I'm just sayin'."

I gasped in shock. "I think you need to leave."

"My name is Ford Hughes, and I was Bettina's life coach." The use of the past tense in front of the missing woman's mother was insensitive. The sharp angles of his face made him look fastidious and like an easily frightened fraud—or someone play-acting. He wore a tie with one of Van Gogh's *Haystacks* embroidered on it in garish colors, deliberately, dangerously pushing the bounds of taste. Not even in a camp way. Probably bought in a museum gift store.

"For the love of fuck," I said. Now, who was pushing the bounds of taste?

But her smirk said she didn't disagree with my sentiment, nor was she offended by the language. I removed his hands, one at a time.

"Who, may I ask, are *you?*" he asked, his hands held up in a goalpost gesture.

I didn't answer him. I turned to the woman I assumed was Mrs. Boscolo. "May we speak in private?" I saw that what she was caressing and twisting was a heavy, gold cross.

She nodded and took my arm, leading me to a mauve flare-armed sofa. "Mr. Hughes, you may let yourself out," she said in a deep, dramatic voice and an Italian accent.

"Please ask your daughter to call me," he said. "Please." Why the pleading tone?

I studied the art on her walls, waiting to hear the door close. Post-Black art hung next to modern figurative paintings, all unexpectedly surrounded by smartly curated and positioned antiques. Apartments with over-sized rooms and high ceilings were rare in modern Manhattan, at least in this neighborhood. Its very survival whispered improbability.

I told her I was Emma Kelly. "You're Bettina Vogt's mother?"

She nodded and held out a hand. "I'm Vanessa-Maria Boscolo." I was sure I had said the triple-barreled name in half that amount of time at the door.

"How are you holding up? Is there anything I can do to help you, Mrs. Boscolo?"

"Please, call me Vanessa-Maria." Couldn't imagine myself doing that, because I had too much self-respect and too little pretension. She wore a navy silk suit and black pumps with a slight heel. They looked suspiciously like those the queen wore. Maybe Stuart Weitzman. Maybe Anello & Davide had made the buttery leather footwear by hand. "Can you give me answers on my daughter's life here? I was told you could." She was back to rotating the cross in half circles.

I blinked in surprise, since what I had in mind when I offered my assistance was along the lines of helping her get information on the investigation. "I never met your daughter." *What had she been told by Taylor Tyndale to get this visit?* "Where was she working?" Linda Ensign thought she worked at the Macquarie Gallery. The Tyndales, Bobbi, and Valerie all said Sutton House.

My question seemed to surprise her. "I thought you knew." Not an answer. I waited.

"The Macquarie Gallery." Why had that been so hard? Wait, if she knew the Tyndales, why hadn't she answered the auction house? "You are the one who recommends caution with newly discovered works?" How would she know that? And, plural?

I looked her in the eye and understood. She knew her daughter was the link between the two paintings, and there was a connection from there to her disappearance, but she would not concede that Bettina was a party to art fraud. I would expect that from a mother. "Do you work as a diplomat? Maybe at the U.N.?" I teased.

"I'm sorry?" Thickening the Italian accent, maybe to feign confusion.

Was her daughter a middleman? Gray man? The Janus figure, who was the trustworthy interface between the forger and the collector?

"The piece the Tyndales want to acquire isn't newly discovered, supposedly." She and the collectors needed to get their story straight. Was the Rembrandt newly discovered, or did it have the patina of being from the Abbott collection? When she said her daughter worked at Macquarie, was it her way of telling me she knew about *Shame*? She would have to mention the painting by name before I would. "Yes, I think we should pump the brakes." The art market has been flooded with works bringing in ten times prices from a year ago. Masterpieces that would have sold for $10 million a year ago were going for $100 million now, and that was before the buyer's premium. What was even more concerning was that these works were being added to collections and museums in half the time. "Did your daughter talk to you about the painting the Tyndales are buying?"

"So they *are* going to buy it?" The eagerness in her voice made me regret my comment. Time to dial it back.

"I meant to say they intend to."

"Bettina is a brilliant artist, but in the last half year or so, she became disenchanted with the art world. Her work celebrated experimentation. Deconstructing to reconstruct. She talked all the time about techno-utopian ideals of innovation and creativity." She was determined not to talk about that specific painting. Instead, she droned on about her daughter's disappointment once she was on the inside and had a paying job in the industry and her regrets about, well, something. She felt art represented institutional power and kept urban centers elite. And how important street art was for communities…. I zoned out when she got to the part about artistic innovation not being appreciated. The works on the walls surrounding us illustrated that aesthetic. Like mother, like daughter. Sorry, but she'd have to finish that walk down memory lane without me.

Where were photographs of the two of them together anyway? There was nothing to tell me about their family.

She believed her daughter was alive. Maybe she was. I hoped she was. Maybe she was hiding her. Did she think I would reassure Taylor Tyndale and they would make that purchase, or did she want me to stop the sale at Sutton House so her daughter would not be involved in a $650 million art scam? Time to interrupt. "What did she tell you about the possible Rembrandt acquisition she worked on for Taylor and Stephan Tyndale?"

She shook her head and twisted the cross pendant. Gazing into the distance, dreamy-eyed, she said, "Bettina was always so sensitive to–."

"I don't care about your daughter's angst. If I learn anything that might help NYPD find her, I will share it with them. Did she talk to you about her work?"

"No."

I stood and buttoned my coat. "You're Italian?" Duh-uh. Of course, she was, but Vogt sounded German. I was fishing.

She rose to her feet. "I'm Florentine." *Florenteen.* "The world thinks all of Italy is one big happy family, but we hate one another. Unification was portrayed as…."

Well, okay. "I do hope your daughter is safe." Not enough to stay here for a history lesson on Italy.

"I was told she would be protected," she said.

She had my attention again. "From whom?"

"From people who are not Florentine," she whispered dramatically. That didn't narrow it down by much.

"Then, protected *by* whom? *Who* said they would protect her?" Maybe whoever it was had her in hiding, and the fake suicide note was part of the plan.

She twisted the necklace and held the cross out, like that was a message I could understand. Not good enough. She could not or would not lead me to the forger.

Chapter Twelve

"Hm." Not good. A plaque with my name was still on the wall by the door to my old office at SIRA. Valerie said it had been converted into a guest office. Or maybe she had threatened the loss of a private office to get me to change my mind. I ended my arrangement to work for SIRA part-time, with international clients when my agency's business grew enough to pay for my routine trips to England.

The minimalist room was the way I had left it. I wasn't someone who decorated her office as a cozy home away from home. My desk was a rare Pierre Paulin writing table, the only Art Deco piece I could tolerate. The loveseat against one wall and the guest chairs in front of the desk were characterless, not statement-making like mid-century could be. An unassuming bookcase held the few art crime reference books I'd left behind.

I texted Elliott to see if the image recognition app had turned up any matches for the bones and flowers design. Was it an icon or emblem? I doubted the unsettling image was a logo. Finding such an odd drawing associated with the artist's name with the FBI's resources should be easy. If the creepy drawing was used in another Julia Belvedere Jones painting, that would be evidence that she painted *Shame*. If they found it on the web but not connected to her name, it might point to the artist who had in fact painted it.

I opened my laptop and created a new document.

"Hi, Emma! You *are* here." Lynya Mitchell, Valerie's uber-efficient admin, leaned in the doorway. She sounded like she'd lost an argument with someone. I told her it was good to see her. "You have a visitor. He insisted you were in your office, and he was right. He's waiting in the –." Someone walked up behind her and she turned. "Uh-h…. Here he is."

"She's expecting me," the familiar voice said.

"It's okay," I assured her when I saw who it was. "Is Valerie here?"

That got a chuckle and an eye roll. "Any minute."

The Macquarie Gallery's assistant gallery manager came in and closed the door, then collapsed into a guest chair.

"What you are playing at, Crawford. Or is it *Ford* these days?"

"How was the life coach thing? Too much?"

I laughed. "Maybe a little. What you said about suicide was over the top."

"I know! But even that didn't rattle any information out of her."

"And that tie is hurting my eyes," I said. "You look pale. Are you alright?" He had earlier, too, but I wasn't able to say anything then.

He loosened his neckwear in agreement with my assessment. "Couture. There's nothing like it, right? Getting into character. I'm not okay. Far from it. Thanks for asking. Haven't slept in days. Where could Bettina be? Were you able to find out anything from her mother?"

I shook my head. "Almost nothing. She thinks her daughter is still alive. What do you think happened to her?"

"On Friday, she told me she was going to commit suicide. I don't know what to think."

I lowered my head and made serious eye contact. "You really don't know what to think? You're sure? No idea? Honestly, Crawford!"

"Sometimes people say it, but don't mean it, right?"

"I don't know. She told you that she was going to take her own life?"

"Her exact words were, 'I'm going to end it all'. What else could it mean?"

"Sounds like you knew her well. That she's your friend. Did you tell Linda Ensign that?"

"She called me yesterday, and I told her that Bettina didn't answer her phone Sunday, and when she didn't show up at the gallery, I called the police. That's all I told her because that's all I know." His gaze traveled around the under-decorated room and back again, careful to avoid making eye contact with me.

"You told Linda Ensign that Bettina was dead."

"Uh, I think I said she committed suicide because I assumed that's what she did."

"Hopefully she's alive."

He put his hands over his face. "Who knows?"

"Her mother told me she was an artist. Any good?"

"Yeah." He drew out the word and nodded once. "I told her about a million times that she was born in the wrong century. She would have fit in with American artists in Paris, like Frieseke, Willard Metcalf, Guy Rose—"

"So there's not a market today for what she paints." I shrugged because that was the least interesting thing about her. "Lilla Cabot Perry," I said.

"Huh? Yeah, her too."

"She's more famous than anyone you listed, but you didn't think of her."

"Okay, okay, but life in the patriarchy wasn't what disillusioned Bettina. Artists think their talent can change what the collecting world is looking for at a particular time. Guess what, it can't. We've all hit a point and had our fantasies smashed to bits. Over and over I told her, what you want to paint won't turn back time to impressionism, landscapes–. "

"I agree, the business of art can disillusion the most stalwart romantic. Wait, Crawford, that's what she painted?"

He chuckled. "Nothing the girl liked more than a good landscape."

"I think her mother lied to me. She said her daughter was despondent because the art establishment wasn't interested in her, quote, techno-utopian ideals. Like she saw herself as a disrupter."

"She said that about Bettina? No, that's not her. Her favorite harsh criticism of a work was that it was *defiantly modern*. I remember once we were looking at a sculpture on the Met roof, and she said to me, "What can you say about it that hasn't been said about electronic music?" She was so funny, and she either is or was my friend, but she wouldn't know a techno-utopian ideal if it walked up and slapped her on the ass. What is it anyway?"

I laughed, and it felt good. "I was hoping you could tell me."

"Yeah, it sounds like something we don't need to know. Believe me, her feelings were hurt because her work wasn't selling. I don't want to claim to know her better than her own mother, but she's just wrong."

"Your take on it makes more sense. Artist-provocateurs rarely paint what you're describing." I was going to have to wrap this conversation up and get back into the outside world, and I started making those motions and sounds. Unplugging the charger from my computer. Long sighs that drifted softly to an end.

"In the fall, she met someone, and just like that, she was happy again."

"Until she wasn't. After all, we're talking about someone who may have committed suicide." I pushed my chair away from the desk.

He sat up straight and lifted his head. "Emma?" He looked into my eyes, like there was a choice to be made, one road or another to be taken. I held his gaze and tried to let him know I would be a worthy custodian of any information he shared with me. He had my attention again. "We were very close." Crawford was gay, so I knew he didn't mean they had a romantic relationship.

"Emma," he repeated. I waited there like I had all the time in the world. He would tell me when he was ready. "Bettina's the forger."

"She forged what?"

"I don't know how many, but several of the *rediscovered* paintings that have shown up in the last few months." I usually hated air quotes, but his sentence needed them.

I sucked in my breath. Most people would need to sit down, but not me. I stood up. Left. Right.

"Which paintings? The Rembrandt the Tyndales want to buy?" I asked.

He nodded. "Yeah."

I was so wrong about her. So much for the common way forgeries got into the art market with a chain connecting someone in the criminal world to a middleman, then to the collector or curator. Bettina Vogt was both the forger and the middle link. "Do you have proof?" My heart rate climbed. Left. Right.

"That one I saw in her apartment. I didn't know what she was going to do with it at the time. I thought it was, like, some kind of hobby. Or she was trying to improve her technique, like the art students you see sketching in every museum in the world, dreaming of being the next Botticelli. Shouldn't their instructors tell the kiddies to set their sights on being the next Damien Hirst?" He chuckled nervously and shook his head.

"If they want to make back that tuition money, they should. Cecily Brown says you don't understand a painting until you draw it."

"Well, that's not what this was. We were standing in her—well, it's a studio apartment, so we were in all of her rooms. She walks over to an easel and picks up this painting of Rembrandt, not on canvas, on metal. I know now it was copper. While we were talking about something, I can't remember what, she peeled off a sticker from the back. Then she goes to the freezer and gets something out. It's another label, and she puts it over where she took the first one off. Weird, huh?"

"Not if you're a forger," I said. She had protected a spot from her simulated aging and then covered it with, maybe, a gallery's stamp. When a gallerist or any authenticator looked under it, that area would look like it hadn't aged the way the rest of the painting or frame had, having been shielded from light and elements. "Though it's rarely done in front of an audience."

"Exactly. Emma, this was my friend standing there in front of me! I guess, on some level, I knew what was going on because I remember thinking that was no way to handle a Rembrandt. Even a fake one." He gave another nervous laugh. "And how would an assistant in a gallery afford a painting so valuable you can't put a number on it?" In a studio apartment with what sounded like little to no security. Yeah, the authentic masterpiece option was off the table.

"Crawford, I can't think of a legal reason for her to switch those labels. Did you ask her what she thought she was doing?" There's no law against copying a Rembrandt, but several against misrepresenting it as such.

"Not at first, because I didn't want to hear the answer. I knew there had to be more to it. That wasn't like her. Or it hadn't been before."

"Before what?"

"Last summer, she fell out of love with the art business."

"Oh, no. Crawford, I know you were her life coach, but still, I don't need to hear more psychoanalysis of her. Don't you have some kind of coach-client confidentiality rule?" We laughed together the way we had so many times when the subject wasn't serious or close to home. "What did she do with the painting?"

"Then?" I meant how did it get to Sutton House, but the next step in its journey would be good to know, too. "She had been looking at it like she was inspecting it. Not like she loved it the way you would if you painted it, with pride. Like she was, I don't know, conniving. She pulled out a little toolbox where she kept new paint brushes, rags, that kind of thing, and rummaged through it until she found a little hammer."

"Like the size used by framers?"

"Yeah. Then she puts the painting down on her coffee table with one edge hanging over the edge. And she whacks that tiny corner." He pantomimed the movement, face scrunched like he hated to do it. I pulled back like the make-believe painting was real and a Rembrandt.

"Wait, which hand?" I asked.

"Huh?" He looked up, mid-whack.

"You're using your right hand. Is that how she did it?" I asked.

He checked his hand and thought before he answered, "Yeah, right hand." My theory of a right-handed painter creating *Shame* still held.

"To make it identifiable?" I asked. That was another trick forgers used. Marking their work so they could later claim that feature meant they were telling the world it was theirs, not by fill in the name of an artist. "Or to help age it?"

He nodded. "I didn't know what she was doing at the time." I shut my eyes. *Oh, Crawford, please let that be true and not something you need to say later in court.* "Next, she goes over to her bed, unmade, as I recall, takes the pillowcase off her pillow, and puts the painting in it. She looks out a window to the street, says she'll be right back, and leaves. Three or four minutes later, she comes back, but without it. I mean, without the painting. She had the pillowcase, which she tossed on the coffee table. I kept asking her what was going on, over and over, but she wouldn't answer me. Finally, I said, 'You're going to sell that, aren't you?'" He put his hands over his eyes and leaned over, his elbows propped on his knees. "You don't know how much I wanted her to deny it. To save our friendship and because it left me having to decide what to do about it." He was in such pain, and it made me despise her. I walked around to him and touched his shoulder. He straightened and covered my hand with his. "That's when she told me she painted the Lempicka *Kizette in a Green Bugatti.*"

"She must have hated me."

"No, she didn't. Strange now that I think about it."

"For someone not to hate me? Ford!" I pretended to be offended. "I'm never going to let you live that name down."

"You know, I didn't mean it like that. Just a week or so before, we were having a drink at the Met in the Great Hall Balcony Café when it hit *The Art Newspaper* that *Kizette in a Green Bugatti* was a forgery, and she toasted you. Not mentioning that she painted it. Wish I had thought to ask her about lying to me, or at least omitting something like that. You're right. Why would a forger—and it pains me to call my friend that—feel like that about someone who had just detected the forgery? Her forgery. If they find her alive, I'll ask her that. I told her I knew you. She was impressed."

"Oh, please." I batted that away. "So, what else did she tell you that evening?"

"Evening? Cute, Emma. Not everyone waits until five for a cocktail." He chuckled. "Like I said, at the time, she didn't let on that she was the forger of that painting or any other. We sat there talking about Art Deco—she knew I wasn't a fan. And that hurts."

"What does? That she didn't tell you she painted it or that she painted something in the Art Deco style?" I teased, trying to help him relax. "Did you fail geometry class? Is that what happened?" Art Deco reflected the glamorization of the industrial revolution. The Coca-Cola bottle was 'applied' Art Deco style, beauty in an everyday design. We laughed, and I leaned against the edge of my desk.

"Art Deco just doesn't do it for me. Nobody's fault," he said.

I smiled at his dry wit. "I'm glad you dropped by, and I'm not saying that because you're telling me everything I needed to know. Good to know I'm not crazy for calling out these sleepers."

He patted my knee. "Aww."

"Did she tell you about any other paintings?"

"Yeah, that same day in her apartment after I called her out, she told me about *Shame* by Julia Belvedere Jones," he answered.

"You mean, *not* by Julia Belvedere Jones."

"Un-huh."

"I wondered when we were going to get to that one." The sight of the lifeless body of the artist, who hadn't painted it, flashed behind my eyelids. I don't know which rattled me more: the world's loss of future paintings by this artist or how my rage took over and made me chase the gunman without rational thought. Figuring that out would have to wait. "*You* knew it was at NMWA. Did *she?*" How deep did her involvement go? Other people had to be involved. I interrupted him before he could answer. "Wait, how did you find out it was there?" Julia Belvedere Jones agreed to handle it quietly. As far as I could tell, neither she nor Linda had made the artist's charge public. That all changed with the murder, not before.

"I don't know. Maybe I didn't know it was there." He covered his ears with his hands.

Body language cliches swirled in the air. Now he was going to start lying to me? "Of course, you knew. It's not like when Linda Ensign called you, you said, *Shame*—what's that?" I had just answered my own question about Bettina, knowing the painting was at NMWA. Of course, she did, and she knew it was exhibited as a Julia Belvedere Jones painting. And she told Crawford.

Now, he pulled on bits of his hair. "I just wanted to help poor Bettina. And now I need you to help me!"

"Oh, God, Crawford. You knew who really painted *Shame* before your last conversation with Linda." One or both of my friends, he and Linda, were in serious legal trouble. Probably him, since two people working at Macquarie knew the painting was misattributed.

"Yesterday was the first and only time I ever talked to Linda Ensign. She called me, looking for Bettina. I was about to tell her what I knew, but she cut me off. I mean, she hung up the phone on me." He twisted in his chair and looked out the window, then turned back to me.

I believe she cut him off to hurry and tell us about Bettina. She was practically in hysterics when she banged on the door with news. She needed Macquarie's Bettina Vogt to clear all of this up and had learned that wasn't going to happen. I didn't buy the part about him being on the verge of telling her what he knew about the painting. "You mentioned art students using copying as a learning tool, but the Rembrandt is the only copy. There is a *Self-Portrait, 1650.* The other two I've been involved with were original, just not by the artists the sellers claimed."

"Yeah. What a talent! I mean, multi-talented. She was, or is, please God, one of those rare people with magic in their hands."

"There are more dots to connect. How did *Shame* get to NMWA, and how did her Rembrandt get to Sutton House?"

"This is where it gets a little woo-woo. And I need you to keep this part on the down low."

"I'm the queen of that."

"Even with your hub being who he is?"

I tilted my head and looked down, telegraphing that this was regretfully so.

"The next week, I went to lunch with a friend who works at Sutton House. I met him in his office."

"Crawford, you sat on this knowledge for a week? Why?" Did not look good.

"It was agony. Please don't tell anyone." I would help him make a deal with the Manhattan D.A.. That's what I would do. "Anyway, you'll never guess what was delivered to him that very morning."

"Bettina's Rembrandt?"

"Yup, it had that bent corner, but it wasn't in a pillowcase. Supposedly, it was delivered by a courier. The paperwork said it came from a gallery in London. He showed it to me. The delivery was signed for by one of his part-time employees, Bettina Vogt, who was, *hello-o-o,* supposed to be working for me at Macquarie."

"Oops," I said. "What are the odds that you, of all people, would be there to see that? I can just imagine the look on your face. What's your friend's name?"

"I'll text it to you," he said.

"Thanks. Don't forget," I said. My chignon felt tight – too tight – and I ran my finger along my scalp beneath it. "Did you tell him what you knew?"

"I told him it was not by Rembrandt, or his workshop, or a follower. Of course, he wanted me to tell him how I knew that when I'd only seen it for, like, a second. I didn't, and we argued."

"Even if he thought you were just giving your opinion, didn't he have doubts? I mean, Old Masters don't just show up."

"Believe me, he's trying to slow this train down. Still! It was delivered so close to the Old Masters show. Everyone wanted it in there. The review process started, and all of a sudden, it was like the clock sped up."

"Crawford, why did you keep protecting her? At that point, you knew she was playing a role at your gallery and at Sutton House, but neither you nor her mother want to talk about that."

He hung his head. "I don't know. She was my friend, and it's easy to get in over your head in this world. Emma, you know that." He sighed and looked up. "Even if you haven't experienced it yourself."

Other than constantly, I've never felt that way. "You were right to be concerned about her. She didn't get money for the Lempicka, but she did for *Shame*, right? It remains to be seen if she'll be paid for the Rembrandt. But, still."

"She was paid for the Belvedere Jones forgery?" he asked, twisting his neck, his voice full of skepticism.

"Someone was paid $15 million. I assumed it was her." Actually, Taylor Tyndale and the *New York Times* assumed it was paid to Julia Belvedere Jones, but they didn't know what I knew. Since the money was frozen, it was doubtful Bettina would ever see it. Could she be the CEO of the newly formed corporation it went to?

"Coming into that much money doesn't track with her mood. Or maybe she was worried about getting caught. That would take the fun out of it." He hoisted himself off the chair. "I need to get back to the gallery."

Not so fast. "Crawford, what does she look like? She's not listed on the website for Sutton House or Macquarie Gallery.

"In her late twenties. Dressed like a teenager."

"Why do you think there weren't any photographs in her mother's apartment of the two of them?" I asked.

"Oh, I didn't notice."

"It was Bettina who talked the Tyndales into offering that crazy high price for what they think is a Rembrandt."

He leaned forward. "How much?"

I used charade hand signs to answer. Six. Five. Zero.

"Six hundred and fifty dollars? For a Rembrandt?"

"Million. $650 million."

"Are you shitting me, Emma?"

I assured him I was not. "Supposedly, her mother told her about this other buyer. I don't think there is one." Could the girl not even trust her mother? I thought about my relationship with mine. No one could trust me, but I could trust my parents. "Did you ever meet the person she started a relationship with last year?"

"Nope. It seemed turbulent. Like he was controlling, then unavailable. I think he was older. Maybe married."

"Why do you think that?"

"He was in the field. I ask you, why else wouldn't she tell me his name? She was afraid I would know him."

The FBI would find the mystery man on her phone or social media. They probably already knew more about Bettina Vogt than her mother did. "But you don't know what he did? Was he an artist, too? Or did he work at a gallery?"

"I never sussed that out. I doubt he was an artist. Not after all the promises he made her. He was going to take her from emerging artist to mid-career to blue-chip. Before you ask, I don't know how he intended to do that. Was he going to get her gallery representation? Or handle promotion?" He threw his hands up. "No idea."

I had another question, but it had to be handled carefully, or I would create curiosity where it hadn't been before. Bettina chose to paint Bathsheba, King David, and Uriah as me, Elliott, and Jason. Why? I couldn't tell Crawford about that. "Did she say she ever met me?"

"Nope. When I offered to introduce you two, she was excited and thanked me. Gotta run. Give me a hug. Talk later?"

I escorted him to the lobby. "Crawford, why did she do it? Most forgers have a grudge against the art establishment, like what her mother wanted me to believe. Do you think she does?"

"I've read that about the big-name forgers. They want revenge! I don't know. Hm, maybe."

"There's this image of art forgers as scamps, pulling one over on the man, but they corrupt the intellectual underpinning of the art market," I said.

He put a hand in his jacket pocket and swiveled his elbow out for me to link my arm in it. "I know, and this was self-inflicted. She, like so many forgers, had the talent. She wanted to make it big, and I wanted that for her."

"Crawford, why are you using past tense?" I unhooked my arm so I could face him. Then I took a closer look into his eyes.

"Am I? I didn't realize I was." He readjusted the horrible tie, giving me a proud papa smirk. "I rise above your mockery."

It was a *you had to see it to believe it* time in the Manhattan art scene. It was fun to experience it with him. He promised to let me know if he heard from Bettina, and I lied and said I would tell him anything I learned. We air kissed at the elevator.

* * *

When I got back to my desk, my phone was ringing. It was Elliott. At least, according to the screen, it was.

"Hi." I waited. "Elliott? Are you there?"

There it was. The hollow sound evil made when it found you. Some part of me always knew he would return. My voice from the void. The one, probably a man, who financed a fundamentalist group with tentacles around the world to attack art last year. The technology he used distorted his speech so well that even the FBI couldn't un-mangle it and get clues to his identity.

I put my phone on speaker with the thumb of one hand and woke up my laptop with the other. The document I started earlier was still there. I clicked on *dictate.*

"Emma!" he shouted. *"Hai fatto proprio una bischerata!"*

Wait, those were clearly spoken words. I didn't know what they meant, but sanctimonious fury sounded the same in any language. He was male, not young, maybe even older than middle age, whatever that meant in today's world. Most of that I'd guessed from our last encounter. Now I knew he was Italian. The next sentence was distorted again, but those few had been clear. Had it been intentional? Did he think my curiosity about his identity would have me squealing with delight over this crumb? "Why did you call?" I asked, assuming what he said was either a threat or a lead-up to one.

"There was a time when my house was not in order. I needed others to do my work. I wanted you, Emma, to be one of them. You failed the test I gave you." As an extra measure, the cadence sped up one minute, slowed the next, which added to the menace. That was new since last year.

"When you asked me to cancel publication of *Art, Religion, and Women?*" Like it had been a polite request. That was the textbook I authored for the class I taught at NYU.

"Yes."

"You said it was the Messengers of Mary fanatics who made that demand." One by one they admitted it in courtrooms around the world at their criminal trials. The lie he told was as disorienting as the shifts in the pace in the computer-manufactured voice, though it was probably hypocritical of me to feel offended. And fibbing paled in comparison to the murders and the destruction of art he was responsible for.

"Their concern was that you wanted to place Mary Magdalene above the Virgin Mary. Mine was broader in scope. You are trying to rewrite art history, and I will not allow that. The fate of the world's masterpieces was at stake. All due to your stubbornness." Re-writing art history? I taught about women in history. He paid Messengers of Mary to vandalize works around the world, and now he wanted to blame me for not preventing it.

80

The psychosis of *look what you made me do* worried me. "Maybe I should express thanks, though. For the new experience. To destroy something irreplaceable made me happier than I have been in years. Think about that concept. Every day, more people are born, more money is made. Art is different." He paused. Maybe he wanted a response from me, but I didn't have one to give. "The monks are in prisons around the world." Was that a sigh I heard? "Thankfully, my family is once again united." Meaning he would get along fine without the incarcerated or scattered group, the Messengers of Mary. "Shall I introduce you to one of them?" I didn't answer, and he went on. "Look out the window."

I did as he said.

"Emma, are you there?" the voice asked.

"What am I looking for?" I saw Crawford waiting for Don't Walk to change to Walk so he could cross West 58th Street. Was that who he was directing me to see? I sucked in my breath. Was he saying my friend was part of his family? Could or would Crawford tell me who this voice from the void was? The light changed, and he looked both ways. But if he was, could I believe anything he had told me? Before he reached the other side, a van parked at the curb pulled into the street. Why was it accelerating when the light was still red? In a sin by the universe, Crawford turned toward the sound or maybe the movement and was watching when it hit him, full force. The impact threw my friend's body diagonally until it struck the door of a car parked on the other side of the street, then dropped to the ground. The killer sped off. That goddamn tie bounced up and then floated back down to his chest.

Chapter Thirteen

I screamed. Of course, I did. Well, I thought I did. My mouth was open. Maybe no sound came out. Below me, people rippled away from the two points: the intersection and the spot where Crawford's body lay. A few made phone calls, others wiped their eyes, some screamed, most ran away. The murder, because that's what it was, would visit them in their day and night dreams for a long time. I let my forehead drop to the windowpane. It was cold and soothing. Maybe I could stay in that position forever. *Oh, Crawford.*

"Emma?" I rallied at the sound of the mechanical voice and drifted over to the guest chair, where I curled into a fetal position. "I know you're there. Did you enjoy seeing what my family is capable of?"

"Why did you do that?" I spoke as loud as I could without alerting Lynya, or anyone working in a nearby office.

"What happened to your friend was both a cautionary tale and your punishment for interfering with certain recent art sales."

"What?" The collision of what was going on in the art world with these new works and this killer felt like Hiroshima in my head. I wasn't strong enough to go up against him again. Why should I have to be the one? I heard an ambulance outside and went back to the window.

He was talking again, or the computer was. "I was counting on the funds from those transactions for – well, let's call it my *big picture*. I've never interfered with your work, your real work – what you live and breathe for." I ran to my desk to look at my laptop. Still recording. "Actually, I admire what you're doing and wish you luck. I'm simply asking for the same consideration. Have I ever lied to you? Or blackmailed you?" Stop. Even if I clipped that section, the FBI would be able to reconstruct it.

"You just lied to me. You had my friend killed because of what Bettina told him. It wasn't just to teach me a lesson. You haven't tried to blackmail me *yet*." He never had. His hit man had tried it. One of my friends shot him dead. That was okay, though. He needed killing. He would have come in handy now. "Why haven't you?" I asked.

"One should always play fairly when one has the winning cards, in the words of Sir Joseph Duveen." Name dropper. "And I do, Emma. Make no mistake. Now, before we say goodbye, you may ask me anything." He didn't add, 'and I'll answer.'

"Is Bettina Vogt alive?"

The sound he made was like a snort. "She strapped on a suicide vest the minute she crossed me."

"She painted the three works for you. Maybe more," I reminded him.

"The Rembrandt wasn't painted as I instructed. It was to have been a seascape. A ship is tossed in a storm, and a member of the crew is a self-portrait. Do you know the one?"

I covered my lips with my hand to keep everything I felt in. The painting he described was Rembrandt's *Christ in The Storm on the Sea of Galilea*. He wanted the world to think that Graham's collection included work from one of the most famous art heists in history. It was stolen in 1990 from the Isabella Stewart Gardner Museum, the largest property crime in US history. Probably mob-related. It was sixty-three inches by about fifty inches, whereas *Self-Portrait 1650* was a fraction of that. And it wasn't painted on copper. Bettina Vogt painted just the opposite and stopped his plan. Who was she? Why would she try to help me? Or was he lying again? If she painted the piece from the Gardner Museum, the minute Sutton House saw the painting, they would call the police. It would never be sold.

"What was the purpose of the fake provenance?" I asked.

"She thought she could paint something saleable and then retire. When I realized what she did, I made lemonade out of lemons, isn't that what you say? Goodbye, Emma." The first words were transmitted at a slow tempo, and the last at double time. As disorienting as his lies.

"Did you also tell her how you wanted *Shame* painted?" Without intending to, I spoke at varying speeds.

"That was fun. Wasn't it, Emma?" My friend lay dead or dying on the street, and he was making sick jokes? "I have to go now. I will leave you with this. If you have suspicions about other works of art that go up for sale, you will keep them to yourself. You will not interfere. Do you understand?" He waited. "Emma?"

"The subjects in *Shame*, Bathsheba, King David, and Uriah were portrayed in a way to draw me in—to get my attention. Now you're telling me to back away. Why? Isn't that a contradiction?"

"I couldn't resist. Anyway, connoisseurship is a bit, uh, performance-y. Wouldn't you agree? No matter. It's beneath us."

"What do you need so much money for?"

"War is expensive."

That was all it took for my mind to choose a road to take. I hung up and closed my office door on the off-chance Valerie had staggered in. I was again a woman with blood coursing through her veins instead of the world's expectations. Left. Right.

My first call was to Taylor Tyndale to say that Graham and Emmaline Abbott still owned *Self-portrait, 1650*, but it was painted on canvas, not copper. She told me I had saved them $650 million and hung up. *You're welcome.*

My next call was to Elliott. I didn't care if anyone was listening in. "That gallerist, Bettina Vogt, *was* the forger. She painted *Shame*, *Kizette in a Green Bugatti*, and the painting Sutton House was about to sell as a Rembrandt. I don't know what else." I told him the Tyndale sale was off. "Not only is it not by Rembrandt, but it wasn't painted by anyone in his orbit. I think Sutton House and Macquarie Gallery will cooperate with your Art Crime Team now." I didn't have Crawford's friend's name to give him, and now I never would.

"God," he said. I heard his chair squeak when his weight dropped onto it. "Looking at it like that, suicide almost makes sense, but not with the note and body not being found in the same place. Don't worry. If she's on the run, it's just a matter of time before we catch her."

They wouldn't find her. Should I tell him? No. There would be too much to leave out. I didn't want to tell him I'd seen a friend murdered. The witnesses on the street would report the hit and run. I would give him something else.

"I visited her mother. She and Taylor Tyndale went to a posh boarding school together. Her name is Vanessa-Maria Boscolo." Then I gave him her address. That might have been oversharing. Was the Voice who she thought would protect her daughter? He or someone working for him promised to turn her career around. To make her a famous artist. Once again, he preyed on his victim's truest desire, then he had her killed.

"Can DNA left on a pillowcase transfer to something carried inside it?" I asked. Without Crawford, there was no evidence that she was the forger. *Self-Portrait 1650* might be resurrected by one of Stephan Tyndale's experts sometime in the future. Maybe the next time as by *a follower of.*

"Why?" I told him the minimum and that it was at Bettina's apartment. He would tell someone to get her address from her employer. He had me on speaker, and he was typing. "I thought I had some good news for you, but it's been OBE." Overcome by events. "We didn't find that drawing of flowers and bones on anything else by Julia Belvedere Jones."

"Copying a drawing that she used would have been a pretty sophisticated move for a forger. I didn't get the feeling Bettina Vogt was that."

"Since she painted the Rembrandt, do you recommend testing it? To see if there's a drawing underneath?"

Doubtful. I told him not to go to the trouble. The copper sheet was probably sanded by the artist to get the sublime effect the *New York Times* described.

"How did you find out she's the forger?"

"I'd rather not say. Do you need that information to have that $15 million returned to the National Museum for Women in the Arts and the National Endowment for the Humanities?"

"I don't think so, Babe, but when they find her, and she's charged, you'll need to testify about how you learned it." Professional. No emotional blackmail.

85

"Fair." An easy promise to keep.

Chapter Fourteen

WEDNESDAY IN SEA ISLAND, GEORGIA

Emma!" Hillary Kelly, my mom, called out to me, waving her arm over her head. She stood by their silver, electric Mini Cooper at the curb in front of the Brunswick Golden Isles airport. We'd flown Delta Airlines from Washington, DC to Atlanta, and after an hour layover, on to the airport closest to Sea Island, Georgia.

"Elliott! Over here." My dad, Hunter Kelly, stood next to a white Ford F-150 parked behind her little car.

They were both baby boomer Leos. Both stood five feet, nine inches tall, and had a medium, solid build. Today, they both wore blue jeans and blue jean shirts. My parents matched. Except for Mom's black eye patch. Dad ironed his pants himself, even blue jeans. That knife-edge crease was a standard he kept. All my life.

"What's this?" I pointed to the truck.

"We were afraid your tall husband wouldn't be able to stand if he rode the twenty miles home in a damn clown car, so we rented this. We're going full-Griswold today." My father laughed and tossed Elliott the keys.

After hugs all around, both of my parents checked me for wear and tear, then smiled with approval.

* * *

I looked over at my mother because she had stopped talking mid-sentence. She drove fast all the time, but had suddenly sped up to twenty or thirty miles over the posted speed limit.

"No brakes! Fuck." This, from the woman for whom using blue ink for social correspondence was a mortal sin. She stamped her foot on the floorboard. "And the accelerator is stuck," she hissed through clenched teeth.

Now, we gained even more speed, closing the distance between us and Elliott and my dad in the F-150.

I steadied myself with my hands on the dash. "Mom, you have to pass them." No choice. "We'll pass on the right. I'll help you." She nodded without looking away from the truck. My phone rang, but there wasn't time to answer it. I assumed it was Elliott. "Ready?" If we didn't change lanes soon, we would ram them or at least clip their bumper. She turned on her right signal indicator. "Three. Two. One." She changed lanes, and we sped past them. We had open road ahead of us, and we hurdled along. She still had control of the little car. "Like riding a bike?"

She smiled weakly. Hillary and Hunter Kelly both retired from the U.S. Secret Service five years ago. They moved to Sea Island, Georgia, in Glynn County and took contractor jobs at the Federal Law Enforcement Training Center in Glynco, Georgia. Glynco wasn't a real city, it was named for Glynn County. Until three years ago, she was a Driver Training instructor at FLETC. She had skills.

Her eyes darted to the exit ramp ahead, then back to the road ahead.

"Are we getting off?" I asked.

"Not steep enough to slow us down." She tried the brakes again. Nothing. We raced past that option. The small car floated over the road.

"Don't you dare," she yelled to someone. An SUV drove down the entrance ramp to the highway. She blew the horn. He pulled onto the road in front of us. We were inches away, and I waited for the impact. It didn't come because she swerved into the middle lane. Elliott, in his truck, moved to the far left lane, then he was in front of us. Wasn't this what we just got ourselves out of? His brake lights came on, and I understood what he was doing. Before I had time to tense, we bounced off his bumper. His brake lights went off, and he pulled ahead a few feet. The metal-on-metal contact was fleeting, but a sound like a buzz saw rang in my ears. He slowed again, and the car and truck hit once more. The sound was horrifying, and this time, my teeth rattled, but it seemed we were slowing down. "Good boy," my mom said. *Boy?*

I heard a car pull up by us on the passenger side. A Georgia State Patrol officer, driving with lights flashing, saluted me and nodded.

"Again," my mother said to get my attention and to warn me, just as we collided with Elliott a third time. Everything quieted. Our engine was off, and we slowed to a roll. Without power steering, she had to practically wrestle the car to the side of the road. The state police car drove off into the distance.

We got out of the car, and my mother walked around to me. I was about to hug her since she'd saved our lives when I was whirled around by my shoulders. Elliott scooped me into a hug and buried his head into my neck. He exhaled, and it sounded like, *haaaaa.* He breathed out tension, fear, relief, exhaustion.

"Everybody okay?" my dad asked, as he jabbed the screen of his phone. "I'm calling USAA." He turned away to speak to the roadside service employee.

"I have internal injuries," I called out.

"Concussion here," Elliott added.

"Wimps," he said.

"Take an aspirin." My mom walked around to examine the front of the car. Jason, preferring to criticize rather than join in, never got used to my family's odd sense of humor. It had taken Elliott only a month or so. He rarely, if ever, coddled me or put me on a pedestal. Maybe that's why, to me, he felt like home.

Dad joined her, and they shook their heads at the damage to the grill. "It was like the little car gave up," he said.

"It didn't give up," she said. "It defeated whatever was done to it." Her glance at him was brief, but not quick enough to get by me. She moved her weight to the left, then right.

"What do you mean?" I asked.

"Hillary, you're being paranoid. And you might be a little sleep-deprived."

My mother inhaled indignation and seemed to grow taller.

"Look out," I whispered to Elliott. "She's about to blow."

And she did. "I couldn't sleep because the motion sensor lights kept coming on all night. How would my lack of sleep make the electronics network in my car go haywire, anyway?"

"Where'd Ricky go? He was the closest state police officer." The look on his wife's face and her hands on her hips told him his attempt to change the subject might have been unwise. "How many times did we go outside to check? Half a dozen. There wasn't anyone out there."

My mom turned on her heel. "Elliott!"

"Yes, ma'am, I mean, Hillary?"

Then she started laughing with the hit of adrenaline and relief. "I don't know what's so funny." She bent and held her waist. "I do have a serious question for you." She laughed more and wiped her eyes. "A hacker could override my car's network, right?"

"Mechanics have been—let's call it *reprogramming* engines to get more horsepower for decades. Today's cars run on computer chips, so you could even do it remotely. Why would anyone want to?" I saw the squint of his eye. Anger did that.

"That's just it," Dad said. "No one would."

We turned at the sound of another vehicle pulling up behind ours. My dad went up to the state police officer and held out his hand. He said something to him that I couldn't hear. Then louder, "Ricky, thanks for coming so quick." The two men walked up to us.

"I wasn't needed as it turned out." He turned to Elliott. "That was some quick thinking." Elliott nodded, and they shook hands, then we went to look at the rear of the truck and the front of the Mini Cooper.

Ricky pushed his hat back and scratched his head. "I don't have to write up an accident report because there wasn't one. An accident, I mean. Mr. Kelly, if you'll let me know what the mechanic finds, I'll follow up then."

"*Suuuure*," my parents said at the same time.

"Glad everybody's okay. Have a nice rest of your day."

"Dig you later," we four said in unison, but we didn't laugh the way we usually did. That was my Dad's stock goodbye. I knew it was coming the way I knew the sun would rise tomorrow.

We didn't speak again until he drove off. "What just happened?" I asked. Both parents looked at the ground and shrugged. "Take your time. I've got nothing to do until the tow truck comes."

"We're going to handle this ourselves. Ricky's fine with that," Mom said.

My dad draped his arm over her shoulders. "We haven't been in the field for a long time, but there are some counterfeiters in the area who might remember us. We'll start by—"

I couldn't let them waste time thinking the person who had sabotaged the car was from their past. My parents hadn't worked either for the government or as contractors since before the pandemic. Too far back for the settling of scores or grudges. And what about the timing? The attempt was made during my visit. I could choke on that much coincidence. The hacker was someone in my Voice from the Void's family or someone he hired. What had I started? "Mom? Dad? I think this was because of me."

The air went still. Breezes, birds, everything.

Elliott ran his hand over his head and looked at the horizon, then turned back. "You may find this hard to swallow, but there are people out there that get their nose bent out of joint when they find out they're not going to get the $3 million they expected for selling a counterfeit painting. Others who get sore that the painting they just paid fifteen million dollars for is worthless." My mom and then my dad turned their heads in slow motion to stare at me.

"Emma? You did that? You were able to find out those paintings were fake?" The pride and love in my mother's eyes nearly broke my heart. What would happen when they learned my secret? Would the big picture of why I did what I was doing justify it for them? I believed all the way to my core that finding *Portrait of a Young Man* and restoring it to Poland did. Would they? Would the world?

I nodded.

Elliott went on. "*And* she stopped someone from buying a fake Rembrandt for $650 million."

"But that's a good thing," my dad said.

"Not to the guy who was going to get the big payout," Elliott said.

Dad looked at him. "You got this?"

Elliott nodded. With the hand not on my back, he pointed to the Mini Cooper. "This is a convenient time for you to have your car in the shop."

"No such thing." Mom finally peeled her eyes off me.

"Your belated Christmas gift from us is a cruise. You should take it now," Elliott said.

Chapter Fifteen

We were on the balmy Georgia coast, and my parents weren't of Scandinavian descent, but their house was decorated in what they explained to me was known as lagom, pronounced luh-gohm, which replaced hygee as an interior design concept, pronounced hoo-gah. The first word meant balance, and the other meant cozy. I didn't know one from the other, but after the day we'd had, I was all in and let myself sink into this sense of quiet and comfort. I stared at the tray ceiling, painted a rich taupe, of the guest room and wondered if going on a cruise would keep my parents safe. Elliott's admin made the arrangements, including their flights to Miami. They were on the phone finalizing everything my parents would need.

He climbed into bed and snuggled close, spooning. "I have to tell you something." I turned my head, and he whispered in my ear. "Bettina Vogt's body was found." I gasped and searched under the covers for his hand. *Careful, for you, suicide was still on the table.* I knew she was dead. Hadn't doubted it for a minute after my caller told me she was. I'd never met the woman, but still, it made me sad. "It gets worse. All they have is her torso—wrapped in plastic."

I rolled over to face him. "Was she found in a river?"

"Yes, the Hudson! How did you know that?"

"That's how a Russian art dealer named Aleksandr Levin was found. He was found in the IJ River, along the Amsterdam waterfront. The Dutch police think he was killed by a Russian gang or the FSB."

"Are you saying this woman was killed by the Russians?"

"No. By any chance, was she wrapped in blue plastic?"

"Yeah."

"So was Levin. I think someone's trying too hard to get you to connect those two murders."

He grunted in agreement. "We're looking for other people she sold her fakes to. Macquarie or Sutton House should be able to help us with that. With the prices she was getting for them, I can't say I'm surprised it would come to this. We want to know who she was working with."

I hadn't told him the Voice was back. "You don't think she was alone? There's no reason to think Macquarie Gallery or Sutton House knowingly helped, is there?"

"Un-uh. But with what happened to Julia Belvedere Jones and then to Hillary's car…. This is more than an art crime. And there's something else. I was going to hold off telling you this for now. We were looking for a male who visited Bettina's mother just before you. Was he at the apartment when you were there? Or was anyone?"

"No, just the maid," I lied and trusted they'd never find Vanessa-Maria. I didn't care about the housekeeper. She was like an actress in a silent movie. Good luck getting anything out of her. How *did* Crawford get that address? Taylor Tyndale gave it to me, but how did he get it?

"So this guy, the visitor, was the victim of a hit and run the same day." We were still whispering in the dark but holding hands tight.

Careful. "But it wasn't an accident? Has anyone been arrested?"

"No, stolen van, and it happened so fast witnesses couldn't ID the driver. A couple of them even thought it was an accident."

A huff escaped before I could stop myself. Un-seeing that van as it sped away was not a thing. Getting to the bottom of this dumpster fire was. He could chase after a cheated art buyer, but I knew it was the Voice.

"Has anyone told her mother?" Who was going to tell her that her daughter had not been protected?

"She's gone. Flew out of JFK to Italy."

"As far as she knows, her daughter is still missing. And she left the country?"

"Yup," he said, snuggling and closing any gaps between our knees, thighs, bodies. "Anyway, the apartment was locked up tight. The woman never really lived there. The landlord let NYPD in. It looked like no one lived there. At first, no one would admit to seeing her. Not the doorman, not the guy at the desk, no neighbors. Security camera footage showing her coming and going Monday and Tuesday jogged some memories. As it tends to do."

"What was it? A high-class VRBO?" How did Crawford know about the address? Bettina would hardly have listed it on her employment application, but maybe she told him.

"Dunno." He was fading. "The NYPD detective said there were a lot of antiques, but nothing on the walls. Was it like that when you were there? Is that what they do with those rentals."

"I saw paintings on the wall." Had Vanessa-Maria taken the artwork with her? "How about the housekeeper?"

He yawned. "Didn't know there was one. I doubt we could find her anyway. I may ask for fingerprints."

Was I on one of those videos? I had made the right decision to tell him about visiting the woman. "Are you going to extradite Bettina's mother?"

"She hasn't committed a crime. Who knows, maybe she'll want to talk when she knows we're looking for her daughter's murderer." As Bobbi would say, "cute." The FBI would never hear from Vanessa-Maria Boscolo. "Let's get some sleep."

"Not yet." I rolled on top of him.

Chapter Sixteen

Elisa Pesarini, Director of the Vatican Museums, returned my call at eight o'clock on Thursday morning, as I sat alone in the kitchen, studying *Shame*'s under-drawing on my computer tablet. The FBI expanded the search from looking for it on a site referencing Julia Belvedere Jones but hadn't had any hits. I knew Bettina Vogt drew it, but what did it mean? It was early afternoon in Rome, so I thanked my friend for letting us sleep in. "I need a favor," I said.

"Go ahead. I need your help with something, too." She agreed readily. After a couple of rounds of *you first, no, you first,* she asked, "Do you remember Colonel Guy Marra? The Commandant of Pontifical Swiss Guards?"

"Yes." Though not fondly.

"He wishes to speak with you. Will you take his call?"

"As long as he doesn't want a confession out of me." She laughed at that. Elisa had the crazy notion that I was religious but didn't know that I was. "What does he want to talk about?"

She didn't answer, and I wondered if the call had dropped. "I would rather he explain it." Her words were doled out one by one. "I will say that someone put a notion in the Holy Father's head which may have frightened him."

"He's the pope. If he has a problem, he should talk to God."

"God doesn't need a favor in return. You do."

"True. Give Colonel Marra my number. I'm about to send you a line someone said to me in Italian. I don't understand what Google Translate says it means. Would you decipher it for me?"

"Why would anyone who knows you not write in English?" she asked, putting the call on speaker.

"I took a screenshot, so you'll see the Italian version and the translation."

"Emma, when are you going to learn Italian?"

"Never. Has it come?"

"Hai fatto proprio una bischerata," she read.

"Google translate says that means 'you really made a biscuit.' What does that mean?"

"Your friend is from Tuscany? Most likely a Florentine?" she asked.

"He's not a friend. Are you saying he's from Florence?"

"Most probably. It's a common expression. It is similar to your 'takes the cake,' but maybe more critical. Like if someone does something stupid."

That fit. He yelled my name before the phrase. And it described how he felt about me discrediting the three works of art.

"When you speak to Colonel Marra, don't mention that I said the Holy Father was scared. He would not appreciate that I used that word about him." There was a protocol for talking about the only elected monarch in the world. She thought she may have violated it.

"Don't worry, Elisa. You didn't make a biscuit." My mother came into the kitchen, carrying a basket of eggs from her chickens and flowers from her greenhouse, so I ended the call.

"Do you want biscuits, Emma?"

I told her that sounded nice and reached for the flowers in the sea grass straw basket. "Want me to arrange these?" She wore a tan gauzy midi skirt and a white button-down with a shawl around her shoulders, looking like a Coastal Grandmother ad in a high-end magazine. Her mother, my grannie, was a fashion designer in 1950s Atlanta. Style was a DNA requirement to be born into our family. Today's eye patch was a winter scene with tiny white flowers. I pointed to my own eye. "New?"

She nodded and handed me two Mason jars and snips to shorten the stems.

"Was that your friend who works at the Vatican?"

"Un-huh."

"I would love to see her again. When she and her family come back to the States they're welcome to stay with us. It's so peaceful here. Don't you agree?

It might be just what she needs with everything that's going on. I thought I'd make a frittata." She flitted over topics in a conversation like a butterfly.

"What do you mean?"

"All those articles in the newspapers about how poorly the Vatican is run."

"There hasn't been anything in the Times for a while. Are you talking about the pedophilia disgrace?" I turned each jar around to check for renegades that might have escaped my clippers.

"As far as I'm concerned, that's their biggest problem, but then there's everything else. Missing money, auditors fired, toxic fertilizer on the grounds making dogs sick, staff shortages, unsafe work conditions. God knows what else."

My parents were devout atheists, and I wondered if that gave her a more negative view of the city-state. "Where did you hear all this?"

"Different newspapers. Google it."

"I will." I picked up my phone. "I wonder why none of that has been in the *New York Times*." There they were. Reputable news outlets around the country showed up in the Google search. Each article I clicked on told of some way the Vatican had gone to hell with itself.

"Poor Elisa," she said.

"I didn't see any criticism of the Vatican Museums. Thank goodness."

"Yet, at least. Where's Elliott?" Mom asked.

"I'm supposed to say he went for a run."

"But he and your father are checking all our security cameras one last time before we go?" she asked, though it was more of a statement.

"Yes, they want to be sure none have been tampered with, disabled or taken offline. The trip sounds nice. Do you mind going?" They would fly out of Fort Lauderdale and cruise to the Panama Canal, with several stops in Central America along the way.

"Not at all. Our fortieth anniversary is this year. It's a lovely way to celebrate. And it's for the best. I'm a much better shot than your father, you know. Should I worry?"

I laughed. "Worry about Dad?"

"Should I worry about what will happen to the guy who hacked our car if he comes back and I'm still here—I think not. It's better that we go." She looked down at my tablet. "Lilies, roses, carnations."

"Not very interesting, are they?"

"They're all funeral flowers. Plus, they are all fragrant, so your house would smell like a funeral home."

"Elliott says those are cadaver bones."

"What's the artist's message?" she asked.

"I have no idea." I shook my head. Was Bettina bringing the dead to be with the living or the living to the dead? "She died a few days ago. I wonder if she knew her days were numbered?" Did Bettina know who she was up against?

"We die when we die. That's it."

"I certainly hope you're not going to talk like that the whole time we're on our cruise," my dad said, walking in the backdoor. Elliott was behind him. "What are you cooking? Smells good."

According to Elliott, Hillary and Hunter Kelly had the same speaking rhythm. "Enough short sentences, non sequiturs, rhetorical questions to fill a Mini Cooper."

I thought the forced cheerfulness in my dad's voice would break my heart. We all knew why they had to leave, and I knew it was my fault. I had brought danger to them. Nothing remotely hygee about it.

The past year, whenever I thought about them finding out how I really lived, I imagined their shock, pain, shame. Now, in this house, I felt certain that at least the last reaction wouldn't be there. The dagger-sharp creases on his chinos told me so.

We talked about everything except what we really thought while Mom cooked. Gentle jokes about long-married couples. Hurricane predictions for this year along the Georgia coast. And 'It's not the heat, it's the humidity.'

My dad asked about the legs of the flight I would take to London, where I had a case, or so I told all of them. "We're lucky. Our flight to Fort Lauderdale and Elliott's and yours to Atlanta are close together. Elliott, how long do you have in Atlanta to make the connection to DC?"

"He's going back home to New York," I corrected him.

"Actually, I have to go back to Washington," Elliott said, sheepishly.

"Why?" I asked.

"Discharging his firearm in a public place, and I'm glad he did," Hunter said.

"I thought that was all settled because Georgia and I were in imminent danger of being killed. The DC Police didn't even take your gun."

Elliott shrugged his shoulders. "I don't know who called for the investigation. One minute, everyone was telling me it was justified. Then, on Tuesday, something happened."

"Tuesday?" I asked.

"Breakfast is ready. Let's sit down and eat," my mother said.

After we took our places around the kitchen table, Elliott said, "I got a call that night from a bud." He picked up his coffee cup for a toast. "To the importance of the heads up."

It was after the Tyndales passed on the Rembrandt. The voice from the void made this happen. I needed to know more about him than where he was from and that he had a very mean family. I needed to know where to find him. I wanted to kill him. Maybe balance was better than cozy? If I couldn't have hygee, then I would settle for lagom.

"Do you want me to stay?" I asked him. I could get out of the affair at the Victoria and Albert Museum.

"No, we need at least one paycheck."

"It won't get that bad, will it?" Mom asked, her brow furrowed.

Elliott took a stack of plates to the table. "Hope not. But, hey, you've got plenty of room here, right?"

We sat down to eat frittata and biscuits, and I thought about three fragrant flowers and three bones from a dead person, or people, drawn by a dead person.

Why did it feel like a message? Had any famous forgers left messages like that? I realized with a jolt that, yes, there was one. The most famous forger of them all—Tom Keating. He called them time bombs. They were known to go off when one rich person sold a fake to another rich person.

Chapter Seventeen

Elliott and I loaded the dishwasher while my parents packed their suitcases. I told him about my theory that the drawing was Bettina Vogt's way of getting a message to me.

"Why you?"

"She recommended me as the mediator with the National Museum for Women in the Arts," I reminded him. "She knew I would see *Shame.*"

"That means she knew you, not why she picked you. I'm asking, why *you.*"

"I don't know." I couldn't tell him what Crawford said about her reaction when news of the *Kizette in a Green Bugatti* fraud broke. She trusted me to catch her. Instead, I told him my theory on the drawings being time bombs, and about Thomas Keating. "Some forgers hide clues to their paintings' inauthenticity in their forgeries."

"They want to get caught?" he asked.

"Keating certainly didn't want to be arrested. He loved to embarrass art experts. Other forgers have used it as a get-out-of-jail-free card. Say you paint a tiny modern object in an eighteenth-century painting. Later, you could say you weren't trying to fool the buyer and that your work wouldn't fool anyone." He hand washed, and I dried the cast iron pan. We talked but kept our voices down.

"But you think she drew the flowers and bones to send you a message, because she knew she was in danger and didn't care if we found out she was the artist?"

"Maybe."

I went back to deciphering the drawing. Its secret had to be in the number three. Three strikes, you're out. Three blind mice. Third time's a charm. The subject was from the Bible, was it the trinity? Three's compa.... Left. Right. Three wise men! Their bones were said to be in the Cologne Cathedral. Cologne. Fragrant flowers. I had to go there. Who? Emma? Or Emmaline? My mind raced.

"Babe?" Elliott touched my arm. "I didn't tell your dad everything. It's not just the DC police who want to talk to me. It's the FBI, too. The Office of Professional Responsibility is looking into Jason's death again. Someone told them their opinion on what the painting was implying happened the night Jason died." The insinuation was that he sent Jason out that night to get him killed. Or maybe, if he didn't know that's what would happen, then he should have. And it was done for Elliott to have his wife, me.

"Elliott!" I tossed the dishtowel onto the counter and wrapped my arms around his neck. Valerie tried to spread that poison, but since she was drunk most of the time, no one listened. She'd finally given up. Or so I thought. "Do you think Valerie heard about the painting?"

He shook his head. "I don't think she would stoop that low." I wasn't so sure.

"She hasn't said anything to me. Are you sure you don't want me to go to DC with you?" I wanted to stay, but I needed him to tell me to go. Until I decided if Emma or Emmaline would be in Cologne, I couldn't tell him that's where I would be and why. I was going to London to work on an art theft case; then I would go to the Vatican. We would leave it at that.

"Absolutely not. After the three murders, I'm happy for you to be far away in a different country." He pulled me in for another hug. His hands on my back were wet, and there was a fragrance of testosterone. "All I need to know is that you don't hold me responsible for Jason's death. I was his supervisor—"

"I have never thought that for a second," I interrupted. "I remember how you and everyone else worked so hard to find the guys that did it."

"Hell, yeah, it was about one of our own! It was all thoroughly investigated at the time."

My phone rang with a call from Italy, according to the country code, thirty-nine. "It's the Vatican. I'm sorry. Do you mind?"

"It's fine. Go," he said.

I took the call in the living room. And took my tablet in case I needed to take notes. "Colonel Guy Marra here." I remembered the large man, with a temper he liked to use to get his way. The day I met him, he was in a bespoke suit that cost what the average Vatican employee earned in six months.

"Good afternoon."

"Signora Pesarini told you what I wanted to discuss?"

"Just that you had some concerns." No need to say who he was concerned about.

"The Holy Father traveled to Greece last year. I believe something happened during that trip that has led to where we are today. He visited the Parthenon after dark, in the company of Ieronymos II, the Orthodox Christian archbishop of Athens." He was also head of the Greek Orthodox Church. "They discussed the Parthenon Marbles."

In the 19th century, the sculptures were chipped out of the Parthenon by Lord Elgin's workers. Most were now in the British Museum. The UK and Greece were holding secret talks on their return. Three fragments, a part of the horse pulling Athena's chariot and the faces of a boy and a man, had been in the Vatican Museum for years. specifically in the Gregoriano Profano Museum, an archaeological museum. Even a staunch supporter of repatriation in this controversy, like me, had to admit they were displayed simply and perfectly, but that was irrelevant.

"Was it during that trip that he decided to return the Vatican's Parthenon marbles?" Some called these the Elgin Marbles, but I preferred the name he and I used.

"If you asked me that question directly after the trip, I would have told you no. While he was there, he asked for forgiveness from God and the people for mistakes of the past. Then, after he returned. a statement was issued that said the donation was a concrete sign of his sincerity." They preferred to call it a donation rather than repatriation. Their word was less loaded legally.

"I think he may have been threatened while he was there."

Had I heard correctly? When I could speak again, I said, "I'm shocked anyone would threaten an eighty-six-year-old. Especially one with a security detail." Or maybe the threat wasn't the kind I was imagining. "What about the article in your Cultural Property Protection Act on the inalienability of collections?" It was illegal to remove items from the Vatican Museum collections.

"We intend to use a different law to return the marbles. The Pope can use what we call supervening powers when urgent or necessary." What I called a legal fiction. "But something else happened that night, other than talks on the return of the antiquities. I believe someone, or something, put the idea of retiring in his head."

"Someone other than his predecessor, you mean? And he's dead, so you can't blame him." That made him laugh out loud. "What would you like me to do?"

"Could you come to Rome? Right away."

"I can be there next week. Can't you tell me more?" I asked. I agreed to come because it was Elisa who asked me to, though I couldn't imagine what they needed me for.

"This is better discussed when you are here," he said. "Not sooner? Where else do you have to be?" I didn't love the pressure he was putting on me.

No one was more important to Marra than the pope. In Elisa's words, the membrane between the two men was more porous than with their predecessors, expressing it as only an Italian could. His protectiveness over his boss was all-encompassing. I would fly to London that night, then Cologne. I didn't know why Bettina was sending me to the German city, but it was more important than going to Rome. I couldn't help the Pope with his retirement plans or with whatever Colonel Marra was hinting.

"I have to go to Toronto first." Why had I thought of that city? "I will see you Monday."

"Monday," he repeated reluctantly and hung up.

Chapter Eighteen

FRIDAY IN LONDON

"Do you mind if I turn this off?" Graham asked before he reached for the car radio.

"Not at all. Haydn is just so Haydn." A memory of Jason popped into my mind. The music would have just disappeared. The radio would be turned off, or the station changed. I never would have been asked. It had not been a good marriage. The drip, drip, drip of disregard. I was always happier when I was away from him. I don't know how long I would have put up with feeling like I was less than a full adult. When I became free, I left all the rules behind.

"Exactly," Graham said with a nod.

Now, it felt good to ride in companionable silence. I needed to think. I'd checked my phone at the airport before I turned it off and saw a message from Valerie. She'd heard from a client, the Wallraf-Richartz Museum, in Cologne, of all places, who wanted to check on their coverage. He was particularly concerned about one very expensive piece of art. A woman had a painting from her collection on loan to the museum. It would be included in a joint exhibition they planned to hold with the cathedral. Could I please go there? **Yes, I could**, I texted her back. She would email me more details. I was going to the Cologne Cathedral because Bettina was sending me there. And now, I would visit the museum, and SIRA would pay for my flight. That was a bonus.

Graham knew I couldn't stay long. Usually, I was in England more than overnight, though. And the time was spent in Bath. I would let him think I was returning to the States. No. Not pressing enough. I would think of something. But *Emma* would go to Cologne.

My last-minute call with Elliott was more troubling. The DC police had lost interest in talking to him about firing his weapon in a public place about as quick as they had gone into it. There was an immediate threat of loss of life. Ditto, the FBI's Office of Professional Responsibility, about Jason's death. There had been an agency-wide, no expense spared, full-court press to find Jason's killers. Elliott hadn't hidden anything. The next day, when the NYPD, along with the FBI, went to arrest the thugs that tortured Jason to death, they were both dead. Kneeling. One shot to each forehead. Close range. Conscious victim. The working theory was that they were killed to keep them quiet. Then why was it handled execution-style? That was the only loose end, and no one spoke of it.

The latest development was that Elliott was being subpoenaed to appear before the House of Representatives Committee on Oversight and Account- ability. *They* wanted to go over the investigation into Jason's murder. It would be a closed meeting and was scheduled for Monday. What was behind this sudden thirst for knowledge? By the United States Congress, no less. There were too many investigations. Like with Stephan Tyndale's thirteen experts. Didn't Washington have more pressing matters?

The only good news he had for me was from his daily call with my dad. My parents were safe and maybe drinking too much. It felt like I was shirking my duty as a daughter for Elliott to take on the job of the daily check-ins rather than me, but he was the one with access to a secure phone. Hard to argue with that.

Graham reached across the Range Rover to me in the passenger seat and massaged my shoulder. "How was your flight?"

"Good. I slept." That much was true. I had let my shoulder-length hair down from the bun at the back of my neck before I dozed off. If I timed it right, I ended up with a soft cascade of hair. A lesson I learned the hard way. On one trip, I forgot. When I woke up, I had bends and curls in my hair that brushing didn't make go away, from it being up in a chignon all night. I wrapped a scarf over my head and tied the ends around my ponytail. A photographer got a shot of this, and within the week, thousands of British women with long hair wore their Hermes scarves that way. Thankfully, the photo was taken from behind while Graham embraced me. That public display of affection was the photographer's object, but the fashion section of the paper saw a different use.

Manhattan had different mood music from London, which was not the same as Bath's. That made it easy for Emmaline to *be* different from Emma. In England, for some reason, the more understated I was with wardrobe and makeup, the more attention I attracted. Before landing, I always scrubbed off the matte makeup and red lipstick and slathered my face with a heavy moisturizer. Something TikTok called slugging. Then I changed jewelry. And just like that, I was Emmaline.

I asked Graham about his two-and-a-half-hour drive from Bath, and he told me about the traffic and road work.

The phone rang, and he answered it on the dash. It was Isabella, one of his sisters. She and Charlotte were forty-eight-year-old twins.

"Tell me you're not staying at the boring Goring," she whined.

"Oh, but we are. Say hello to Emmaline."

"Hullo Emmaline," Isabella called out.

"Hi. We like being boring. And it's a beautiful hotel."

"Your friend, Emma Kelly, has been in the news a lot lately." Whenever I was asked if I knew her, I said we had met or that our paths crossed from time to time. The question usually came with a look at Graham like, if you had to marry an American.... "She is a one-woman happening!" She sighed. "Why don't you want to stay with me in West Brompton?" Why would anyone want to do that? I thought. "Or stay with Char in Knightsbridge. Yeah, do that."

"Sorry, but no," Graham said, no discussion. That was the role he played in the family dynamic. "You'll join us back at The Goring for a late dinner after the V&A?"

"Uh, well, about that. Char and I thought we could go to Tramp. They're

107

members, and it would be so much more fun."

"Not a chance," Graham said.

"Would you at least consider moving our dinner to burgers at Bar Boulud? It's French enough."

I rolled my eyes and mouthed, no. "That's the restaurant in the Mandarin."

"See you tonight at the V&A. You'll bring Mother with you, right?"

"Yes, she's already here." I hadn't thought of their mother, the fearsome matriarch Caroline, who had foregrounded duty her whole life long. I was expected to fill that role in the future. May she live forever. If she was joining us, it would definitely be the V&A and Goring. Certainly not Tramp and burgers anywhere.

"Don't be late." Graham hung up before she suggested any more changes to the evening's plans.

We pulled up to the valet, and someone opened the car door for me. Someone else took our luggage from the boot. "Graham, do you have your EpiPen, or do you need this one?" I motioned to the glove compartment. He was allergic to bee venom.

"I have one in my kit bag," he said. "Want to walk in Hyde Park after we check in?"

* * *

"To Speakers' Corner or along The Serpentine?" Graham asked as I pulled on my gloves. "Might be more private away from the water." It was so cold that there were few people milling around anyway. He took my hand, and we wandered along the path north.

"How would you feel about going to Cologne tomorrow?" he asked.

I hid my surprise at now having three reasons to go there and pretended to give it some thought. "Do you think Bear and Zora will forget me?" The two Giant Schnauzers were my constant companions in Bath. I needed a beat to consider if Emmaline could or should go to Cologne rather than Emma, as I planned.

"They can go for another week without you spoiling them." He kissed the top of my head.

"Wait." My heart skipped a beat, and I let go of his hand to clasp them together. "Is this going where I hope it is?" He had contacts in museums and galleries in major German cities. They were to report any rumor about the Raphael that came their way. "Has someone heard or seen something concerning the Raphael?" That was how we referred to *Portrait of a Young Man* like he had only painted it and then said, 'no more.' I'm done.

He laughed. "Afraid not. Have you heard about the plans for the block-buster show at the Wallraf-Richartz Museum and the Cologne Cathedral of paintings depicting the three kings honoring the Holy Family?"

I told him I had. The exhibit would run for four months and was scheduled to start early next year. "They've asked to borrow Lazzaro Bastiani's, *Adoration of the Magi* from The Frick."

"Well, I learned there will be a test in preparation for the exhibition."

That sounded like the dry run that had made SIRA's policyholder nervous enough to confirm his insurance coverage. Bettina's drawing told me to focus on the Cologne Cathedral and the Tomb of the Three Magi. Now, the museum and cathedral had a joint project.

The Wallraf-Richartz Museum was one of the main museums in Cologne and near the cathedral. The collection grew with donations of art, both large and small. After two large donations of contemporary art, the collection was split. The Museum Ludwig was established to house 20th-century art. In 2001, the Swiss collectors Marisol and Gérard Corboud put their vast Impressionist and Post-Impressionist collections on permanent loan to the museum. The institution was renamed Wallraf-Richartz-Museum & Fondation Corboud—not much to ask. The museum now held the largest Impressionist collection in Germany, including treasures by Morisot and Renoir. In 2008, restorers found a Monet, which was donated in 1954, had been painted with a colorless substance to mimic aging. They kept the non-Monet, with their four authentic works by him. It seemed no museum was immune from forgers.

In this ambitious collab, one by one, paintings depicting this Biblical story would rotate to the cathedral, where the relics of the Magi were, while the others were exhibited in the museum.

The two parties sought commitments for the loan of some of the world's most important paintings. Last year the Frick Collection in New York announced they would close for renovation. Some of their collection moved to a temporary space known as "Frick Madison," but not all. Ordinarily, the institution could not lend its art because of their founding documents, but since the works had to be relocated anyway, there was an opening. The German curators saw a possible opportunity to borrow Lazzaro Bastiani's *Adoration of the Magi.*

"The Frick wants assurance—not insurance, that was a given—that should they decide to loan their painting, it would be safe," Graham said. The idea of insurance for something irreplaceable had a logic problem. It might even make the piece more vulnerable to being stolen for ransom. "The plan is to have an as-of-yet undisclosed artwork transferred from the museum to the cathedral. Representatives from The Frick Collection will be there to observe. That would be interesting to see, don't you think?"

"Yes, but why would anyone put a masterpiece through that?" I asked. He shrugged. Or was it a masterpiece? All I knew about the piece from Valerie was that it was a painting. Without knowing the substrate, what it was painted on, I couldn't know its vulnerability to temperature, light, or moisture. Most accidental damage to art occurred during shipment, compared to, say, a museum visitor tripping and falling against a sculpture. Why gamble with fate and circumstance?

"If The Frick envoys can be convinced it could be done safely, they will lend their painting. Your National Gallery of Art is expected to follow with their Botticelli, *The Adoration of the Magi.* But if they give it a thumbs down, even museums that had promised art might change their minds. I planned to have my lawyer take care of something for me in Cologne, but now I can check into it myself. That's always better. I want to tell you more about it, if you want to hear it."

"Please do."

"I learned about the tryout for the exhibit through a call from an old friend there. It'll be delightful to see him again. And to introduce him to you. He told me there's something curious about the woman who owns the painting they plan to use."

Was he talking about the SIRA client? Had Valerie given me a name? No. Could it be? "Like, why she's okay with her painting being a decoy?"

"There's more to it." He looked around and over his shoulder. "She was the one who suggested the test to The Frick and to the Wallraf-Richartz—

"Your friend is at the museum?"

"No, he's at the Cologne Cathedral, but it seems the curator at the museum was telephoned by this Italian woman suggesting the painting they had on loan from her be used to prove to The Frick executives that their plan to safeguard the works during transit was sound. He wasn't familiar with the painting—and he certainly would have been. It's not exactly the Met or Louvre in size, with all of their stored works. She told him it had been there three years and where it was stored. When he looked for it, voila, it was right there where she said it would be."

"How would the lender know where a painting was stored?" I asked.

"And an overseas collector, at that."

"I can see why he was suspicious," I said.

"He can't find a record of the loan, either. Even if you assume the record keeping isn't all it should be, it's a bit much to swallow."

"Hm, if she suggested the experiment, I guess it's only fair she offer up her own painting for it," I said. "I have a suggestion."

"Please."

"Many insurance companies require a documented pre-loan discussion. He could look for a record of that, at least."

"I'll call him now." He pulled his phone out and placed the call. I pulled my collar close around my neck and walked ahead to think about connections between this and the Bettina Vogt forgeries. She was sending me to Cologne. Could this be why? My own phone rang. It was my US phone, and I had to decide if I should answer it. Why had I brought it? I wanted to know if there were leads in the murder investigations of Bettina Vogt and Crawford, but I could have waited until I had privacy to find out. The reason I had that phone with me was that by the time the footman finished introducing us to our hotel suite, like we were buying it, instead of sleeping there one night, there had been no time to hide the damn thing.

Graham never stayed on a call very long, so I wouldn't answer. Then I saw it was from the Vatican. "Hello."

"Signora Kelly? Emma?"

It was Colonel Marra. "I wanted to confirm your visit for Monday."

"Of course. I look forward to seeing you." I didn't really, but I took pity because of the obvious tension in his voice.

"We would like to pay you for your time in addition to reimbursing you for your airfare."

"That's not necessary. But there is something I wanted to ask you for." I came up with this idea on the flight over. I planned to ask when I got there, but it made more sense to do it now so if the request was approved, they could cut through their red tape and locate the documents I was interested in. "Would it be possible for me to review something in the Vatican archives? I would like to see Cardinal Faulhaber's diaries."

"Ah, yes, does this concern a certain painting by Raphael which is lost?" That was a euphemism. *Portrait of a Young Man* hadn't wandered off during World War II. "Elisa Pesarini told me of your interest in it."

I forgot to track how close Graham was and looked over my shoulder. He was walking to me. I had to get off the call.

"Those should be in our archives. We can do that. What time is your flight?"

"Thank you. That would be wonderful. I land at ten o'clock. Are you sending a car—?" He hung up. Well, well. I didn't know if Faulhaber had even kept a diary, much less where it was now. That was an audacious ask. Should I feel guilty?

I reminded myself that the request had been granted to Emma, not Emmaline. The Vatican didn't know she existed. On Sunday, I would fly to Rome, but Graham would think I was returning to the US. I would tell him anything I learned from scouring Faulhaber's diaries and come up with some explanation on my source.

Graham and I traced *Portrait of a Young Man* to Lake Schliersee. In May

112

1945, Hans Frank, the wartime General Governor of the colonized middle section of Poland, was arrested in Upper Bavaria, where he had a home. He and his wife, Brigitte, were in possession of the Raphael at the time. One of his sons, Nicholas, remembers the Americans moved the family to an apartment after the father's arrest. In one account, he said they didn't take things with them. Yet later, he described Brigitte selling their possessions to buy food. Sometimes bartering. He says, especially jewelry. The Raphael wasn't mentioned until he later wrote that the painting was "Probably hanging in some farmer's kitchen having been swapped by mother in 1946 for some eggs, butter and a pork roast."

Cardinal Faulhaber visited the family, gave them much-needed food, and even hosted them at his residence. Frank and he were frenemies, but when the trial began, the visits to him in Nuremberg ended. The prisoner threatened to tell all about the Vatican and Nazi's "secret agreements." Still, Faulhaber interceded with Pope Pius XII, asking for clemency for Frank. It wasn't known how hard he tried. In October, the Butcher of Poland was *re-baptized*. Graham and I assumed it was by the Cardinal. That is until I found an interview in *Al Jazeera* where the son says the service was performed by an American priest, Father O'Connor. Graham took on researching him.

Were either Cardinal Faulhaber or Father O'Connor aware of the painting? Faulhaber had to be. We traced the Cardinal's movements, relationships, finances as well as we could, which was not a lot, but probably more than any of the other researchers.

Brigitte was not suited for the hard times the year 1946 brought. Though she regularly pressured Faulhaber to appeal to Pope Pius XII to ask for clemency for her husband, neither Graham nor I thought she would exchange the painting for it. She needed money.

So his diaries were in the Vatican Archives, or maybe the library and I would have access to them thanks to Colonel Marra. I would read those from 1945 to 1946, maybe later, too.

By the time Graham got through researching the American priest, he would know more about the man than he knew about himself.

Were we finally closing in on the most important question? Did the Vatican have Raphael's *Portrait of a Young Man?*

Graham was back and reached his hand out to me for us to walk back to the hotel. "No record of a pre-loan meeting. Curious-er and curious-er." His word choice was light, but his jaw was clenched. "I found out it's *The Annunciation* by Zanobi Strozzi. No one is to know that."

"Fifteenth century, Florentine painter." I rubbed my forehead. "Why that painting? I thought the subject of the exhibit was the Adoration, not the Annunciation."

"They're not the same?"

I practically screamed a laugh. "Do Church of England members know nothing that's in the Bible?"

"You're not exactly a regular attendee, Madame." He grabbed me and tickled my ribs.

"Alright, I admit that probably one hundred percent of my religious education came from art. Let me enlighten you. The Annunciation is when the angel Gabriel told Mary what was going to happen. The Adoration was when the wise men went to see the newborn Jesus. Good thing C of E wasn't around then. They wouldn't have shown up. So why are they using this particular painting?"

"Perhaps they will use it for the test and not the exhibit," he said, tilting his head.

"Do you think it's real?" I asked. *Careful.* All he would know about the spate of forgeries was what he read in the papers. Not that Emmaline had been involved. Was there a connection between what was happening in the States to this? The collector's actions raised suspicions. Other than that, was there a problem? It was time to take my own advice and look at the actions of the people involved without accusing the painting. Was the woman a fraud? "Has an authenticator seen it?"

"Yes, but he's not ready to give his opinion. They can say a work was bought last week in Chelsea in a minute, but to say it *is* by the artist claimed takes longer."

I nodded. "Moving it for a demonstration bothers me. An art museum of any size has had accidental damage happen to works in their custodianship.

Traffic, bumpy roads, and weather conditions are all at play during transit. Graham, you're squeezing my hand too hard." I stopped and turned to him. "It's not the painting you're concerned about."

"Sorry, darling." His lips were curled in a sneer I hadn't seen before. "I'm mad as hell." We walked again. "I didn't want to worry you, but what I haven't told you is that we are listed as a previous owner of her painting." How angry would he have been if he knew about the plan to implicate him in the Gardner Museum theft?

"We or you?" I asked.

"They're the same, darling."

"I'm thinking of the timing. If I'm listed too, the fake provenance would have been constructed recently."

"Of course." He relaxed. "We haven't known one another for three years." He pumped his fist in the air. "Why didn't I think of that?" He kissed the side of my head. "I should call him back." He reached into his pocket.

"Wait," I said. "Will she be there tomorrow?"

"She's determined to be. She insists." I raised an eyebrow, and he took my meaning. "I'll tell him to let us surprise her."

The American equivalent would be if you bought a house that once belonged to a movie star and then you met him or her. "I would *love* to go to Cologne," I said. SIRA wouldn't have to pay my airfare, and they would never know why. "Her reaction should be priceless."

Chapter Nineteen

"Feast your hungry eyes on me." That wasn't what the commanding, yet boyish in a young Robert Redford way, Dr. Tristram Roberts, said to the guests at the Platinum Circle Winter Fête. It was what the Director of the V&A's hands, in the pockets of his tuxedo jacket, conveyed. The one bent knee. The way he hovered over the podium. I wondered if he had a story. Maybe. Not as interesting as mine, but he could have a secret hidden here and there. Or maybe he was bored. No, he had an audience. He was loving this. I, however, was standing there but eager to be in Cologne or Rome. In motion.

"Time to get serious. Sorry." Frowny face. *The fun part is over.* He threw his head back and laughed at his own joke. He wasn't funny, but the crowd was kind. His introduction of Dr. Antonia Lawson, the museum's Director of Development, smacked of passive-aggressiveness, and he may have sabotaged her remarks for a cheap laugh. We would see. I scanned the room full of donors. They were here thanks to her and the staff she led.

She straightened her mother-of-the-bride formal gown and walked to the mic. Then she smiled and cleared her throat. "Sir Graham has been a trustee of the Victoria & Albert Museum since 2015." Good for her. She hadn't thanked her boss for a warm introduction. "He was knighted—hard to believe it was a decade ago, in the New Year's Honours for services to the Arts and Philanthropy." She twittered. Standing ramrod straight in his tuxedo in the LED candlelit reception hall, Graham was certainly handsome. She paused and timorously motioned to each of us. Why would someone in her position, for decades, be a nervous public speaker? Had Tristram

116

Roberts' unfunny joke gotten to her? He glowered at her from the other side of the stage, annoyed at her case of nerves. If she saw him, it would only make her more ill at ease. "He and his lovely wife, Emmaline, have funded numerous projects including, but certainly not limited to, major gallery renovations here at the V&A. Their collecting interests are wide-ranging but focus on Old Masters, medieval tapestries, and Byzantine art. Sir Graham holds an MA, with honors, and a first-class BA, also with honors, in Law from Mansfield College, Oxford University. He is Chair of Oxford University Investment Committee." She looked up from her notes and blinked twice. "But, Emmaline, it is you we are here to celebrate this evening. It is my distinct honor to name you an Honorary Senior Research Fellow of the Victoria & Albert Museum."

I stopped myself before I snorted a laugh. Where were my paragraphs? Of course, Emmaline had none. Was that what caused her anxiety? That she couldn't make a long speech about me? I smiled at Dr. Lawson, and she immediately relaxed. I wasn't offended, just the opposite. I had done it. There was no digital life. I was an art advisor who worked so discreetly that her client list was unknowable.

"Please join me," she said, as she held an arm out in our direction.

I hesitated. Buying time. I looked and found the lowest wattage light. I was no longer afraid of grainy newspaper photos. They weren't the threat. Facial recognition software was. My dress was a distraction for humans, but not for technology.

A stylist had sent my dress and jewelry for tonight's event to the hotel. The top of the sleeveless, midnight blue gown was fitted, but from my hips down, it was pleated. With each stop, white satin inner pleats glowed through dark panels. Dressing inconspicuously hadn't worked in my favor. Maybe this would.

Graham took my hand and walked me to the podium, shoulder to shoulder. The microphone, perched on the podium, was ablaze with pink-gold light from above. Of course, the audience, the media, and the V&A expected me to say a few words of appreciation. From the semi-darkness, I looked square at the crowd and smiled. Lips closed. Not the New York smile. Would that placate their hungry curiosity, or was this how it all ended? The Raphael I was meant to find, *Portrait of a Young Man,* was still out there. Graham and I still had to locate it and return it to Poland. The audience waited. They needed more from me. No, from Emmaline. I could think of no way to avoid that pillar of light. I would stand back from the microphone. If anyone asked me to move closer, I wouldn't hear them. "Thank you," I mouthed.

Then Graham took a step ahead. He was at the microphone. I was in the shadow. I was safe for now. "In honor of this special evening, Emmaline and I are offering a work that is so special to us for long-term loan to the V&A." It was my anniversary gift. Two men wearing dark suits walked onto the stage from opposite directions. They pulled back the curtain on the wall at the back of the stage and secured the velvet cloth on ornamental silver hooks. The dramatic contrast of white gloves on crimson was visually stunning. Rembrandt's face looked at us, or for us. A moment of perfection. So rare. I felt happy. Like I could afford to pay what my big picture cost me. Pleasures like this kept me going.

The crowd gasped, then surged. Pulled forward by the power of the art. The small painting now had its own security staff, and the two men and two women moved in from their posts along the wall. "*Self-Portrait 1650* by...." He stopped there to tease the crowd. Then laughed. "By either you-know-who or an artist, or artists, in his workshop." Gentle laughter and goodwill swirled like the floor was carpeted in dry ice. "As you can imagine, my wife and I talk about art a lot. Recently, over lunch, she explained to me how men such as forger John Myatt and fraudster John Drewe have tampered with the V&A's records, and of course those of other museums, to the point where researchers will find it virtually impossible to tell fact from fiction for years to come, if ever." Graham was a former MP and very good in front of a crowd. Had we had that conversation *over lunch?* Breakfast would have smacked of intimacy. We would lose special-ness if they came that close. Over dinner, it would make me sound like a party-pooper. Lunch was just the right word. "And for this, Myatt served four months at his majesty's pleasure and Drewe a mere two years. Discovering this painting's secrets will be up to the researchers here. We look forward to their answer, but take as much time as you need."

Tristram walked to the podium, stepping in front of Antonia. "Emmaline, would you say a few words?"

I smiled. Rather than moving to stand in front of the microphone, I pulled it to my side of the podium so I could stay in shadow. If I kept my remarks brief, the lighting engineer might not be able to adjust in time. "When a relatively low-cost *circle of* painting is upgraded to *artist's hand*," the work hasn't changed, but its value in the market grows exponentially. Even when there is no criminal intent or even the desire to deceive, market forces create a bias toward attributing the work to the more famous artist. Not to, say, a woman artist." The last bit was said with a conspiratorial, here-we-are-together-in-this-sisterhood look at a few of the women in the audience. "We must guard against bias leading to misattribution, as well as nefarious motives." The spotlight tracked me. Time to move. I walked to a nearby server with a tray of drinks and took a champagne flute. "Generations of Abbotts have taken good care of the painting at Emrick Hall. Let's toast them." There.

"Here, here." I held up my glass to Caroline, sitting at a table at the side of the room. She wasn't able to stand for long periods of time, and the museum had made this accommodation for her and a few of her contemporaries. The room erupted in cheers and applause. Maybe a first for London's Victoria & Albert Museum. Graham hugged me, and I turned to look safely over his left shoulder as people with cameras surrounded us on three sides. Dr. Antonia Lawson smiled and clapped from the other side of the podium. I took her arm and pulled her to us for a very public hug.

She was slightly unnerved but obviously delighted. Graham patted her shoulder before shaking Tristram's hand. I motioned to the room of high-top tables, all covered with ten or so LED candles in varying heights. "It's perfect. Did you choose the décor?"

"I, uh…" she stammered.

"That's how it was seen by Rembrandt and his contemporaries. The painting was meant to be seen in candlelight." The flattery was a small act by a vigilante.

Because of Graham's deed, the copper impersonator in New York was forever vanquished. No question. It would never be purchased by a collector on the off-chance of who *may* have painted it. Rembrandt Harmenszoon van Rijn smiled. He could rest in peace.

The National Gallery would not be happy that the V&A was chosen. Later, I would ask Graham if any ruffled feather soothing would be needed over there. If it was, I would do it from a distance, with notes and phone calls.

I pulled away from them and drank in the ugly beauty of the small painting. Good God. I had a few seconds before politeness required me to move for others to get a look at it, or I was overpowered, whichever came first. Rembrandt looked out at the viewer. Over. Powered. There was a loss of paint here and there, but it was in very good condition, partly because it had rarely been moved or shipped. He painted this, if he had, in his mid-forties. Oil paint was slathered on. Daubs of white. Splotches of black. The nose almost protruded from the canvas. He was lit from the top left of the painting. It was the face of man with *appetites,* after time did what it does. In 1650 he was forty-four-years-old and seemed to be questioning everything. Everything. The artist gazed over the shoulder at the viewer, which created a dialog. It increased the painting's intimacy. In his life, he overspent, going into bankruptcy. His wife died after giving birth, and later, he had an affair with the baby's nursemaid. To end it, he had her committed to an asylum. His last years were hell. In the painting, he said, "I'm human. Look at what a mess I've made of this life." His later self-portraits were ruthless. This one was pitiless and eternal.

I stepped to the side, out of its force field, so I could think. If it had been painted on copper, would it have had more impact? Certainly, the colors would be more intense. His finely detailed brush strokes and whisper-thin layers of oil paint would not have sunk into a nonabsorbent surface, especially if it was coated with tin or lead first. In a painting about living and aging, luminosity would have become glare. The choice of canvas was so Rembrandt.

The plain black frame looked to be the original from the 17th century. In the flashiness of the 19th century, some Dutch collectors replaced these with gilded frames, which were popular at the time. It was a shame since they made Rembrandt's work recede, and any gold in the painting looked yellow.

My husband took my hand. "Emmaline, it's time to meet the others for dinner."

Chapter Twenty

The Goring was less than two miles away, but Graham had two limos waiting to take our group of seven back to the hotel. His mother, Caroline, rode with us. She sat behind the driver, wearing a black silk pantsuit. She and her daughters had a ritual of checking out my midsection every time they saw me to satisfy themselves that I wasn't pregnant. Other than on that one topic, she had little curiosity about me, but she was obsessed with Graham.

"Well done, Graham," she said. "Both of you."

I smiled. I would have loved to talk to someone about how misattribution of a painting by someone as beloved by his country as Rembrandt was close to a crime against cultural heritage. I was lost in my thoughts as we pulled away from the kerb. Suddenly, the rear passenger door opened, startling us all.

"*Gawd,*" Caroline screamed from the other side of the car.

"*Gad,*" the driver said as he braked.

Graham, in the middle, reached across to shield me from whatever was out there in the night and from falling out with one arm. He hovered over his seat, ready. Age had not diminished his strength nor slowed his reaction time.

"I'd rather ride in this car, if it's no bother," Charlotte's husband, Dr. Sheldon Martin, said, jutting his head in. Graham relaxed back into his seat. "They want me to face the back," he whined.

"Shel, Shel." His wife was behind him, pulling the sleeve of his tuxedo. "Get back in the car. Please."

He planted his hands on top of the car, and his skinny arms framed his long face. "I will not be moved."

"Do something, Graham. He's making a spectacle of himself," his mother said.

A driver tried to pass and used his car horn to let us know he was annoyed. "Sir, I'll have to move," the driver explained to Graham apologetically. "We're in the way of traffic."

Graham pivoted to the back-facing seat. "Emmaline, do you mind?"

I laughed and got up. "You may have to help me with this dress."

"Avec joie." He took my waist and turned me around to sit close to him. "Get in, you two," he said to Sheldon and Charlotte. "He could drink for England," he whispered to his mother and me.

I looked at Caroline and moved my head half an inch, side to side, and she winked. Sheldon didn't drink often enough. That was his problem. On the rare times he did, he got shit-faced and handsy. Graham caught our exchange and glowed with pleasure. They had no idea how very unlikely this friendship was. I dreaded hurting her.

Charlotte took her brother's place in the middle, and then Sheldon accordioned his gangly body into the car. He slouched sitting, like when he stood. Was he beaten down? The way I had been while I was married to Jason? Should I feel sympathy for him? The Abbott family could be overwhelming, but I had never seen Graham treat him with anything other than respect and amity. The contrast between the two men could not be more striking. Graham had a cosmopolitan air and a commanding personality. Sheldon was vaguely sketchy.

"Emmaline, tell me something." *Shum-thing.* "Was every single person in the Dutch Golden Age ugly?" *That* was what he witnessed in the museum? Freedom from Spanish Catholic rule triggered cultural pride, and artists celebrated Dutch life and identity in their paintings. It was a time when the tiny country leapt ahead in prominence on the European scene. In art, science, and commerce. Independence did that.

"Vermeer's subjects weren't like that," I said.

"You know *Girl with a Pearl Earring*?" he countered.

The painting was called other names for more than three hundred years. That can happen in different parts of the world, or from a modern translation, or a new owner. *Mona Lisa* and *Girl With a Pearl Earring* were good examples. But since ours was not destined to be an assumption-challenging debate, fueled by intellectual vigor, we could go with the more familiar title for it. Sure. Less than a decade ago, a Dutch astrophysicist argued that based on specular reflection, the earring was probably polished tin. Yeah, I'd heard of it. "That's not a portrait; it's a tronie—" I said before being interrupted.

"When a mum brings in a kid presenting like that, I think, uh-oh."

Charlotte stared straight ahead through the windscreen, as far into the distance as she could see, and then some. Which offended her more, the comment about children or his untutored taste? Hard to tell with her.

"Now you're being cruel, *Sheldon*," Caroline said. The emphasis on his name shut him up. Our car full of people froze.

"You may be thinking about *Portrait of a Young Woman*. Or about something by Judith Leyster, another Dutch Golden Age painter," I said into the heavy air.

"Yes," Caroline said. "For my money, just as powerful at Rembrandt."

"She painted people, warts and all, with no idealization," Charlotte added.

"But that's different from a tronie," I said.

"Never heard of her," Sheldon said.

"I'm not surprised. For years, her work was attributed to Frans Hals or her husband, Jan Miense Molenaer." We would fake pleasantness, and it would be ours. "She and her husband used the same models and art materials, and that contributed to the misattribution." Leyster was a woman artist lost to history for two centuries.

"Talk art to me, baby!" Sheldon yelled out at me, spit flying. He thought he was funny. He was wrong.

"Maybe we should have walked," Charlotte said. She patted Sheldon's leg. Hard. Bordering on a slap. "The cold air would've sobered Dr. Martini up." Her little joke served the same purpose. He tensed and sat up straight. No longer jabbering on. I was thankful for small favors. We might, for once, be spared the Beatles trivia he liked to drop into conversations ad nauseam.

Like "'Fool on the Hill' is profoundly classical. Wouldn't you agree?" He was from Liverpool and thought that gave him the right to bore us. Funny, he didn't have that distinctive Liverpool accent in his speech. Maybe he'd misplaced it in the years of medical school and beyond.

"You found a martini?" Graham asked, intentionally misunderstanding and bringing him back into the fold. "Good man. All I had was champagne."

Back at The Goring, uniformed footmen approached both cars. Yalta was straightforward compared to deciding if Caroline should get out on the far side of the car where she sat, or scoot over the seat.

Graham took my elbow. "There's another photographer, Emmaline. Let's go in. It's enough to make one miss News of the World." The now-defunct tabloid was known as *News of the Screws* or *Screws of the World* because of its coverage of celebrities, scandal, and gossip.

"Who are you wearing, Mrs. Abbott?"

I ignored the man who'd shouted, and we walked up a few steps to the hotel doors, held open for just the two of us. Charlotte and Isabella were not shy around cameras, and they had their business—taking foreign visitors on shopping tours—to promote. We left them to it. They made the most of Graham's new celebrity, enjoying the profits, which I'd unintendedly brought him. It made everything harder for me.

Eventually, the others joined us at the bar; then we were taken to our table. We dined on branzino al sale and fava beans with ricotta, garnished with lovage and nasturtium flowers. I talked, and I laughed, and I was there and not there.

Chapter Twenty-One

SATURDAY IN COLOGNE

T he flight to Germany in the private plane took less than two hours, but with the rain and turbulence, it seemed longer. It wasn't cold enough to snow, but almost. I wore drapey winter white slit-leg pants—the sides opened to my knee—with tights, short boots, and a white Burberry raincoat. Someone from the charter service met us at the top step of the aircraft boarding stairs with two golf umbrellas. The chivalrous young man gave Graham one, opened the other, and held it over my head as he escorted me in. He was too close. The proximity bothered me, and I walked faster. I was a runner, but that would be weird.

My Voice from the Void hadn't called since Tuesday. Maybe he felt the message he sent when he tried to kill my mother and me spoke for him. Was it too much to hope he was dead?

We got in the waiting car for the drive from the Cologne Bonn airport to the cathedral. The pounding rain and weekend traffic made for slow going, so I looked out the window at Germany's fourth most populous city.

"How far is it to the cathedral?" Graham asked.

"About sixteen klicks," the driver answered, and my husband nodded.

In a few miles, the twin spires came into view. The cathedral was on par with Notre Dame and Chartres Cathedrals. After a few more turns through the downtown area, our car pulled up to the main entrance, which faced west. The altar was on the east side. The tradition of a liturgical east end probably came from the Jewish tradition of praying facing the direction of the Holy Temple in Jerusalem. Two men in cassocks, more large umbrellas deployed and held aloft, met the car.

"I thought we would be, like, tourists," I said.

Graham didn't answer, but the driver snickered. As we walked across the courtyard to the porch, one of our guides talked to us like that's exactly what we were.

"Construction of our Gothic cathedral began in 1248. Its official name is Cathedral Church of Saint Peter and is the most visited tourist site in Germany," he recited. "It is the largest twin-spired church in the world, second tallest church in Europe, and third tallest church in the world. It took nearly seven centuries to build. The completion coincided with Europe's industrial revolution. Pollutants from industrialization caused acid rain, which attacked the calcium carbonate." I looked up at the blackened building and tried to imagine it pristine. There were more scaffolds than I could count for what must be ongoing restoration work. "So our cathedral has been under constant attack from one enemy or another since it was consecrated." The sentence trailed off. Awkward. He opened a massive door with its bronze angel doorknob, and I saw he was biting down on his lower lip. He was afraid he had offended the Brit and the American with what he meant as a statement on clean air.

"Including fourteen hits by Allied bombers, I believe," Graham said. "Those dark days are far behind us, aren't they?" He patted the man's shoulder, twice, cordially.

"You made that less awkward," I said to Graham when the door closed behind us. "In Germany, history is so close you bump up against it. In the States, you have to look a long time to find it."

He smiled, but before he could say more, a man with military bearing, dressed in a business suit, approached us. "My friend," he called out.

"Horst, so good to see you." Graham shook the man's hand. They were about the same age and height. "Emmaline, Horst here is the assistant to the cathedral provost."

He took my hand. "Horst Krogemann. So very nice to finally meet you.

I've heard so many wonderful things." He was British, which surprised me because of the name. Small groups of worshipers dotted the church. We moved away from the massive doors so that tourists, maybe they'd made a pilgrimage or were just trying to get out of the rain, could come inside. "In case you are wondering about an Englishman with a German name, my paternal grandparents were German, but I was raised in England where my mother's family lives."

Graham slapped his friend on the back. "One day, when we were *lads*, mind you, my best mate here informed me that Spanish cedar wood was best for making cigar boxes. We were, what? Five or six? I ask you, Emmaline, what child knows that?"

"The kind that is trying a little too hard to impress!" Horst answered. "I guess I heard my father or grandfather say it at some point."

We all laughed, and I wrapped my hand through the crook of Graham's arm. It was hard to imagine him at any other age. To me, he was only the age he was now.

A woman with shoulder-length, glossy black hair walked toward us. She wore a black dress with a full skirt and black knee-length suede boots. Graham's friend's eyes darted to the side, the way people did when planning their escape. When he saw that wasn't possible, he said, "Sabine, may I introduce you to Sir Graham Abbott and his wife, Emmaline?" She looked us over and smiled. I saw recognition of our names or maybe Graham's face. Would she associate us with her painting?

She shook our hands. "Sabine Gaddi." She laughed and pointed to a group of men standing to the side. "My painting is the guest of honor today. They're from The Frick." Two of the men wore business suits. An older, lumbering man in jeans and a leather jacket, probably meant as a signifier of what, maybe toughness, slouched near them. Muscle? My eyes lingered a beat as I compared him to the others. He wasn't particularly handsome, and he had the odd habit of huffing like he was smoking without a cigarette.

What if one of the men from The Frick knew me or, rather, knew Emma? Why hadn't I thought of that? I turned my back to them and looked at the stained-glass windows along the north wall. The oldest windows were from the 13ᵗʰ century. Some of the windows along the north side were original. Others had been removed in the 18ᵗʰ century. Others were the replacements after World War II. The most famous in that category was on the south transept, and designed by Cologne artist Gerhard Richter.

"Please tell us more," Graham said to her, giving her another chance to connect his name to the painting. If you owned artwork that had at one time been in a renowned collection, you knew it. The discipline not to name drop was rare.

"It's *The Annunciation* by Zanobi Strozzi." Her Italian accent did the artist's name justice.

I turned back around but kept my head down. "He was from a wealthy family that rivaled the Medici," I said to Graham. I didn't know if he was familiar with him.

"Oh, I think not," Sabine declared.

"You don't believe he was from *the* Strozzi family?" I was always ready to learn, and she would have read extensively on the artist because of her painting.

"The Strozzi family did *not* compare to the Medici."

She beamed up at Graham and Horst. Flirting.

"Was your painting ever known by another name?" I asked.

"No," she answered. Definite. No question. Full stop.

"But Strozzi's *The Annunciation* is at the National Gallery in London," I said. "It's not currently on display, but they have it." The different name option would have been a good out.

Horst's eyes widened, then a smile started.

She seemed rattled. She would be unless there was an explanation, like the artist painting multiple versions, like Van Gogh's *Sunflower* series. Or LdV's *The Virgin on the Rocks*. One of those was at the Louvre, and the other was at the National Gallery. I've heard artists say that returning to a motif or a subject was thrilling. The only wrong answer for Sabine was none.

When it was obvious she wasn't going to take any of the lifelines, Horst asked, "Why did the curator at Wallraf-Richartz not know the painting was in their collection?" Accusing, but not. Her glossy-purple smile dropped, and she glared. Annoyed that he was not in the market for what she was selling. Or at our straightforward, some would say blunt questions.

"The painting was originally attributed to Domenico by *Bernard Berenson.*" She pronounced the name of the art historian, critic, and connoisseur like it had a bad odor. Later in life, he was in cahoots with a dealer for their financial gain. It was true that Berenson had assigned all Strozzi's paintings to Domenico di Micelino. And Domenico's to Giusto d'Andrea. "That confused the matter," she said. That may be the understatement of the last century.

"I assume the painting is covered by the museum's insurance policy while it's there, and there will be another policy for the exhibit?" I asked.

"I presume so," she said, over her shoulder, wandering away. She studied the ceiling, the stained-glass windows, the art on the walls.

"That's right," Horst nodded.

"Do you have insurance while in transit?" I asked.

"That I don't know." He ran a hand over his mouth and looked over at the group in the corner. He pivoted, closing in our trio, to a private group to confer.

"Even the best-laid art transport plans need it," I said.

"I couldn't agree more. I'll find out right away."

I whispered, "And you should get it through the shipping company."

Graham leaned in, his hand resting on my shoulder. "Should you postpone until you're sure the current policy will cover today?" He thought he kept his volume low, but his hearing loss from military service was bad, and his voice still carried far.

"What is this?" Sabine was back. "There's no time for this. The test is today."

"And it will be," Horst assured her. "Emmaline, have you seen the Shrine of the Three Kings?"

I had, but I knew an excuse to get to a spot for a private conversation when presented with one. "Allow me." Graham and I followed him up the aisle toward the altar, leaving Sabine behind.

The cathedral had the traditional shape of a Latin cross, and when we got as far as the transept, the shorter section of the cross, Graham asked, "Any word on the authentication?"

"So far, not so good." Horst shook his head but didn't look up since he was typing on his phone. "It makes no sense that it might be anything other than a fraud. Why would you fake the provenance if the painting's not a forgery?"

"If you didn't come by it legally, you would," I said. "Remember all those anonymous Swiss collectors?" A laughable, but not funny, number of Nazi looted works of art made it onto the market, supposedly sold by someone in the neutral country. Millions of art objects changed hands during Nazi rule, adding up to some twenty percent of Europe's treasures.

"You think it might be Nazi-looted art?" he asked Graham rather than me. Old school.

"No idea, but something's not right," Graham answered.

"I hate to ask again, my old friend, but you are certain it was never in your collection? I would understand completely—"

"Quite," Graham answered. He reminded him about the date problem.

"Apologies. Just had to ask." It took a lot more than that to offend a rich person.

"Horst?" A tall, thin man wearing clerical robes walked toward us.

"Monsignor! Let me introduce you to my friends." He good-naturedly patted the man's back. "Monsignor Guido Assmann is my boss."

The Monsignor waved his hand in the air. "Ahh, Horst. No one is your boss."

Horst wagged a finger. "He is over every employee here. We are thankful to have him at the helm."

This got a wide smile from the Monsignor, and he pointed up to the ceiling. "I would say someone else is in that position." We laughed gently, respectfully. "Where is Frau Gaddi?" He was, as we say, looped in and seemed suspicious of her but not overly concerned. That was a mistake.

"We were creating distance so we could speak privately," Horst explained.

Monsignor Assmann nodded. "I will take us where she will not follow." He walked past the high altar, and we climbed the few stairs, then on towards the golden shrine.

He walked next to me and looked like he was trying to think of something to say. At the top of the stairs, he blurted out, "You are, uh, glamorous. I believe that's the word."

"Thank you." *I think.*

Graham chuckled. "One magazine said her strong glamour was subtle magic. I would agree with that." I shook my head, and we walked on.

The area was enclosed by a black iron fence. Horst took a key from his pocket and handed it to Monsignor Assmann. "Would you care to do the honors?"

The monsignor opened the ornamental gate, and we went in. Horst stayed behind.

Every day, about twenty thousand people looked through those bars at the shrine housing the bones of the three wise men. Now, we heard whispers of *who are they?* all around us. I glanced at Graham, and he grinned, as happy as I was at our luck.

Horst ended his phone call and joined us. "According to my last text from the museum, they want to go ahead unless there is a reason to postpone." He scratched his chin and gritted his teeth. He was a worried man. "There are two routes from Wallraf-Richartz Museum to here. What we call the west route is along Tunis Street. The east route has more turns. No matter. Having alternates is what's important." He looked at his watch.

The monsignor rubbed his hands together and smiled. "Will it be coming in on blues and twos? Or hole-and-corner?"

"Sounds like someone watches crime shows on the telly," Graham said. Not rudely, and not paying much attention.

"Hopefully, neither. I left a voice mail message telling him to delay. And if the truck had already left, for them to stop at Museum Ludwig and check in with me." He looked around, then whispered, "That's our enroute safe harbor to use in case of trouble."

"Time to start your private viewing," Horst said. The triple sarcophagus was raised above the floor, and though we had a better view than anyone else, we looked through a clear box. The shrine was shaped like a basilica. "It's made of wood but covered in gold, silver, and a thousand gems and pearls." On one side, two stunning cameos were inlaid near the Virgin's head. Jesus looked about two years old, but we wouldn't quibble. Dazzling.

I looked around the cathedral. "Monsignor, what do you think is happening, or will happen here?" I asked.

"Maybe nothing." He looked over my shoulder. "I see the best in everyone, even her." I followed his gaze. Sabine sat in a pew near the front. It looked like she was reading on her phone. Was he right, or was he naïve? If he was right, Bettina Vogt had played me hard. Possible. Friends didn't plant seeds of doubt about your husband with the police or with the Office of Professional Responsibility. But she had been ordered to paint the malevolent portrayal in *Shame*. Maybe she didn't know what she was painting. Or what it would unleash. And she hadn't followed his instructions on the Rembrandt hoax. What about the mistake in *Kizette in a Green Bugatti*? Was that intentional?

If I could keep my lives separate a little longer, I could tell Elliott that. Maybe it would help with the internal investigation.

The priest didn't know about any of that. And I doubted he knew about the forged provenance for this work. His opinion was based on the little knowledge he did have. He was wrong. We waded knee-deep in evil.

Horst moved to the side and took a phone call, covering his mouth with his hand. He hung up and said, "He didn't receive my message. It's here. I'm going to meet the truck. Guess I have to take Sabine with me."

We filed out of the enclosed area. He motioned for her to meet him on the right side of the altar. After one last look at the Shrine of the Three Magi, we walked down to meet her.

"See? No need to stop at Museum Ludwig. *The Annunciation* made it here. Where will it be hung?" I turned in time to see Horst's confusion at Sabine's comment. Graham looked at his friend intently; he caught it, too.

"We've been advised the painting should be allowed to acclimate to our air and temperature before we do that," Horst answered.

"The painting should stay in the shipping container for twenty-four hours," I agreed. "Monsignor, would you show me, well, whatever you think I should see?" I asked.

"Excellent idea, Emmaline," Graham said.

The monsignor said something and took my arm. I didn't speak German or any language other than English, but it was probably "okey-dokey." He led our little group around to the side where tourists marched by the shrine of the Magi.

"Enough talk. Kit up and move out," Horst said. After a quick goodbye from Graham, he, Horst, and Sabine left for a hopefully secure spot to meet the painting.

"I never tire of studying the Richter stained glass window," Monsignor Assmann said to me, as we joined the crowd in the queue now winding behind the altar. "You know he used eighty shades of color that were used in the nineteenth century for it to look to us – you and me, Emmaline—the way it was meant to."

I took a look back at the shrine. The line inched along so we wouldn't be at the Richter window for several more minutes. I wanted to learn more about the altar. "Are the relics really of the Magi?" It was kind of a trick question. We know the men weren't kings. They may or may not have been wise.

"We've always known that bones of three men are in there. Each a different age. A DNA analysis shows they are of Middle Eastern descent. It also houses the relics of three martyrs: Felix, Nabor, and probably Gregory of Spoleto. It's over two meters long, and still, it must be crowded in there." He chuckled. "Of course, scientific analyses are only permissive. You're smiling. You are familiar with that, aren't you? I read you are an art advisor." I nodded sweetly, remembering I had tried to explain the same concept to Taylor Tyndale. Thinking of herself as a future owner of a Rembrandt had meant more to her. "What really matters is that it is wise to seek Him." He reached for my hand, and I let him take it in his.

"I do try to seek good," I managed to say.

"I believe you do."

I pulled my hand away. "I think the choice of an agnostic for the commission was inspired," I said as we walked slowly to the south transept. The work was commissioned in 2003 and unveiled in 2007. "How long have you been here?"

"Twenty-five years in June."

"So you remember the controversy?"

"Ahh." He swatted the air. "Everything Germany does is controversial, but we deserve that. Do you know why?"

"I'd love to hear your take," I said.

"Because for a time, we stopped questioning. You must question everything you are told." That sounded odd coming from a man in his line of work. "And of course, when in 2004, Richter said, 'I can't believe in God, but I think that the Catholic Church is marvelous,' he was easy for me to support." He laughed out loud.

When we reached the stained-glass window, he let it do the talking. It didn't need words. When he was ready to move along, he said, "I'd like you to view the church from up there." He pointed to a platform on the opposite side of the church, so high I had to crane my neck to see it. "But I am afraid my old knees can't climb that many steps any longer. I'll wait downstairs, and you can tell me how you liked it when you come back down." I agreed, and he looked in the direction of the front doors, then around us. He seemed like a man used to a lot of care. "It's still raining, so we can't go that way. Hmm, I wonder where Horst has gotten off to." He looked around once again. No Horst. I felt someone watching me. Now, he had my head on a swivel, too. There was no one nearby. "Let's go this way. I believe I can find it." He led me to a side door and seemed surprised when he saw it was raining there, too.

"Monsignor? Monsignor?" Our tour guide was trying to get his attention. "Can I help?"

"Ah, yes, please." He told the young man where I needed to go, but that seemed to confuse him.

"If I escort her, I can't stay with you. That's what Horst said for me to do."

"If you can just tell me where the stairway is, I'm sure I can find it," I said.

Both men were relieved. The route he described to get to the stairs to the balcony was so convoluted, I began to think it was a tour guide full employment scheme.

Chapter Twenty-Two

Anticipation of the view grew with each step up to the balcony. The half wall at the top let light in, but the stairwell was shadowy.

"That means fuck all to me," Graham yelled. "You *will* tell us who you are working with."

I froze at the top step. "Graham! Don't kill her." I didn't know how voices carried in the cathedral's stratosphere, and I didn't want that to echo around to the tourists below or down to Monsignor Assmann. I didn't want any of the faithful looking up at the woman suspended backwards over the railing. Nor what kept her from dropping three hundred feet below—my husband's clenched hand on her throat, or a fistful of her dress in Horst's.

I had never seen this side of Graham and must have looked confused. He was physically strong for his age, or any other, and self-assured, but never violent. His expression when he looked up was sad, like he had disappointed me.

"Emmmmaaa…" Sabine pleaded. If she called me Emma instead of Emmaline, it would mean she knew everything. "liiine."

"Give her a chance to answer a few questions," I said.

Horst looked to Graham, who nodded. The men pulled her upright. She slumped forward, her hands on her knees, to catch her breath.

Then Sabine stood up and turned toward the half-wall, one arm on the railing and one down by her side. Or was she reaching into the folds of her dress? When I heard the first shout, I looked down to the nave. A purple velvet curtain that hung above a painting in one of the chapels was on fire. In my peripheral vision, I saw Sabine pointing with something. A metal stick?

Horst yelled something about calling a fire brigade. She moved her arm to the left. Another curtain burst into flames. She pointed the weapon, whatever it was, to the next chapel. The fire traveled horizontally along the wall.

"She's starting the fires!" I ran at her.

Graham turned me around by my shoulders. "Emmaline, we have to get you out of here." I struggled to free myself from his grip and took in the carnage below.

Within seconds, the blaze took the wine drapery and carpet in one chapel, then the wooden altar of another. The flames blocked just one door, a side door, but most of the people below panicked. Some stampeded up the aisle to get to the main entry doors. They screamed, ran, pushed. I looked for Monsignor Assmann but couldn't find him.

Horst pulled Sabine around to face him. The force, or maybe the shock, of the undercut to her jaw, unclasped her hand, and she dropped the weapon.

A shout in German came from the direction of the entryway. The big guy in the leather jacket wobbled, standing on a pew, as he cupped his hands and used them for a megaphone. He yelled something in German over and over. In breaks in the screams and shouts, I made out his words. Now, he spoke in English. Maybe it was a translation of what he yelled before. "These doors are locked! The front doors are locked!"

From my vantage point, I could see that wasn't true. Bits of sky could be seen over and over as tourists and worshipers opened the doors and fled. "No! They're not! The doors aren't locked." I yelled as loud as I could, but we were so far above them no one heard me.

I found Monsignor Assmann in the melee. He had climbed the steps to the pulpit, waving his arms. I couldn't hear his words, not that I would have understood what he said if I had, but his hand and arm gestures were easily interpreted. Obviously, he called for calm and for them to go to the main doors. They didn't hear him, no one even looked at him. Flames raced alongside the running people. The priest dropped his flailing arms. Suddenly, he ran to the back of the panicked crowd and tried to make his way through. Those closest to the main door and safety heard the man's shouts first and made the worst choice possible. They reversed direction. The flow of people churned down the middle aisle, and I lost sight of Monsignor Assmann.

I was back in Graham's grasp. He took me to the back wall and lowered me enough for my feet to touch the floor.

Sabine dropped down to her knees.

"Stand up," Horst ordered.

"Just a—" There was a look of hatred on her face, but she took his extended hand. When he pulled her up, she fell against his chest. Or that's how it looked to me from my vantage point behind them. The truth of what she did was written on Graham's face. He let go of me and pulled her away from his friend. That was when I saw the bloody knife. She stabbed Horst in the chest a second time. The last thrust was into his lower torso since that was all she could reach. Graham slung her off the balcony with such force she flew out rather than down. I ran the few steps to look over. The fall hadn't killed her. She lifted her head from where she lay sprawled on a pew.

I sprinted down the steps to her two and three at a time. The walls on either side of the stairwell were paneled in dark wood. I hadn't noticed their pessimism when I happily climbed them minutes earlier and a world ago. I smelled smoke, and I heard fear. Was Bettina a malevolent force bringing me here to burn to death? Her portrayal in *Shame* could end Elliott's meteoric rise in the FBI, an institution he loved as deeply as I did art. It may already have since, in DC, an accusation was as lethal as a conviction. You were only a virgin once. I needed air. But not following orders on the Rembrandt forgery saved the Abbott art collection from tarnish and suspicion of a connection to the works from Gardner robbery. And it had cost her her life.

I was finally at the bottom of the stairs. I retraced the path through the maze, relieved I remembered it. The smell was worse inside the church, but there was more oxygen. I saw one of Sabine's black boots hooked over the back of a pew and ran to her. To get through the people, I climbed and vaulted over the benches.

"The front doors are not locked. Be calm. You will all get out. Make your way to the front or any of the side entrances." Monsignor Assmann's loud voice came from the lectern, and he was now aided by a microphone.

I pulled off my coat and wrapped it over Sabine. "What did he promise you?" I said into her ear.

"Eternal life." *Shit.* "Just to be part of the family." She winced. Her jaw was already swelling where Horst hit her.

I jumped at the next loud crash. A marble mantel fell off the wall of a side chapel onto the floor, knocking over a wooden cross. I needed to hurry and get us out of there. I thought I could carry her. I didn't *know,* but I was about to find out.

"You are in his family? Who is he?" I put an arm under her neck and, as I took a deep, smokey breath, the other under her knees.

"It's not he, it's *we.* The Medici." She smiled rapturously but shuddered as she faded away. I put her body down.

Had the idea of being part of an ancient family seduced her? Once again, the Voice from the Void preyed on desire.

Chapter Twenty-Three

At some point, Graham, his pinstripe suit from Savile Row wet with his childhood friend's blood, handed me off to the driver. I argued that I should stay with him because he had just seen Horst's murder, and he'd countered by saying he had avenged him. Now, I was in a suite at a luxury hotel. No idea which one. There was a view of the garden. I sat on the bed and looked out at holly bushes and empty urns between reading articles on my phone about the disaster.

According to the internet, fourteen people died at the cathedral. The causes were smoke inhalation, specifically poisoning from inhaling toxic fumes; one man had a heart attack; another fell in the melee and died from a traumatic brain injury. The number rose to fifteen or sixteen depending on whether you included Horst, actually a murder victim, and Sabine, who they said died from a fall. In the earliest reporting, a media outlet said she was a terrorist who jumped from the balcony after the destruction she caused. That article quoted Monsignor Assmann. Suicide, so no heaven for her. Almost immediately, named and unnamed sources debunked the claim that she started the fires. She was terrified by the fire, panicked, and fell to her death. She would be greeted at the pearly gates. In both versions, Graham was a hero. Motorcycle jacket guy was long gone. Horst had been in the wrong place at the wrong time. The Frick would loan Bastiani's, *Adoration of the Magi* to the museum to honor the fallen. At least that much was true.

I had the television on, but the sound was muted. I reached for the remote on the bedside table, but before I shut it off, I checked CNN and BBC. Both were reporting live from the cathedral. I wasn't in any of the video clips either station played on a loop. That meant they didn't have CCT footage. Yet.

My white raincoat lay on a chair, folded with the sides together. I grabbed it off Sabine's corpse so it couldn't be used as evidence for any of the several investigations the attack on the cathedral would surely spawn. The authorities might wonder about Emma's DNA all over it.

I went to the website of the hotel I'd stay at in Rome. I changed my reservation. I would arrive a day early. Next, I changed my flight.

The driver knocked on the bedroom door before opening it. "We need to leave for the airport."

"Where's Graham? I don't want to go without him." I was to fly back to London and from there to the States. He would fly commercial if he had to.

"He'll try to get to the airport before you take off. I hate to rush you, but, uh, that's the way it is. The flight plan was filed." I was being spirited out of the country and away from anything tawdry, like a statement to the police. That worked in my favor.

Anonymous sources gave their contacts in the media some version of though the woman was insane, Emmaline, the angel, ministered to her in her last minutes. Had she said anything? Not a word. "You see," Sir Graham Abbott said, "my wife has nothing to add.'

A low buzz came from my handbag on the bed next to me. "Maybe that's him. I'll be right there." I held up the phone in my hand to help him think the call was coming in on it. Like a good hint-taker, he closed the door and waited for me in the sitting room. I had given a soft Kusshi makeup bag a flat bottom by adding a secret compartment. That's where my US phone was. The tone signaled a call from Valerie on the Emma phone.

"Emma? Thank God. I'm so relieved. Are you in Cologne?" she shouted before I could say hello.

"Yes." Had she been worried about me? It was out of character, but still kind of nice.

"The goddamn painting was destroyed in the fire. Have you been to the cathedral?"

Well, well. The painting was the target all along. The inferno in the nave was set to lure the fire brigade there. I got that, but had Sabine's remote fire starter, or whatever it was, had the range needed to go beyond the nave? The signal would have had to go through walls, too. It was doubtful. Someone else had lit up that crate. Was the painting even in it?

"No." I was a terrible liar and did it surprisingly infrequently, but it was needed now. "Do the police know how the fire got to the painting?"

She yelled out an exasperated sigh. "I guess they have old wiring all over."

"What?"

"Look, I need you to do something."

"What were you saying about old wiring?" I asked.

"Never mind. This is important to the company, and we'll pay your art recovery rate." I had to smile at my mistake about the reason for her call. She gave me the details she'd learned from the head of the Wallraf-Richartz Museum about Strozzi's *The Annunciation.* He had told her about the manufactured provenance. I called it title laundering.

"It casts doubt on the artwork's authenticity, but so far, the analysis hadn't proved that. If it's real, SIRA will be out $500 million dollars. Minimum. You need to find out that it's a fake."

I chose to ignore that last bit. "So, this is about insurance fraud," I said. "Or money laundering?"

She paused. Had she followed what I said? "Maybe, maybe not. Just prove it's a fake."

"You know me better than that, Valerie. Did you say $500 million? Who approved that policy, and who valued the painting that high?"

"Mmmm," she said. It was her.

Would that painting be so close in price to what the Tyndales were willing to pay for the Rembrandt, at $650 million? Art prices were already 'keep your appraiser on speed dial' hot, but when late Microsoft co-founder Paul Allen's blue-chip collection went up for auction in late-2022, the world of international wealth and culture was caught by surprise. His Seurat sold for $149 million and his Van Gogh for $117. A Gauguin and a Klimt each went for over $100 million. *Established* art was a safe haven in times of uncertainty. And that's exactly where big money went in this fraught economic period, the war in Ukraine and shifting global alliances. Got it, but still $500 million for a painting by Zanobi Strozzi?

"But Valerie, since the owner of the painting started the fires, why does SIRA have to pay at all?"

"Huh? God, I wish! Did you hear something?" Before I could answer, she said, "Ancient and faulty wiring caused electrical fires. The policy is new, so we wouldn't be liable for wildfires, but that's not what this was. As much as I would love that lifeline, the facts don't fit." Traditional exclusions in fine art insurance policies were war, civil unrest, nuclear accidents, restorations gone wrong, and something referred to as a work's "inherent vices," which meant natural decay because of the materials the artist used. SIRA now added loss due to climate change to this list of exclusions for new policies. As one of the few fine arts insurers writing new policies, collectors accepted the change, along with the higher premiums, plus deductibles, which fine art policies hadn't seen before. "This was like a house fire."

The hell it was. I knew what I had seen, or rather what Emmaline saw. "Who said that's how they started?" I asked.

"The *Times*, and I guess everybody." By that I assumed she meant the American press, but who planted that misinformation? "There's a priest at the cathedral trying to say something about the woman that jumped from the balcony starting the fires, but she was on a *balcony* and not anywhere near the painting. He's just covering his ass. The place was a death trap."

"Is there anything left from the painting?"

"Nothing but ash." Ouch. When an insurance company paid the claim, it owned the painting. For example, if a stolen painting was recovered. SIRA didn't want to own a handful of ash.

"Not even from the frame?"

"Nothing."

"Then I don't need to go there." Not that I would have. "I want everything the museum has. Photos, x-rays, and not just the reports written from them." The tests the museum did when they had the painting in their possession were all there would be. Ever. The clock had stopped for scientific analysis. I had no intention of wasting my time on the painting's authenticity other than a quick email to London's National Gallery to check on the well-being of their painting with that name. *The Annunciation* was my trail back to the Medici family whenever it was created. "Who will be my contact at the Wallraf-Richartz Museum?"

"You have two, the director and the scientific advisor to the directorate. I'll send you their names. How soon can you get there?" She took a drink of something. More than likely alcoholic.

"Valerie, it's like six in the morning in New York, right?"

"Drew and I have been celebrating with the Tyndale's." I imagined her kind, long-suffering husband's broad face and smiled. "Stephan is relieved as hell that he didn't look like a schmuck over that Rembrandt. After a few drinks, he was bragging to everyone in the club about how he'd outsmarted Sutton House. They're so grateful to SIRA. They asked how you tracked down the real *Self-Portrait 1650* in a private collection?"

"Research. Contacts. The regular way. Don't forget to ask the museum director to send me all he has on the painting. Have they interviewed the van driver?"

"Dunno."

"Or the guards who were assigned to stay with it?"

"They didn't hang around! They ran from the fire. I guess they'll all be questioned." She yawned into the phone. "I need to get some sleep."

"Was the painting taken out of the shipping crate?"

"No. Well, I don't think so." She was drifting. Getting bored or about to pass out.

"Is there anything left of the container?" I asked.

"More ash." So it wasn't fireproof. That was convenient for someone.

"They would have taken photographs and video of the painting in the packing container while it was still at the museum. I want to see those, too." Of course, those could be faked, but even that could be used in court. "Have them get CCT footage of the truck en route."

"Are you sure you don't want to go over there?" she whined.

"No need. I don't know if I can trust the museum's leadership. I hope I can rely on their information." Actually, there was no reason not to trust Horst's contact at the museum. I had gone over this morning's sequence of events. He hadn't listened to Horst's message, didn't even know about it, but Sabine did. One or both phones were tapped.

"Whatever. Just don't waste time looking into arson."

"Who's the beneficiary of the policy?" I asked.

Ice clinked in a crystal glass. "The payout would go to a law office in Jersey." I squeezed my eyes shut at the nonchalant tone. More like a shell company. "The true owner's name probably won't appear anywhere." SIRA would never, ever be able to say *the owner* started the fire. "That's why I'm saying not to waste time on that. We need to know it's not *The Annunciation* by Zanobi Strozzi."

"Now I understand." The painting was owned by a network of offshore closely held companies. They would have secret bank accounts all over the world. Bits of money came out of them to buy the painting, and when SIRA paid up, the funds would go back into those tributaries.

"I need a new laptop. Can you transfer me to Lynya?" If I was going to be both Emma and Emmaline for the next twenty-four hours, I needed a virgin computer.

"Misplace yours? Or was it stolen?"

"Maybe it'll show up."

"Sure." She cackled at my carelessness. "Guess what else the Wallraf-Richartz Museum director told me? Emmaline Abbott was there at the cathedral. Do you know her?"

"No."

"Well, she's in a hospital, I mean *in hospital*, in London for mental distress. Sedated. She was *there*! Lucky girl." Then shouted for Lynya to pick up the call.

Chapter Twenty-Four

When I picked up the raincoat, the buckle clanked against the wooden end of the chair's armrest. No, there was something in the pocket. What had I left in there? I needed to get rid of the coat so I had better check all the pockets. I gasped when I saw the steel cylinder. Sabine hadn't convulsed before she died; she had moved her arms to put whatever this was in my raincoat pocket.

* * *

On the way to the airport, I asked the driver if blood could be removed from the lining of the Burberry raincoat. He thought it could. I gave it to him for his wife. He said there was no wife, but his daughter would appreciate it very much. I reminded him to get it professionally cleaned right away. He said he would.

"Leave me at Terminal One."

"Your plane takes off from General Services." He looked at me in the rear-view mirror. Would I cause trouble? Would he?

"I'll get something to eat first." There was something I needed to buy that they didn't have in the terminal reserved for private and chartered jets.

"They have meals on board—"

"Thank you."

He nodded. Not a sore loser.

I left the coat in the car and took the plastic bag for hotel laundry and my handbag into the terminal.

Graham didn't join me at the airport. I hadn't really expected him. He met with Horst's family in Germany, then put in motion arrangements to return his friend's body to England after the murder investigation. We would pay for anything they needed. I would fly from London back to the States. I didn't mention that I would go to the Vatican first.

Inside, I read a long list of stores in the airport terminal. Luxus-Ledergeschäft? The small photo of the smiling cobbler wearing lederhosen looked promising, and it was nearby, so if they didn't have what I was looking for, I would have time to try other stores. Or maybe not. If I had to buy an airline ticket to get to the duty-free shops, a suspicious amount of time would be gobbled up.

The smell of leather met me at the store entrance. I was in the right place. I quickly chose gloves, adult size, and a child's leather jacket and paid with my AMEX. "I need a gift box for the gloves," I said to the sales clerk. "How about the size you use for a tie?"

"You want to surprise someone?" she asked.

I nodded. "He'll never guess *this* gift." We two conspirators shared a laugh.

From there, I went to the ladies' room. I got to work as soon as I latched the stall door. Wearing my new leather gloves, I took the instrument Sabine had used to ignite the fires out of the bag from the hotel and studied it. It looked like a hair-curling iron or maybe more like a dildo. After I rubbed it on the leather jacket several times up and down the arms, I put it in the gift box.

Deliver to the police or Monsignor Assmann, Cologne Cathedral, I wrote in immature block letters, dotting the i's with circles. Nothing subtle. Like an American speaking to a non-English speaker. On my way out of the airport, I reported an unattended package left on a seat. You're welcome. Can't be too careful.

Chapter Twenty-Five

SATURDAY NIGHT IN ROME, ITALY

The drive from the Leonardo da Vinci airport to the Hotel Della Conciliazione, a boutique hotel on a cobblestone street off of Borgo Pio, went as smoothly as it could for someone in a rented Fiat 500 who didn't speak Italian. Google translated the name of the powdery-grey-green color of my car to *green dew*. It reminded me of a cleaning product. I was fine on the A91, but the Cristoforo Colombo exit was tricky. I pulled into the hotel's garage just after four in the afternoon. The handsome young man behind the reception desk wore a black linen suit that was a uniform. In his case, the man made the clothes. It was faded from being cleaned probably a million times, but with his smoldering good looks, the renovated old hotel looked young and hip.

I was about a hundred meters from St. Peter's, and the area was beautiful in the late afternoon sun. A run would do me good, but I had work to do. Thanks to Lynya, a new M2 chip, MacBook Air waited for me. The display was 13.6 inches, but it was 224 pixels, supporting a billion colors that I needed. I took it and went up to my room.

Valerie's text read **You got lucky. A prist or somethng shwed up wth a fire igniter thingy. Was arson. Pay out on hold pnding ivestigation. How did yu say you knew?**

It was the typed version of slurred words. It buoyed my spirits to know I didn't have to prove the authenticity of a painting that no longer existed to stop millions of dollars from being used for this war the Voice wanted to start. Zanobi Strozzi scholars could take the authenticity question and run with it.

It was late morning in Manhattan. I dialed the number of a very powerful friend on the off chance that I could reach her on a Saturday. Florence Bracewell was the President and Chief Executive Officer of the Metropolitan Museum. Her calls were transferred to her admin, who checked with her and then put me through.

"Emma! Outstanding work on calling out those forgeries."

"Thank you. *But* the job's not done."

"There will be forgers as long as there's an opaque industry filled with high-priced, usually easily transported objects. Look, I'm having brunch with Ted Hunter, my armorer, at the moment."

"Emma, keep up the good work," a male voice called out.

"Please thank him and tell him that I intend to." The Met had an armorer on staff. Full time. An armorer.

"When can you come in for us to talk?" Florence asked. "I'd like your take on this shift toward acknowledging the gray areas with attribution." For some paintings, especially those over a hundred years old, there was no way to achieve absolute certainty about its provenance. In a market where value was inextricably tied to attribution, the difference in Expert A's and Expert B's opinions was worth millions. Joseph Duveen and others had weaponized that power.

"I'd like to talk about that when I get back. I'm in Rome for a few days, but what I need to ask you can't wait."

"Launch," she said.

Florence was brilliant and successful, but her management style was the opposite of what was taught in B-school. She inspired terror. When in doubt, she bullied. She never let a subordinate forget a mistake. I helped her last year when a certain philanthropist was murdered in Gallery 901, in the Modern and Contemporary Art Section of *her* museum. (And that was how she referred to the Met.) Though we didn't know it at the time, that was the opening salvo in a world war on art. I arranged for her to be the public face of getting museums to protect themselves long enough for the Vatican to disavow the Messengers of Mary. It added to her renown and saved me from unwanted, though flattering and possibly financially profitable, publicity. I hoped I wasn't about to squander that goodwill with my bizarre plan.

"I recently learned that at least some of the recent sales of out-of-the-blue masterpieces were orchestrated by the same person or organization. I want to pause all art sales to stop their flow of money." Dead air. "Florence, are you still there?"

"You want to bring a five hundred and eighty billion dollars, with a b, b as in *balls*, market to a screeching halt. Am I understanding you correctly?"

"Yes, but only temporarily."

"Fuck a duck. For how long?"

"I don't know."

"You don't know." Her staccato delivery scared me. "Even if we stopped these, let's be generous and call them incorrectly attributed masterpieces, from entering museums, like what happened at the National Museum for Women in the Arts, for instance, what about the rest of our problems? I suppose next, you'll want to take on looting, theft, trafficking, money laundering, terrorist financing, sanctions violations, insurance fraud, tax evasion, and market manipulation."

"I—"

"No, don't answer that. And we would do this, how?"

"If the Met and its board announced that it was going to take a break, maybe other museums and the major auction houses would do the same." Lame. Ridiculous.

"Why would they?'

"Because you are the Met," I said.

"Wonder if we can get a couple of big-name collectors interested? Taylor and Stephan Tyndale should be with us. How about Sir Graham Abbott and his wife? They almost had their names mixed up in this." How did she know that?

"I'll contact them."

"Good. Now, a little free advice from me to you. Sleep on this. If you still want to pursue it, call me back tomorrow. You can help me draft emails to Candace and Tony." Candace Beinecke and Tony James co-chaired the Museum's Board of Trustees. "If I don't hear from you, I'll assume you came to your senses."

We hung up, and I emailed talking points for her use. *The authentication space in today's art market is in trouble. The nature of the process has always been subjective; populism tells people there's no such thing as an expert, and, of course, there's the high prices that we love and hate equally.*

I was tired and afraid of making mistakes. I wanted to stay away from the name Medici, at least for now. It could burn me, or at least keep me from sleeping. Maybe not all roads led to Florence, but enough of them had to cause a traffic jam. It was there that artists first used copper as a substrate. Just a few years later, the trend moved to Rome, where it was most famously used by Flemish painter Paul Bril, whose work, especially his use of light, influenced Rembrandt. Had Bettina's art history nerdery gone that deep? Was that how she knew which deviations from the Voice's instructions to make to keep it plausible? He had her killed for it. Then, there was Elisa's information on the Florentine expression.

I couldn't stop thinking about how horrible it would be if the Abbott art collection included masterpieces from the Gardner robbery. It would kill Graham. With the investigations and media scrutiny, there was no way my secret would stay safe during that. If we found the Raphael, it would not be seen as the selfless labor of love it was. It would look like reputation restoration. I believed the Voice when he said his motive was amassing a large amount of money, but had it been two-fold? Did he also want to destroy Graham?

I took a T-shirt out of my suitcase. A hundred years ago I left the Goring with two suitcases. One held the evening dress and jewelry I wore on Friday night. It went back to Bath, where the housekeeper, Tia, would care for it. The other piece of luggage went on the plane with us to Cologne, ready for when I returned to the States and the work world they thought I inhabited.

After scrubbing the day, the fire, the deaths off my face, I dropped onto my back on the plush bed. The room was small by American hotel standards, but not by European norms. Maybe twelve feet from wall to wall. The drapes were grey, and the bedding was white. The parquet floor was cold. The sheets were ironed. Ironed. I breathed in and felt myself getting lighter. I thought better when I was surrounded by minimalist interior design.

My eyes exploded open at the sound of my phone ringing. Both phones were on the bedside table. It was dark outside, and the Eternal City was buzzing. The US phone flashed. I picked it up and saw I had slept for almost two hours.

It was Bobbi. "Thanks for calling me back."

"Okay, genius, you were right about the Rembrandt." She was cheery and teasing. "Though I wish you hadn't been."

"Why?"

"Because I would have loved to take a selfie with it. Wouldn't you? Taylor could rent it out for just that. I knew you would get to the truth. By the way, did Valerie give you the good news?"

I sat up and propped against the oversized pillows. "She said the Tyndales thanked SIRA."

"She didn't tell you they recommended, and Florence agreed for the Met to put you on retainer? Congratulations! You've made it, my friend."

"She didn't mention it, but when have you ever known Valerie to talk about anyone but herself?"

"True."

"I spoke with Florence Bracewell earlier, and she didn't mention it either." Or maybe she thought that was the reason for my call. It was an honor. I appreciated the confidence it showed in me, but was it something I wanted? Would it bring publicity? I didn't want my photo on their website. Did I really want to work for Florence Bracewell? The answer was that no one did, but everyone wanted to work for the Met.

"She'll have one of her scared rabbits send you the offer and contract." Good, I had time to think about it. "Where are you?" Was there any reason to lie to her, my friend? "You know, you make me nervous when I ask you that, and you hesitate."

"Sorry. Do you remember the computer voice calls I got last year?" I asked.

"Uh, yeah. He financed the Messengers of Mary and Ali, the hit man." She was one of the few people I knew with true bravado. It wasn't bluster if you earned it by fighting human traffickers year after year in a city like New York. The hell of it was that she won time and time again, but they kept coming.

"He's back."

It was her turn to be speechless, so she whistled. Finally, she said, "Wait, didn't they put that group out of business?"

"He's behind the recent forgeries."

"And the movement of money or attempts at-. Oh."

"Yeah."

"How can I help you? Not saying I can, though. Anyway, making money by painting a pretty picture and signing it DaVinci or somebody and selling it to some rich stiff is squeaky clean compared to where I thought the money was coming from."

"He almost killed my mother."

"Your mother? Why didn't you say so? Let's go after him."

"I don't know if she was the target or if I was. It was after he had other people killed. The body count is getting pretty high. One was arguably the greatest artist of our time-."

"You're talking about Julia Belvedere Jones?"

"He admitted to being behind that one, but I don't have evidence to prove it."

She chuckled. "Don't worry about that. Evidence is for other people."

"Uh, riiiight. And the next was a gallerist who was a friend of mine, and the third was Bettina Vogt, who I think was trying to help me stop him."

"He killed Bettina Vogt, the girl who worked everywhere?" she asked.

"Yes. The police are looking at the collectors she cheated. And that makes sense."

"You know what they say, the problem with cheating the rich and powerful is that they are rich and powerful."

"But it wasn't a collector," I said. "It was him."

"Are you sure?"

153

"I am. He told me."

"I don't know if talking to him is such a good idea, but for now, let's talk about why he went after your mother. The three people you listed were in the art world, one way or another. She's not."

"Because I have cost him serious coin," I said.

"You stopped the $3 million dollar sale of the Lempicka. Then, the fake Rembrandt. Let me see, that's—"

"Don't forget the Julia Belvedere Jones painting. That $15 million is frozen. The total is six hundred and sixty-eight million dollars. And I think he may be trying a five hundred million dollar insurance scam, but he won't get it."

"Whoa. If he gets that, it'll be over that "b" number. Let's not kid ourselves. That's a lot of money."

I laughed out loud. "Bobbi, absolutely no one is arguing the other side of that."

"I'm assuming since you haven't told me his name, you don't know it."

"I believe he is in the Medici family." Did I sound crazy? I couldn't tell her what Sabine Gaddi told Emmaline. Would she believe me? It sounded like something Valerie would say. That level.

"Does he want to buy a palace or something?"

"He said it was for a war." Officially crazy. In Valerie-land.

"Does Elliott know about all this?" Now, her tone was all business.

"Yes. Well, most of it. Okay, some of it. He had the account with the proceeds of the Belvedere Jones painting sale frozen," I answered. "He has a lot on his plate right now." I told her about his summons to appear before Congress at a hearing by the House Committee on Oversight and Accountability on Monday.

"Congresswoman Tessum is the Chair, right?" It sounded like she was writing something.

"Yes, but that's an odd bit of trivia for you to throw out."

"You're going to keep pissing Mr. Medici off, aren't you?" Changing the conversation.

"I plead reality," I answered. "I'll do all I can to keep him from putting misattributed art into collections. And that means standing in between him

154

and his big paydays."

"Good girl. We need help."

"Whoever he plans to go to war against would be a logical partner, but I don't know who that is."

We agreed I needed more information and talked a little longer. I felt refreshed after my nap and got up and looked out the french doors to my balcony. It was a beautiful night for a run. I put on a pair of leggings and a fleece jacket over my tee and tucked my passport into a pocket. Before I left, Emmaline emailed Florence Bracewell wholeheartedly endorsing a temporary freeze on art transactions. In the morning as Emma, I would email her to confirm the moratorium. I would sleep on it as she asked, but I would not change my mind.

I took the stairs, rather than the elevator, for a warm up. Outside the hotel, I looked left, then right, and chose the direction of the Vatican. In the first step, I felt a lump in my jacket pocket. From habit, I had brought my car keys. I wasn't going out for long, so it wasn't worth the time to take them back to my room. I'd put up with the thump against my leg.

I thought about the Voice saying connoisseurship was performance-y. In the crisp night air, I composed wounding comebacks. I had seen art experts put a stethoscope up to a painting. That was an act.

At the end of the block, as I waited to cross the street, something bit me. "Ouch." I slapped the back of my neck and wondered about mosquitoes in winter.

Chapter Twenty-Six

"Prego affrettarsi." Antony hoped the Brit knew that phrase was sarcasm. He considered himself facile at languages. All it took was learning about three hundred words in a new tongue and presto.

"I'm sorry, but my Italian is limited."

Was this tosser pretending he didn't know a warning when he heard one? He guessed they didn't teach that at boarding school. Or maybe, by some miracle, Antony had lived to be so old that other men no longer feared him.

"She put up a fight when I put her in the van, but then she passed out and hasn't moved since. You need to hurry up and get here," he said, teeth clenched.

"You're telling me she's been out for almost twenty-four hours?"

"Yeah, more or less." Antony shrugged.

"Did you use the correct dosage?"

"All of what was in the syringe I got from the hospital went into her." He was a professional. He didn't need this. "Whose bright idea was it to bring her to a church on Saturday night if she needed to be outta sight for two days? Like, you do know what this place is like on Sunday, right? There was a mass at 10:30 this morning, and then the place filled up with tourists. She's here now, so don't pee your pants." Antony had given her a little something from his personal *farmacia* and left her in the parked van until everyone had cleared out. From the tchotchke peddler in their gift shop to the priests. They were finally all gone.

"This has all been very last minute. I think she changed her travel plans. How is her breathing?"

"Ehh." He raised his hand, palm up, like the guy on the other end of the call could see him. *"Non lo so*. I don't know."

"Well, go and check."

His big feet hurt, but he walked over and looked through the peephole he had drilled through the wood door, which was also old. "Yeah, looks like she is."

"I will take an early flight in the morning and be there around eight."

"No way you can come tonight?"

The man on the other end of the call hesitated. Had he changed his mind about when he would get here? He heard voices in the background. Maybe he was waiting until he could talk again. "I can't get away until tomorrow. Look here, I'm a little concerned about her going so long without water."

"I know he wants her alive, but if she dies on me, you'll still owe what we agreed. Next time you talk to your boss, ask about my latest invoice." Antony loved using words like that in connection with his work.

"I'll be there in the morning. If she wakes up, give her a little water. A small amount at first."

"She won't. And that's not my job, so you better get here."

Antony had been paid for the hit and run in New York but was owed for taking care of the forger. Dismemberment extra. He hadn't decided if he would charge them for killing the artist in DC since he contracted that out. Poor Vince. Too bad. The kid was his cousin. He asked him to be there with him for his first job, and he'd told him he would be. But he had left early. Like when things went sideways. Not happening. Rule number one was to never be where you're expected.

He rolled up his leather jacket for a pillow. Then he lowered himself back on a bench that must be a thousand years old and thought about a dream he'd had years ago. In it no house in the entire world had indoor plumbing. Outdoor loos everywhere you looked. And the stench! So, kid, missing the rest of your life in this world wasn't such a bad thing.

Then he slept.

Chapter Twenty-Seven

I was on a floor. One of my nightmares was waking up and not knowing where I was. That was now. It was even more horrifying than I imagined it would be. I wasn't in either house. Someone brought me to wherever this was.

I remembered going out for a run. Cobblestones, shops, and streetlamps. A brick wall. Vatican City was behind it. I was cold and alone. But hadn't I just heard a noise? Someone else was here.

The dark and my mind dangled two options in front of me: pretend to be asleep until I knew more, or run for my life now. Paralyzing terror, more powerful than anything I'd ever felt kept me from choosing.

A scraping sound. That was what woke me. A door closed. A man bellowed, "You kidnapped the wrong goddamn woman!" The volume, or maybe it was the gauziness, told me he was in a different room. British. Angry. Jumpy. Was I back in England? "Do you realize what you've done?" I knew that voice. My eyes grew accustomed to the dark, and black became grey. I turned over to see one pinpoint of light. The effort of that slight movement exhausted me. If I wasn't careful, I would go back to sleep. I focused on that word, kidnap. It was neighbors with words like ransom. Had that process started? If it had, with whom? Elliott or Graham?

"Yo, watch your tone. That's Emma Kelly. I got a *photograph*." He had said my name. Well, one of them. It was all the motivation I needed to stay awake. This voice was gravelly, octaves lower than the first man.

"What photo? No, I don't care. That's Emmaline Abbott in there. You idiot! You kidnapped the bloody wife of one of the richest men in England.

158

He is someone you do not want to make mad." This man was younger, or maybe he led an easier life than his friend. Who was he?

"*Calmati,* Doc." That sounded Italian. "The *photo* I have is the one on her passport." He chuckled at his own joke. I had stuffed my passport in a jacket pocket when I went out.

Doc? I sat straight up like a swimmer, breaking through the surface of the water to air. I knew who he was. The younger man was Sheldon Martin, Charlotte's husband. Why would a pediatrician kidnap Emma Kelly, a woman he didn't know? Why would he kidnap anyone? Ransom money. Could he be the voice from the void? Hard no. He was more vapor than man, while Sheldon was all too human. And why had I connected *him,* the Voice, to whatever this was? He hadn't contacted me in days. There was this sculpture that SIRA insured, which decayed for no apparent reason. It was what it was, and it didn't matter that we never connected the dots. He was my only enemy. That's why. Once I accepted that, my head began to clear.

"She is my wife's sister-in-law, I'm telling you!" Sheldon was saying.

"Go back in there and look again." The older man was toying with him. Did Sheldon realize that? Doubtful.

"And have her recognize me? No way." The voice moved. He was pacing.

"Just look through the peephole. You can at least do that, can't you?"

I quickly laid back down and faced the wall. When I did, the pain kicked in, hard, but I didn't make a sound. My left hip and shoulder hurt, but then so did my back and neck. As I lay there, I inventoried body parts, including between my legs. I hadn't been raped.

"Yeah, it's her," Sheldon said.

"Her who? Which one?"

"It's Emmaline Abbott." Silly Sheldon had only pretended to look. The idea of him as a criminal mastermind was laughable, but earlier, when he came into the room, he saw my face, and that made him just as dangerous to me.

"Look, Doc, how do you figure into all this anyway?" I heard someone strike a match.

"What do you mean? Uh, are you supposed to smoke in here?"

"Your boss pays me, but you're the only one I talk to." The words had to fit around the mechanics of lighting a cigarette and that first fine puff.

"He's a distant relation, not my boss." Was Sheldon saying he was a Medici? Martin didn't sound Italian, but Martini did. That was why he had reacted the way he did in the car outside the V&A when Charlotte called him Dr. Martini. Was that his real name?

"Whatever you say." Patronizing.

Next, I heard movement I couldn't identify, then something small and plastic rattled together. "What are you doing?" Sheldon asked.

"You stay here. I'm going to her hotel to ask for—what's her name again?"

"Emmaline Abbott." The tone he used was not a compliment. "Her husband is, uh, nobody." Why had he stopped short of naming Graham? A rare, for Sheldon, perceptiveness lived in that half sentence. I would like to believe it was appreciation or respect, but his tone suggested an awareness closer to fear.

"I'll ask at the hotel if she's staying there. I say that woman is Emma Kelly."

"I'm telling you, she's not."

"Whoever she is, I'm moving her car." An image of the keys to the rental car tapping my hip as I jogged floated in my head. I felt in one jacket pocket, then the other. They were gone, but my room key was still there. "You figure somebody has reported her missing. The first place the cops will look for her is the hotel. If it's not there, it'll buy us some time. It'll make 'em wonder, did she go off shopping? Maybe sightseeing in the Eternal City. If she's *your* person, she won't need it since she won't be driving again."

"What do you mean? You're going to kill her?" he whined. I wanted to tell him to grow up.

"We can't let her walk out of here, can we? He said to keep Emma Kelly where no one would find her for two days, but don't hurt her. He never said anything about keeping anybody else alive."

"I don't know. It *would* make my life easier. I mean, maybe," Sheldon sputtered. Idiot. It hadn't been a question or a decision for him to weigh in on, but a sadistic offer of power to the powerless. "I have to think about it." Graham, with no wife or heir, was a wet dream for all four of them. How

160

convenient.

"You do that. Think away."

"How do you know which car is hers?" Sheldon's voice was stronger. He was even more stupid than I thought.

"Click, click. I'll just walk through the garage." The rougher man said with a chuckle, then he was gone.

So, we were somewhere near my hotel. We were either in Rome or Vatican City. Had we gone over the Tiber? I didn't know. Had we driven over a bridge? Was that a memory or a dream? Crossing bridges gave me the same bliss flying did. It was a time when no one could find me. I didn't remember feeling that.

The soles of Sheldon's expensive shoes whispered on a path back and forth in front of the door. At some point, his phone rang.

"Hi, Char." That's what he called Charlotte, and she called him Shel. They thought they were cute. Or something. He listened to her and said, "Yeah, the flight to Glasgow was fine. The university programme is running behind schedule." *Shedule.* "I should still be back tonight. Call you later." Pause. "Kiss, kiss you, too." If they were going to kill me, why couldn't they have done it before I had to listen to that? We weren't in Scotland, and Shel was a bad boy.

Now that I knew approximately where I was, the next question was how I could get away. And what would I do then? Sheldon had seen me. He didn't know I had identified him. What would he say when we were together again? Which was always with Graham. What *could* he say? "Were you, by any chance, kidnapped in Rome last week?" If—and that was a big if considering what I'd seen of his utter inability to see what was right in front of him—he figured out I was both Emma Kelly and Emmaline Abbott, would the fool dare blackmail me? He was the type who would try. Did he need money? Or had the Voice found another weak spot to press his thumb down on?

I got up off the floor. Legally, I had more on him than he had on me. He was involved in kidnapping me for God knew what reason.

Chapter Twenty-Eight

Antony took a taxi to the Hotel Della Conciliazione and waltzed in with what he believed to be a charming smile, carrying a large bouquet of flowers that he could not have named with a gun held to his penis. The television in the lobby was on but muted. A boy and girl, bored but behaving, stared at it. He froze. Then, he pulled out his phone and pretended to check the screen. Shook his head. Silly me. Walked back out.

Putting the doc's mind at ease about the name of the woman he kidnapped didn't mean squat now. He had seen himself, leather jacket and all, on the telly. His photo with *Wanted Antony Pullella*, under it was next to one of the woman he was working with. He turned down the alley that ran along the side of the hotel and took off the treasured jacket and the waste of twenty-euros-thank-you-very-much flowers. The weather was cold, but he had on a sweater underneath and didn't look out of place. He was too mad to feel the cold. Christ, his picture and name were out there. This all needed to go away. He'd been more visible this week than in the last decade. He wanted the money he was owed, sure, but what he wanted more was to stay out of prison. He felt his heart beating in his chest. He was taking all the risks. From the hit and run in New York to that shit show in Cologne. Hold on a minute. They knew he was at that cathedral. Maybe he died there? He was *wanted*, which he wouldn't be if they thought that. He was scared and, for once, didn't feel the hard cobblestones through his Italian shoes.

He thought about what else he'd seen on the television screen while he walked around the block. They had a photo of his remote fire starter. He guessed they found that in the cathedral, but why had they linked it to him and not...? What was her name? Something that started with an S. Maybe it started with an S. His prints weren't on it. Hers were. What about that old dude? The one who threw her off the balcony. He couldn't believe the old guy had it in him. Maybe he could grass him up? He had never done that in his life, but the guy looked like he could afford it.

Fires were his specialty, but no one knew that. Until now. Now, the cops would look at him for everything from an inferno to a campfire. His career was over.

He stopped to light a cigarette and scrolled through his news feed. Sixteen people died in the cathedral fire. What else? She had an accomplice who lied about the cathedral doors being locked. Well, that wasn't good. He had ad-libbed to buy time when what's her name stopped before all the chapels were on fire. Guess this meant he wasn't seen as a good Samaritan the way he planned. Another article said she was maficso since she spoke with an Italian accent. Sure, let's go with that.

Hold on a minute here—not all the bodies had been identified. Good. He could use that.

Over the years, as he made bank, he had set up a few retirement possibilities. A cabin here, a beach shack there. He was finally getting out. Maybe he would go live somewhere around people. Maybe he would meet someone. Get married. He had a son, who, according to Facebook, now had a son of his own. After a few years, when it was safe, he might call him. He'd do that as soon as he could answer simple questions like a normal person. For example, 'Where do you live?' Yeah, that's what he would do. He'd get his son's phone number and call him. Or visit? Too much? He'd telephone first and see how that went. Easy does it. He spent his years making plans, some very elaborate, and implementing them. That's not what this was, though. Or maybe it was. Maybe his kid would say, "Hi, Dad." Wouldn't that be nice? First, he would tie up loose ends here in Rome. The 'Antony died in the fire at the cathedral in Cologne, Germany story' would only work until all the bodies were identified. It would buy him days, not years. What he was about to do would be permanent.

He looked around and went in the back entrance to the hotel's garage. It was small, one floor, so he found the little car after a couple of clicks of the key fob. A source of irritation was getting out of the garage without a ticket, but that was resolved by backing up and then driving at the flimsy aluminum bar at the exit gate.

He had to laugh thinking about how the video of this would look to the cops as they searched for Emma Kelly. That was her name, right?

Chapter Twenty-Nine

The older man was back, and this time I saw him through the hole in the door. He laid the keys to my rental car on a small table by the door.

"Where've you been? The hotel is, what, two miles from here?" Sheldon whined.

"The church will open up soon. We better get out of here." He walked toward my door, and I backed up. Now that it was light, I saw my door didn't have a lock, or even a knob. Something metal slid against the door. A latch? That he had opened. I looked around for something to use as a weapon. Anything. Along two walls, there were several types of clerical vestments: chasubles, stoles, dalmatics, and others I couldn't name. Nothing I could use to fight him with, but I could hide. No, not without being trapped against a wall. The guy was big, but I guessed not fast. I would fight, then run.

When the door didn't open, and I didn't hear anything from the outer room, I went back to my post to watch them.

He stood in front of Sheldon. "I have one more thing to do before I go." He wasn't coming in. At least not yet.

Sheldon let out a high-pitched yelp. The large man had him by the front of his shirt and was about to hit him with his fist. With the guy's hundred-pound weight advantage, it was sure to be a knockout blow. The pediatrician's eyes bulged as he squirmed to get away. He writhed like a fish on a line. I almost laughed when I saw what Sheldon was trying to do. Only an aristocrat would be audacious enough to try a Bertie Wooster and Jeeves move like that. He swung lower and lower, using momentum and agility until he was low enough to grab his opponent's penis and balls with those long, scrawny arms. The man roared, loosening his grip in his surprise. Sheldon pulled free and ran to the door, grabbing the car keys on his way out.

"Noooo," the man bellowed, chasing after him.

They were both gone, and my door was unlocked. I wanted to wait and think, but they could come back any minute. I looked around to see if I was leaving anything behind. I would decide later if I—either Emma or Emmaline—had been there. I was leaving nothing behind but a little DNA.

I opened the thick wooden door with its antique hinges and stepped into a sitting room. What I hadn't seen through the hole was a sofa, upholstered in emerald green linen, with carved legs, two pink and green striped silk armchairs, and an incongruous wooden bench. The massive, unadorned antique sat to the side. The man said the church was about to open, but this piece of furniture was the first sign that I was, in fact, in one. And which church? Rome had over nine hundred.

I looked out at a short hallway, senses on high alert for a trap. It was empty. What was all this for? They hadn't held me for two days. If my bladder was to be believed, not even close. Their fight wasn't part of a deception. Sheldon was truly shocked and scared when the man attacked him. At least one of them would be back. But why had he unlatched my door? My passport was on the table by the door, and I put it in my jacket pocket, where my hotel room key was.

I stopped and put my ear to the first door I came to in the hall. The ancient wood caressed my face. "You're safe," it whispered. I jerked away. Maybe the drugs were still in my system, maybe not, but I couldn't stay where I was. I opened the door.

The next room was round, made of brick and concrete and sculptures. Sun shone down from an opening in the domed roof high above me, seemingly for the sole purpose of transforming marble and other decorative stones on the walls and floor into a controlled riot of yellows, pinks, greys, and whites. My breath caught somewhere deep inside me. I was in the Pantheon, where Raphael's tomb was. The reason my captors chose this spot, I'd have to figure out later. The men were gone, so I ran between the high altar and the few wooden benches provided for worshipers and twirled around with my arms outstretched. The temple was half an American football field in diameter. It was the largest unsupported concrete dome in the world.

The genius of its design and how it had been used, cared for, and loved for nearly two thousand years were the reasons the Pantheon existed today. The theory that the name meant it was built to worship *all gods*, was replaced with the more likely view that it would be used for emperors not yet deified since Romans held this honor up until after the ruler's death. Later, the deified emperor Hadrian, of Hadrian's Wall fame, was honored here. There was another temple to him down the street, but all that was left of it was a marble slab on the exterior of a modern financial building. When the Roman Empire became Christian, the Pantheon became the Church of St. Mary of the Martyrs. It was remarkably well-preserved because it was a living building.

I stopped and rubbed my face, then shook out my hair, trying to get rid of this pastel-dreamy state I was in. I couldn't go back into the world until I knew what waited for me there. Without a phone, how could I find out? There was a chance neither Elliott, who thought I was in London, nor Graham, who thought I was in the U.S., had reported me missing. I didn't know. There was *so much* I didn't know. Some people could tell the time of day from the sun coming in from the oculus, over a hundred feet up. I wasn't one of them. All I knew was that it was light outside. I remembered it was Sunday morning, before church services.

What should I do about the Sheldon problem? I doubted he had told his wife, or Graham, or Caroline, definitely not her, about seeing me. How would he explain his role in whatever this was? Left. Right. He wouldn't dare try to blackmail me. Would he?

The explosion knocked me down. When I hit the marble floor, I landed on my sore shoulder.

Chapter Thirty

There are idiots and then there are idiots, then there are people like this guy. Antony felt sorry for any patient of his, if he was even a real doctor. The plan was to knock the guy out with one quick pop, letting the girl watch. What was her name again? She would see him go and come out of her closet. She'd take her keys and the first time she unlocked the car, she'd be gone. Along with half the city block. The first explosion would probably wake the doc up. Maybe not. He'd added three follow-ons. If number one didn't kill him, the second or third would. He wouldn't know it, so it didn't really count as murder. If the doc made it that far, he would go outside, and the fourth in the chain would do him in. Probably, debris would hit him. That was one part of the genius in the plan. He'd recovered his jacket from the alley and left it on the sidewalk. The cops would declare him dead. Retirement would begin.

Now, he had to stop this idiot before he clicked…

Chapter Thirty-One

I saw Munch's *Scream* behind my eyelids when I blinked because I, too, held my hands against the sides of my head. My mouth hung open. Could I lose my mind from fright? I thought you *can* get out of here. Then, just the opposite. No way I was going to save myself. The loss of the ability to reason terrified me most. I wanted to run, but I also wanted to curl up and never stop screaming.

Maybe the second explosion wasn't as powerful. Or maybe the ringing in my ears tamped the sound. I was able to stand after whatever the air did to me the first time, but this blast may have knocked me down for good. Instinctively, I broke the fall with the heels of both hands, protecting my shoulder. The smallest bit of grit embedded there felt like broken glass, so I quickly lowered myself onto my elbows to relieve the pain. I faced the high altar and craned my neck to look around. By some miracle, those bronze doors, probably added in the fifteenth century when Rome came out of the dark and into the Renaissance, held. Did the Corinthian pillars on the portico still stand? The granite was stolen from Egypt and brought in ships across the Mediterranean Sea, but had they ever had to endure anything this bad? God. Would there be more? Were these bombs? Gas line explosions?

If I was going to die here, I knew where I wanted my body to be found. The tomb of one of the greatest artists of the Renaissance, Raphael Sanzio, was on the right wall. I crawled forward on my stomach. He asked to be buried in the Pantheon and in that very spot for a reason. That was where the last light of the day coming in from the twenty-seven-foot diameter oculus landed.

He became more appreciated and famous after he died. Three centuries later, he was a rock star. So much so that Pope Gregory XVI had his tomb opened. The skeleton was confirmed to be the artist's. Better not to overthink how that determination was made. Certainly not with DNA analysis, like Monsignor Assmann had access to for the Magi.

I could rest when I got to it. These days, it was behind glass, but I could see it. Almost immediately, I was exhaling puffs of air through my lips from the pain in my right shoulder, now both hips, hands, wrists, head. Plaster rained down on my legs and back.

I was within sight of the Madonna of the Rock statue above Raphael's tomb. He had commissioned his pupil, Lorenzetto, to carve it. Giuseppe de Fabris's bronze bust of the artist was in the alcove on the left. That's what I was looking at when the third blast rang through the Pantheon. I dropped my face into the crook of my elbow and covered the back of my head and neck with my hands. My own touch reassured me in a simple, stupid, inborn way. Staying alive didn't matter—the twenty-foot thick walls would protect me—getting to the artist's sarcophagus did. He was born and died on Good Friday. He was thirty-seven, and I was almost that old. I crawled again. That was the last of them, I thought. Three, a trinity, was complete. Three wise men. Bettina's three fragrant flowers and three bones. I pulled myself along the marble floor, faster now. Closer with every new wave of pain and every exhale.

I crawled under the velvet rope and touched the glass covering the ellipse. The brickwork of the original niche had been replaced with marble. Grey, black and white. Cold. A decorative floral wreath and two doves were added. So many times in this last year, I imagined, no, I *did* talk to Raphael. I assured him I would never stop looking for *Portrait of a Young Man.* I rolled over onto my back and closed my eyes to rest. He would have to understand.

Chapter Thirty-Two

T he gust slid me along the polished marble and gilt floor. Flat on my back, I flew through the square and circle designs on the floor. My body knew there had been another blast. I scrambled to get back to Raphael's tomb, grasping for something to grab with flailing arms. One hand ran over a drain built into the floor to catch the rain and the rare snowflake. My running shoes futilely pounded the floor. Because of the round shape of the room, I knew a wall would finally stop me. When it did the impact restarted the pain in too many body parts to count. This time the bronze doors, over fourteen feet wide and almost twenty-five feet high, blew open with a vengeance. Every Roman ruler, centurion, farmer, courtesan, and every young girl and boy on the cusp of becoming a woman or man was awake from twenty centuries of sleep and ready to rage. They told me I was silly to think a gas main explosion caused this. Bombs. Detonated.

Beyond the roar that swept through, I heard chaos and the sounds of destruction out in the Piazza della Rotunda. The distinctive wail of Italian emergency vehicles. Screams. Shrapnel flew horizontally into the Pantheon. I twisted onto my belly and crawled, all in the same movement. Back to Raphael.

Larger pieces of debris flooded in now, along with waste paper, coffee cups sucked dry and singed leaves. I reached the marble surround and huddled against it. I held on with one hand and again covered the exposed part of my neck with the other. Soon, everything was quiet again, but the rubble hadn't settled. Bits scraped and slowed and swirled over and behind me, around my feet. Something substantial hit my back, and I screamed. It wasn't very heavy, but I knew it was long because I felt it down to my thighs. With one hand still on the glass wall protecting Raphael, I rolled over to see what it was. A car door lay there, like it was waiting for me to do something.

I stared at it. I knew that paint color. It was called Green Dew. Recognition, then dread. I was on the floor next to the door of my rented Fiat. The upholstery had several rips. An accordion-folded map was wrapped through the door handle, like I'd gone back in time by a decade or so. Thankfully, it was rented by Emma. If it was mine, and that was a big if, all I had to do was report it.

The glass where my left hand rested suddenly felt warm, nearly hot. I snatched it away and jerked my head back to see if there was a fire in the niche with the crypt, but there wasn't.

"Run!" The command from the voice in my head was kind but unequivocal. Nothing I needed to fear.

I was up, and the wind was literally at my back. I sprinted, looking for an opening. Not the room where I'd been held. There hadn't been a route to the outside from there. I couldn't go out the front through the porch in case there was another explosion, so I ran around the rotunda looking for an exit. There were windows, no doors. The cries for help, moans of pain, orders shouted in Italian from outside the vestibule grew louder. One of the additions to the back of the building had to have a door. I half ran, and half slid through corridors, a kitchen, and store rooms. Time and again, I was fooled by light from a window until finally I saw a door. I made a plan to break through it, but someone had already beat the door open. Maybe a person, maybe the pressure from the blasts. Maybe Sheldon. Had he gotten away? The other guy was big and slow, and Shel was motivated, so maybe.

Chapter Thirty-Three

I walked out into hell. Dante would have been hard-pressed to describe this world. Broken glass littered the sidewalk and street. I watched my running shoes crush and scatter it, but I couldn't hear anything. My hearing returned, and then it was gone again. Or maybe I only imagined the way noises should sound and thought my hearing was restored. Curtains flapped outside the squares that had been windows before the explosions. A few people wandered along the street, dazed, but most stood stock still like they thought they were in a field of landmines. If they moved, it might trigger another blast. A shutter, painted baby blue, slid down the side of a building, and a man jumped when it crashed. Maybe they were right to stand still, but I turned left and walked along the back of the Pantheon. Because Raphael told me to. Insane. No, he said to run. Could I? For him? The search for his lost painting had given meaning to my life, so to thank him, I would try. After the first footfall, pain shot from my hip down my leg and took my breath away. How had I run out of the Pantheon? Had adrenaline masked the pain? I would have to walk. The end of the back wall would be my goal. I made it and looked up the side street. From there, I could see a gathering of people at the front corner of the Pantheon. They weren't frozen in shock; they were riveted by something happening in the piazza. That was my next target to walk to.

If I didn't speak, I wouldn't stand out or be memorable to people when they were questioned about what they saw that day. Instead, I thought. Why did I assume the car door that blew into the Pantheon belonged to my rental car? There were lots of Fiats in Rome, though that paint color was odd. Mine was parked at the Hotel Della Conciliazione.

As I moved along the wall, I heard a blowing, crackling sound from the sky. My hearing was returning. This time, I was sure of it. After I took a few more steps, I saw the top of a pillar of fire. It was in front of the Pantheon. I needed to get to the hotel, but first, I wanted to see what was in the Piazza della Rotunda that could burn with a blaze so tall and fierce. I limped the rest of the way along the side. The smoke smell was more intense, more synthetic, here.

When I got near the front, I saw police cars and ambulances blocking the side streets leading up to the piazza. I walked to the side of the crowd gathered there and looked through the columns on the portico. I inched forward, trying to get lost in the group. What was left of a small car burned. A FIAT. A funny shade of green. I went back to calculating the odds. Not only was the passenger door missing, the back of the car had blown off. I could see inside the blackened, melted hull.

Was that how I had gotten to the Pantheon? Had I driven it? I wouldn't have parked it there. I turned, and every car I saw was dented and scorched, not as bad as this car, but most of them were probably totaled. I told myself I didn't know it was mine.

I looked around at the people I stood with. The car wasn't what the crowd was there to see. Six or eight officers in tactical gear, head to toe, faced the ancient church. Helmets with visors covered eyes that were focused like lasers on the Pantheon portico. The two in front knelt, serious-looking guns pointed straight ahead at something or someone. Those behind them held shields.

I couldn't ask my fellow onlookers what the hell was going on. And I had no idea what they told one another in low voices. A young man had a cell phone in his hand and turned the volume up. In English! God bless this guy! A voice reported that witnesses saw two men run out of the Pantheon shouting at one another in the seconds before the first bomb went off. Sheldon and the other man?

The account went on to say bombs were placed outside the Pantheon, and the Carabinieri suspected more terrorists were held up inside. A group—no one had taken credit yet—was involved because of the additional blasts, and the size….

"Shhhh." The rest of the dressing-down the group leveled at him was, of course, and unfortunately, in Italian, but their gestures alone warned the guy that his cell phone could trigger more explosions. Could it? He turned his little instrument of death off. Hand on his cheek. *I didn't know.* Nods. *Of course, you're right.* Hand in prayer position. *Thank you for telling me. Won't happen again. So sorry.*

There might be more bombs that would detonate. Why in the hell were we standing here, then? Was that why Raphael told me to run? No, it wasn't. The S.W.A.T. team, or whatever they were called here, was on the move. Their first two steps were a march, then those holding shields put them on the ground and pulled out their sidearms. The team broke into a run. Up the steps onto the porch, through the columns, and inside the rotunda. What was happening? Wasn't a church a sanctuary in Italy? No, that wasn't a thing any longer. Anywhere. Should I yell that there was no one inside? No, they would see that for themselves in seconds.

Gunfire rang out. I thought *thank you, Raphael.* More shots than I could count, but it was over in less than a minute. Had someone hidden inside? Or maybe taken refuge from the blasts? Police radios squawked from inside the Pantheon and from the police cars on the side streets.

I needed to get to the hotel and away from cameras. Every second I delayed was too long. At the hotel, I would find my little car sitting in its parking space in their private garage.

I scanned the courtyard for a route. A few charred pieces of clothing lay on the ground. That was when I saw the bodies. People cried over them. Where were the emergency responders? I'd heard sirens. I saw an elderly couple sitting on the ground, holding one another, and I limped toward them. I didn't have a phone, so I didn't know how I could help, but it seemed wrong to walk away. How could I be so self-absorbed to worry about media attention if my rental car was one of those destroyed?

Someone somewhere laughed. Someone else yelled something in Italian using a microphone. I stopped and looked to see who it was. Police cars and ambulances were parked, blocking the side streets. He repeated himself. Who was he talking to? I walked again. "Stay back!" This time, the man spoke in English. The order came from a uniformed officer, who stood by his opened car door, a handheld speaker in hand. They were ready for more bombs or whatever caused all of this. "We will assist them. Leave the area."

I turned for one last look at the wife and husband. I smiled. They nodded. Then I walked down a narrow side street and started the mile or so trek from where I was in the heart of medieval Rome to my hotel. I knew the general direction I needed to walk. I would cross the Tiber River, and that was west....

A row of scooters in front of an ice cream shop were knocked to the pavement like dominos. Vacant-faced owners righted them or pulled them apart. One teenage girl cried, looking at her white Vespa. A man and woman came out of the gelateria, both shouted to anyone who would listen. Her hands were on her hips, and the man pointed at something near their door. The mangled hatchback from the hired car had pushed café chairs up to the wall of the building, and now it lay there. The logo of the rental car company wiped away any hope or doubt I had left that my car wasn't destroyed in the attack. One door was inside the Pantheon, the body of the car was at the piazza, and here was the hatchback. Were there more car parts yet to show up? Had I left anything inside? Sunglasses or a scarf? Didn't think so.

At the end of the block, men and women with stretchers and medical bags ran past me in the opposite direction. They were going to the Pantheon. We crossed streets wherever we wanted because there were no cars there. Their pace was in sharp contrast to people huddled together or against buildings, looking in the direction of the Pantheon, not at one another. Like a bad version of Mecca or Jerusalem. If they spoke at all, it was in hushed tones. Had they been on their way to church? My watch had stopped, but it felt like it was still morning. Hadn't the man told Sheldon the church would open up soon?

Roadblocks and cops stopped traffic from crossing the Tiber River. Cars lined up. Drivers stood by their cars and scooters, asking their neighbors what happened. Shrugs, and talking with their hands. Maybe this or maybe that. More shrugs. I walked by a line of cars.

Finally, I reached my hotel. The handsome young man I'd seen when I checked in was at the garage exit with another man who took photographs with his phone. The gate was smashed. Surely, a minor matter compared to an attack of this magnitude.

A handful of hotel guests and employees stood outside. Fixated on the column of fire. No one noticed me when I walked through the small lobby. The TV showed the Pantheon, racing police cars, crying people, destruction, and dozens of small fires on a loop. After they ran the tape and went to a reporter on the scene, the giant flame was there in the distant background.

I took the elevator down to the garage level. The space where I had parked my goofball little rental car was empty.

My room was both welcoming and unfamiliar at the same time. One of my cell phones was plugged into the charger. It was almost ten o'clock. Knowing that seemed like progress. I called the rental car company and reported that the car had been stolen. Had I notified the police? No, I hadn't. They would take care of that, preferring to communicate directly with law enforcement since the car had a locator on it. Would I please confirm my contact information? She recited my phone number and address in Manhattan. I told her, yes, that was correct. Did I need them to deliver another car to me at my hotel? No, I didn't, but thank you. Did I have the keys? No, they were missing. I had them in my pocket when I went for a run. I didn't know when I lost them. Probably stolen, she tutted. Pickpockets in Italy? I was shocked. She felt certain they would recover the car. They would be in touch. I wasn't to worry.

There had been several calls from Elisa. Another came in just as I hung up.

"You did get into Rome, didn't you?" she asked.

"Yes, I'm here."

"Will we see you soon?" I needed a shower. And I would have thought Vatican employees got Sundays off. Whatever.

"Would she like us to send a car?" Colonel Marra asked in the background.

"No, it would be quicker to walk," I said. I picked up a bottle of water and chugged it. Then, I regretted it. Was that heartburn? The walk to the hotel

177

had gone a long way in reviving me. My shoulder and hip still hurt, but my joints felt looser. I felt more like myself.

A minute later, I had hot shower water running down my back. I leaned my head on the tile and imagined slapping Colonel Marra. Hard. The reverberation would travel from my hand up my arm to my sore shoulder, but it would be worth the pain. Maybe the smack would be heard in the anteroom of Elisa's office. Maybe the sound would ricochet off St. Peter's Basilica, which her office in the Vatican Museum complex overlooked.

This was the man who was hell-bent on me coming to Rome. So that I would be kidnapped. Who else knew I would be in Rome?

The realization that I couldn't tell anyone what had happened hit me as hard as I wanted to hit Marra. There would be no way to talk my way out of saying Emma was kidnapped and Sheldon saying Emmaline was.

Was the bombing related to my abduction? Was Colonel Marra behind the bombing, too? Was the Vatican going to war against Italy? And where was Sheldon?

Chapter Thirty-Four

MONDAY IN VATICAN CITY

There were five of us in the Elisa's office. Colonel Marra made a point of looking at his watch, and then at me, like *where have you been?* My friend wore a modest black knee-length, long-sleeved dress, and he wore a black suit. Bespoke. Expensive. He held his hand out to me. "Welcome."

I stared at it and realized I had to respond, so I reached out and shook his big paw. None of this made sense. Why did he seem annoyed? I was one day early, *and* he had me kidnapped. A reason for a hall pass if ever there was one.

"My rental car was stolen." Wouldn't hurt to get that information circulating out and about. After that shower, by which all other showers must be measured, I rolled my hair into a chignon and applied the Emma special: three layers of red lipstick. I was passable on the outside but a mess on the inside.

"No," he said and repeated the word over and over in that Italian way. *Sorry, but I said it was.* "Was this within the walls of the Vatican?"

I shook my head. "From the hotel parking garage."

"God! Emma!" Elisa said. "*Stai bene?* Have the *polizia arrestata–?*" In her distress, she jumped back and forth between languages. "I doubt the police have the staff to respond to anything other than the attack." She and Colonel Marra, like all of Rome, were in mourning, and regrettably, I had added to her worries.

"The car rental company is handling all of that," I assured her.

Marra nodded emphatically. The subject of my car had been covered well enough.

When I came in, they were watching an update on the bombing on a small television on a bookshelf. According to the crawl, the political elite exulted in the building's design strength and predicted the Pantheon would stand another two thousand years. We turned back to it now. A man in tactical gear was speaking, and I pointed to the screen. "What is he saying?"

"They originally thought the bombs had been laid in front of the Pantheon. They know now that it was a car bomb that the terrorists used."

He took a question from the scrum of reporters, and Elisa laughed at something he said. She translated what was going on for me. "He was asked about the gunfire inside the Pantheon. People saw them charge in with guns blazing. The police mistook the sunbeam from the oculus for a person and fired away."

Thinking about the scene I witnessed there, I began laughing. I didn't want to because there was nothing funny about bullet holes in the walls of the Pantheon, and I tried to stop. I couldn't. I wasn't myself.

The others stared at me. Who could blame them? "I guess it is funny that they shot at air," Elisa said in my defense.

"Shooting at sunlight," someone said and laughed too.

When I composed myself, Elisa took my arm. "I have an office set up for you to use to review the journals you asked to see." Good. That meant I could still spend time with Cardinal Faulhaber's diaries.

"Colonel Marra, thank you very much." I still had no idea what they wanted from me in return, or if it was anything I could do. I did, however, know how they limited access to their precious archives.

"Eh." He cleared his throat. "I'm sorry, but we must hurry," he said, pushing his eyebrows as low as they would go. "We're all going to a mass called for the victims of the Pantheon Attack. We must leave soon." That explained the way they were dressed. Or did it?

"You just happened to have a black dress at the office?" I asked Elisa.

"I do keep one in my closet," she said in almost a whisper. With an eighty-six-year-old boss, that was what you did. She looked at her colleague. His lips were in a tight line. Each understood why mourning clothes might be needed at any time, but it was painful for Colonel Marra to imagine that day would come. This sensitivity was a part of the man I hadn't seen before. He moved through the Vatican like a cruise ship. Everyone moved out of his way. That was what the Titanic expected too.

The crisis had a name now. I thought about the bodies in the piazza and that couple I couldn't help. He led us out into the hallway. His shock over the carnage answered one question. Colonel Marra was behind my kidnapping but not the bombing. The two weren't related.

The guest office, two doors down, didn't have a view of the dome of the basilica because there wasn't a single window in the room. When I realized I wouldn't be able to see outdoors, it became harder to breathe. The space had half as much oxygen as I needed. There was a guard posted outside. Should I scream to him? He wasn't there for my safety; he was there to protect the valuable and vulnerable archival material. All I wanted was more damn air, not the cold opulence that pervaded the Vatican.

We went in, and Colonel Marra closed the door. God, no. Besides him, Elisa, and me, two young men in clerical collars and black suits were with us, and they had to breathe, too. The room spun, and a large photo of the pope on one wall buzzed by. My slacks and blouse felt tight and constricting. I was too warm. I was trapped. Think about anything. Anything except suffocating. On the back wall, there was an eighteenth-century watercolor, the Gallery of Maps. At that time, the galleries were open only for the pleasure of the elite. Now, six million tourists a year visited, looking for the Sistine Chapel, many unaware of the Vatican Museums' seventy thousand artworks spanning five millennia. Left. Right. Deep inhales. Factoids.

Colonel Marra's gravelly voice cut through to me. How long had he been talking? "I asked you to come to Rome because the Medici have plans to take over the Vatican." Had I heard him right?

The pronouncement was weighty and could have used a warm up sentence or two, but it grounded me. Should it have come as a surprise? In my head, I heard how Sabine had said the name, the ecstasy on her face. This was why Bettina Vogt sent me to Cologne. This was the war the Voice needed money for.

"This has nothing to do with the return of the Parthenon Marbles?" I asked.

"No," Colonel Marra answered.

"Or what was said to the pope?"

"That was all true, but you do not have to concern yourself with it," he said.

I took a deep inhale. "Let's start from the top. Who are you talking about when you say The Medici? Gian Gastone was the last Medici duke. He died without an heir." It was true. He was wild, gay, an alcoholic, and probably impotent. He and his wife hated one another. None of those bode well for fertility. My head was clear. I was back.

"Oh, but Giovanni was *not* the last Medici. You are correct that there are no Medici heirs, but there are Medici descendants," he said.

I went behind the handsome table in the center of the room and sat down. I took in the expression on Marra's lined, tanned face, as well as the others. Pinning hopes on me. To do what? I knew little about the Medici, but this sounded like a family feud. I wanted to put my head down. So tired. And, though I had showered, I smelled bad. At least I could breathe again.

"I would like to show you something, then we will leave you alone with Cardinal Faulhaber's diaries." One of his assistants handed him a leather folio. He walked around to stand by my chair and opened it on the polished surface in front of me.

He fanned the clear plastic sleeves, and the moving air puffed my hair. When the pages settled, I saw they contained newspaper clippings. I touched the top article with a fingertip. "I don't know what this says."

"No Italian," Elisa explained.

"Look at the others," he instructed.

I turned page after page. The images told me each article had something to do with the Vatican or maybe the Catholic church. Thankfully, some were in English. From an American paper. Or from a UK or Australian publication. I had seen some of these before. On-line. In Georgia. I knew there were reports of mismanagement and worse at Vatican City. The last articles were on the fire in the Cologne Cathedral. "You were blamed for this, too?"

"Sí," Elisa and Colonel Marra said together.

"Since it happened on church property," he added.

"Were any retractions printed saying the fire was intentionally set and not caused by the building's wiring?"

"Sadly, no," Elisa said.

"I sympathize, but I don't know how I can help you." My spirits were so low I could hardly help myself. I didn't know how long I could pretend to be alright.

"This is a smear campaign." Colonel Marra leaned on the desk, his weight on meaty hands. Man-spreading. Trespassing.

Was he trying to intimidate me? Big mistake.

"Why would anyone do that? You all do such a good job making your own bad publicity. Wait, I shouldn't have put it like that. Pedophilia is the sin of all sins, and media coverage is sunlight."

"What about all the rest?" he said.

I appreciated being spared the party line about all they did. "It does seem like overkill, and it's suspicious that it portrays you as an institution that can't do anything right," I said.

He smiled. "So, Emma, you admit we are good for something?" He looked at me the same way he had last year. No extra curiosity.

"You are the custodians of the greatest art collection the world has ever known." How much had been bought with guilt, I couldn't say. "For centuries, you've kept it safe and, since 1932, mostly accessible to the public. The world, past and future, owes you a debt for that." Had I imagined the dropped gaze when I said safe? Why? The thought that one inch of their three and a half miles of galleries was at risk was bad. Battery acid bad.

He nodded. "This isn't media sunlight." He picked up the book and tucked it under an arm. "You may say it doesn't look like propaganda. Just remember, propaganda doesn't work if it looks like propaganda." I nodded in agreement, and he went on. "This is realpolitik, power, and money."

I rubbed my forehead, but it didn't help with my remaining brain fog. We were no longer talking about the newspaper clippings. That much was clear. "You are the Vatican. Aren't you supposed to value ideals?"

"That's a luxury I don't know that we have. This is designed to call for a new order."

"That's the signal inside the noise?" I asked. If he knew the reason for these media attacks, I wanted him to say so now.

He looked at me, visibly confused by the phrase.

"I'll translate later." Since we came in, Elisa had hardly spoken except to tell Marra to keep it in English, but her eyes hadn't left me during the exchange. Now, she moved closer and handed me a pair of white gloves. "For now, we will leave you alone with these. We have to go. Take your time. Do you need anything?"

Two pens, two sharpened pencils, and three notepads in that annoying European length waited for me on the table next to the worn leather-bound diaries. "Water?" The young man closest to the door disappeared almost before I finished saying the word. "Elisa, I can't imagine how I can help with, uh…" I pointed to the binder of clippings Marra held onto so tightly.

"We'll talk later," she assured me.

Someone returned with a silver tray with a glass and carafe of cold water. They all turned to leave. Colonel Marra stopped at the door. "Again, Emma, thank you."

"For what?" I had Faulhaber's diaries in front of me, but I hadn't paid for the privilege yet.

He motioned for the others to leave. "Signora Pesarini, please stay." He approached the desk again. "Thank you for the…shall we call it the unofficial embargo on art sales?"

The hit of adrenaline put air in my lungs, and hope almost pulled me out of the chair when I finally understood what he was saying. "I wasn't sure it would work." Even though I hadn't called Florence Bracewell back, she must have put the plan in motion.

"It certainly has. When your Metropolitan Museum said it was you who had requested it, the art world took notice. Sotheby's, Christie's, Sutton House, and everyone in between. And quickly, everything was in place before banks opened this morning."

What banks were open on Sunday? Those in the Middle East, I guessed.

"We have something to go over with you later that will prove how important this pause is to anyone who cares about art," he said. "Now we must attend the Mass."

I watched them leave, then I grabbed my phone. It was Monday, not Sunday! Son of a bitch. Had I said anything crazy to Elliott? When he said he was on his way to the airport, I thought he was flying down the day before to be in DC for an early morning hearing. Or to the woman at the rental car company? The police might want to hear that call.

Marra hadn't been behind my kidnapping or even known anything about it. The Voice was. The Voice had me held for two days, so I couldn't call that saint, Florence Bracewell, back to confirm I still wanted the embargo of art sales. He knew about that from a tap on my phone. Son of a bitch.

Chapter Thirty-five

I found the volume of Cardinal Faulhaber's journal that started on January 1, 1945. I used Google Translate for about five minutes before I had to admit just how tedious the man's notes were. He logged in painful detail what the weather was like each day and what he ate for dinner each night. I told myself I had to suffer through this everydayness if I wanted the same level of specificity on what I was interested in. That was everyone he visited or was visited by, and who said what. Wait, maybe I didn't. I would use keywords. I ran my gloved fingers over the lines, looking for Frank or Franc, or Brigitte, or Raphael.

In 1939, pompous and mediocre Hans Frank was appointed governor of the middle section of Poland, which Germany had set up as a colony. He installed himself in a castle in Cracow and decorated it with all the country's artistic treasures he could get his hands on. One was Leonardo's *Lady with an Ermine*, which American troops returned to Poland in 1946. Another was Raphael's *Portrait of a Young Man*, which still has not been restored. In 1945, Frank ran for his life from the advancing Soviets and took the paintings to their house in Upper Bavaria. It was there when he was arrested in May. Then it was gone. His wife, Brigitte, used some of the artwork for bribes, others she sold. When I met Graham, he was investigating SS leadership, in particular those looting art for Hitler's planned museum. I took a different approach and went after every red flag name known to have traded in art stolen by Nazis after the war. Who sold *Portrait of a Young Man* for her? I looked for a connection between Brigitte and someone who worked in a local gallery or auction house between May 1945 and early 1946. Or someone

186

who knew someone.

The cardinal visited Frank in prison regularly until the trials at Nuremberg began in November 1945, and a delegation from Poland met with him and *advised* him to stop. Advice he took. He also stopped lobbying Pope Pius XII to ask for clemency for Frank. To retaliate, the prisoner threatened to go public with what he called the Vatican and the Nazi's "secret agreements." Then, for some reason, after he was sentenced to death, Cardinal Faulhaber pled Frank's case with the Vatican, and the Pope interceded with the Allied Control Council, asking for clemency. What made Faulhaber change his mind? The reversal was stunning. The Pope's request, made just before the time limit on appeals, wasn't successful. It was denied, and Frank was hung on October 16, 1946.

Brigitte Frank was mentioned in the diaries when Faulhaber saw her. I noted each date for the wall of notes Graham and I kept. Visits with Hans Frank were described with details of his mood and a little about what they discussed. The *Portrait of a Young Man* was never mentioned. He autographed the front cover, "+ Faulhaber."

I stood and stretched and opened the 1946 volume. An hour later, I was celebrating New Year's Eve. My shoulders ached, the left more than the right. I didn't find a smoking gun, in that one either, but I hadn't expected to. At least I had notes of Brigitte's movements for that period of time, including who else was at the dinner parties Cardinal Faulhaber hosted.

There was one more book, bound in honey-colored leather, not the brownish-red cover used for 1945 and 1946. I was getting antsy and hoped this would go quickly. The handwriting was different. It wasn't written by Cardinal Faulhaber. I looked at the inside front cover. "+Hudal."

A knock, actually a tap, on the door, brought me back to the present.

"Excuse me," Elisa said. "We're back from the Mass. Have you started the third volume?"

I held it up to her. "This is someone else's diary."

"It was Bishop Alois Hudal's." Her words were parsed out slowly like there was a message hidden between the letters.

"One of the organizers of the Ratline?" It was an escape route for Nazis after the war. Hudal's network helped Josef Mengele, Adolf Eichmann, and many less prominent war criminals, get to South America. Instinctively, I wiped my hands on my pants.

She nodded. "I just emailed you something I think you'll find interesting."

I checked the emails on my phone and saw a message with a large attachment. "What is it?"

"It's Hudal's diary translated and transcribed in English," she said with a tentative smile. It wasn't the look of someone who had just given a friend a generous gift. More like someone about to ask for a favor.

"Thank you, but he was Austrian and was based here in Rome during the war," I argued. Did I need it?

"Still, I think you'll find it a good read." She narrowed her eyes.

"Okay. Thank you," I repeated. Her implication was staggering. Had *Portrait of a Young Man* been taken to South America? It wasn't *impossible*, but so unlikely.

Bishop Alois Hudal used the Ratline to spirit Nazis out of Italy, sometimes by obtaining identity papers for them from the Vatican Refugee Organization. Some were interned, and others had not yet been captured. If Hudal or Faulhaber were paid with *Portrait of a Young Man*, it would not be shipped to South America. It would be in or near the building I was in now. Hudal offered to get Hans Frank to South America, and he declined. One source said the offer was made by others who were *highly placed* at the Vatican. He turned them down, also. When Frank was arrested, he told his children that he had nothing to fear because he was turning over his diaries to the Allies. He had no reason to give Hudal the painting. If Brigitte allowed it, and he gave Faulhaber the painting, what was it in exchange for? I remembered how Sabine said, "Eternal life," when I asked her what the Voice promised her. Was that what Hans Frank wanted to buy with the Raphael?

I thanked Elisa and told her that I looked forward to reading the document and in English. I stacked the Hudal diary on top of the two Faulhaber volumes, a visual for my rising debt to her. "Now, can you tell me why I'm here?"

"Lunch first?"

"Sounds good," I said. When had I eaten last? Saturday?

CHAPTER THIRTY-FIVE

"Then follow me."

"I need to check my emails. Can you give me a few minutes?"

"Of course, I'll wait in my office. Do you know how to get there from here?"

"I doubt it," I admitted. The layout of the Vatican Museum was very complicated.

She laughed. "I'll come back for you in ten. Sì?"

"Perfect."

I picked up the phone I'd laid on the desk, but when she was out of sight, I retrieved my UK phone from my makeup bag. There was a text from Graham. **Need to talk to you. Soonest.**

Chapter Thirty-Six

I closed the door and placed the call. The terse message was out of character. Did he know? Was this it? Was it all over? Maybe I wouldn't go back to Bath. All I had there that was incriminating was a burner phone hidden under a bike seat. The clothes they could have. I didn't have to call back, but I already was. If he asked for an explanation, I would give it. I stood up and waited for whatever was coming. Left. Right.

Graham answered on the first ring. "Emmaline, darling, good. We're in quite a state here."

"Are you alright?" Recalibrate. Left. Right.

"Sheldon has been killed in Rome."

I gasped. Really. Not acting. I was truly surprised, though I couldn't say why. Obviously, he wasn't able to get away from the other man. A man used to violence. Not exactly a divergence of opinion on a medical matter with a fellow pediatrician. "How?"

"There was a terrorist bombing outside the Pantheon. He was on the sidewalk nearby. Poor fellow. Wrong place at the wrong time. Charlotte is inconsolable. She called Mother when she got the news, and we drove back to London. We're here now."

It was okay to be surprised at his brother-in-law's death, but not at the Pantheon bombing. That was on every cable news station on the planet. I made sympathy noises.

He lowered his voice. "Darling, do you remember him saying anything about going to Rome when we were all together Friday night?"

I pretended to think back over that evening. "No-o-o."

190

"Mother swears that on the phone, Charlotte said that this couldn't possibly be true because Sheldon was in Glasgow. Then, when we got to the apartment, she said she knew all along he had gone to Rome." Translation, he was possibly having an affair, and I want it covered up.

"Poor Charlotte. How are their children doing?"

"I don't know. They are both on their way here." Each sister had a daughter at *uni* and a son out in the work world with a job you couldn't say with a straight face. What were the odds that both young men were thwarted by a lack of talent? "Can you come home soon?" he asked.

"Of course. I'll look for a flight." I told the lie he wanted to hear. I would try, but my situation was, uh, fluid. "Has anyone claimed responsibility?"

"Not that the papers are saying."

"Give Charlotte and your mother a hug from me," I said.

"Emmaline, I do love you." Where had that come from? The death of a childhood friend and now his brother-in-law would take a toll.

"Graham, I mean a *real* American hug." He chuckled. I held back tears. I could handle anything and everything except goddamned gratitude.

191

Chapter Thirty-Seven

I powered off that phone and put it back in the secret compartment of my makeup bag. My next call was to Elliott. We had talked once already this morning, actually the middle of the night for him, when I checked on my parents. He had been on his way to JFK for a six o'clock flight.

"No call for two days, and now two in one morning," he teased. I was still adjusting to having lost a day. I heard a lot of noise in the background. Music, laughter, talk.

I opened the office door. "Don't tease me. My morning is going from bad to worse. I may have to stay in Rome longer to deal with that rental car."

"Even if your car hadn't been stolen, getting out would be a nightmare. They briefed us on the bombing. Have they closed the airport?"

"I don't know." I hadn't thought of that. I hoped not. "Has anyone claimed responsibility?"

"Oh yeah. Too many to count. Not a single one is credible, though."

"You sound happy. Did the hearing go well? Where are you?" I asked.

"I'll put it like this: I am having a beer with my attorneys at National Airport right now."

I looked at the classroom-style clock on the wall. "Are you kidding? It's not even nine o'clock there."

"The hearing was done, and we were out of there in five minutes flat," he said.

Then, the questions spilled out of me. "Does that mean it's all over? What happened? Oh, Elliott, I'm so relieved."

"Guys, I can tell Emma what happened, right?"

I heard several people say, "Sure" and "Go for it" in the background. He was, after all, their boss.

"I'll put you on speaker. This is how it went down. The hearing started at eight o'clock sharp in a Rayburn House Office Building hearing room. I sit. I have four *excellent* attorneys with me." Cheering from the background. "They sit. We look like an aging 1990s boy band, all dressed alike." I laughed at the image.

"Excuse me!" a woman's voice called out.

"Sorry, but just that look," Elliott said.

"No, I think we should start one for real," someone else said. "We could be the new NSYNC."

"Backstreet Boys," another yelled out.

"Boyz II Men." How much had they had to drink?

"Then things get weird. Not a little. A lot." Hearing his talk about his day was domestic bliss and worked like a salve. "Members of the committee file in. They sit in their *big* leather chairs. Congresswoman Tessum takes her place in the middle. Suddenly, she looks like she's seen a ghost in the back of the room. She goes white, like she's going to faint. I turn around, and there isn't anyone there that looks like they shouldn't be. Some staffers. A few interns, I guess. Nobody special. She says, "Elliott Baldwin." Then she looks down at her notes and reads—she has to read it, because she didn't even know my job title!—"as assistant director in charge of the New York City field office...." She looks at the back of the room again and says, "I'm sure you have more important matters to spend your time on back in New York. This meeting is adjourned. Please accept the apology of the committee." Then she stands and walks out. The other members of the committee realize what just happened, and they get up and leave, too."

"What did you do when she said that?"

"I thanked her. What else could I do?"

A voice in the background yelled out, "I guess you could have refused to accept her apology."

Laughter. "Just don't let it happen again!"

I heard less background noise. He had taken the call off speaker and was walking away. "Maybe you can shed some light on this next part."

"Me? I wasn't there."

"This handsome kid stopped me when I was walking out and whispered that Bobbi said hi. You know anything about that?"

"I may have told her about the hearing," I admitted with a snicker. "Our imaginations can take it from there."

"Knock, knock."

"Is that Elisa I hear?" Elliott asked.

"I'll put you on speaker to say hello," I said.

"Hello, Elliott," she said, smiling and miming hugging herself and swooning. *So handsome,* she mouthed.

All mine, I mouthed back.

"We will be sending her back with one of our problems. She may need your help with it," Elisa said to the phone on the desk.

"I am her devoted servant. You know that," he said. We all laughed. Left. Right. Breathe. "Winter is almost over, and we haven't skied once. Remind Fabio about that." That vacation would never happen. Much of the Vatican Museum's collection of art and antiquities was unprovenanced. If my journey to the Raphael led me there, so be it. I knew that. Elisa knew it, too.

For now, we could pretend.

"The kids are giving him a hard time about not skiing with you." She was the mother of three. "They are fascinated with the FBI. I try to tell them how wonderful the carabinieri are, but they won't listen to me."

He laughed, but let it die out. "Seriously, Elisa, I want to express my deepest sympathy for the loss of life from this morning's car bomb attack. I know the president has spoken to your prime minister and offered help with intel and whatever Italy needs."

She thanked him for the sentiment, and we said our goodbyes. "Just a sec," he said. Someone in his office was speaking to him.

"Here, read this," his colleague said. No more joking around. No background noise at all.

"Emma, can you take me off speaker?" His tone had done a one-eighty. I shrugged to Elisa and did as he asked. "Those bombs were in a rented car. The company has told the carabinieri who rented it. Sweetheart, it was yours." Buzzkill. He yelled to someone in the background to get him a flight to Rome. So much for their good time.

"Do you think that's necessary?" I asked.

"I'll let you know. Keep your phone close, okay?"

I almost promised I would fly home, and I wanted Elisa to think I was flying back to the States from our visit, but I didn't have a return date yet. I still had to go back to England for the funeral of one of my kidnappers.

I knew someone had stolen my rental car and drove it to the bomb site. Why was this last link, that it had been turned into a car bomb, so hard to fathom? The terrorists could have used any car. But they used mine. My phone tumbled in slow motion to the floor. "I, I don't feel well—"

"Emma!" Elisa screamed.

Chapter Thirty-Eight

A white linen tablecloth fluttered down to the small oak table in front of the window in Elisa's office, where we would eat our late lunch. The dome of the basilica presided in the distance. Like when the Rembrandt was unveiled at the Victoria and Albert Museum, it was visually a perfect moment I hoped to remember forever. Time sped up as two suited waiters covered the surface with plates, cutlery, stemware, delicious-smelling food, and, natch, wine.

"Do you faint often?" Colonel Marra had joined Elisa and me for lunch. He implied it was a character flaw and gloating that he'd been the one to suss it out. They were both still dressed in black.

"No, never." I hadn't eaten since Saturday. Elliott's news that the bombs were planted in my rental car was more than I could take on an empty stomach.

"The horror of this morning's attack affects everyone differently," Elisa said to him, a gentle reprimand. She patted my arm. "You gave us quite a scare." She led me to the table. "Here, you need pasta."

I sat, I smiled, I ate, I appreciated her care, but I pondered, too. The Voice wanted Emma held for two days. Someone else wanted the explosion to kill me. No, it was Emmaline they wanted dead. Was that why the kidnappers, or at least one of them, left my door unlatched? The older man, the one who wasn't Sheldon, planted those bombs. I'd heard him say he was going to move my car from the hotel garage. Then why did he hang around? Why come back inside the Pantheon if you had just parked a car with that much explosive power right in front? Was it a suicide bombing? No, that didn't track. He came back to kill or maybe incapacitate Sheldon. How much time passed between the two men running out of the room and the first explosion?

I looked down at the plate of pasta with red sauce. Funny, but I didn't feel hungry. It was like every function in my body except thirst shut down. I ate slowly and wondered what the blow back would be, now that the Italian police knew whose car it was.

"Elisa, I like your new haircut," I said, sensing it was time to make conversation, or invite suspicion on my mental state.

She reached up to touch her brown chin-length hair. Still a bob, but several inches shorter, tucked behind her ears. "My daughter calls it a Sloaney 'do. Should I be offended? I have no idea."

"It's London chic," I assured her. "Just don't get a flip phone. I hear that's popular with Sloane Rangers these days."

Chapter Thirty-Nine

After we ate and they drank wine and coffee, we walked through a labyrinth of long, ancient corridors, staircases, and elevators to get outside. We were on our way to the basilica. For some reason, neither of them had spoken. Elisa kept a close eye on me for another fainting spell.

Finally, in a patch of sunshine where I could have lived forever, she spoke. "Last week, a rather elderly canon died. His name was Canon Monsignor Michele Boscolo."

There was a click of recognition at that name somewhere in there, but I couldn't reach it. The pain in my shoulder was back.

She went on. "You may have heard the name in connection to the Euphronios Krater and the Met?" That wasn't how I knew the name Boscolo. I had a closer connection.

The Met bought the Greek vase used for mixing wine with water by the important painter and potter Euphronios for a million dollars in 1972. It was thought to have been excavated in 1971, so the sale contravened Italy's 1909 law against the export of culturally important items. Eventually, in 2008, the Met returned it to Italy. "A copy of the Euphronios Krater was found in Boscolo's effects."

"I read that." The story was like a soap opera. "His copy was dated in the nineteenth century." I laughed. To make Boscolo's copy, someone had to have seen the 515 BC Euphronios Krater. The vase wasn't excavated in 1971. It was excavated at least in the 1800s. They were thinking about asking for it back.

"Yes," Colonel Marra confirmed, adding three more *yesses* for good measure. "Meaning the vase the Met had may have been excavated before the law was enacted. But that's not what we want to talk about."

"Wasn't Boscolo investigated for trying to sell fake antiquities a few years ago?" I asked. When I said that name, I was rewarded with another flick of recognition, but I didn't know what it meant. This didn't feel right.

"The case was dropped," Marra said, protective. Pouting. Discussion closed. Moving on. The Vatican went silent on the whole affair. "In 2020, he donated his collection of almost seventy works to the Fabric of St. Peter."

"What is that?" I asked.

Elisa spoke before he could. "They maintain and conserve the basilica. Those works were stored at Monsignor Boscolo's home near here." She pointed to some indistinct spot to our right. I took that to mean he lived in Vatican City.

We stopped at a door on a private side of St. Peter's Basilica. Work to replace the Constantinian structure with the basilica we see today, began in 1506. After almost fifty years and a string of alpha-architects, including Raphael, Michelangelo was pressured to take the job. He devoted himself to it until his death in 1564, and it was completed by his pupil, Giacomo Della Porta, after two more years. This was an area I'd never seen, as often as I had been here. The air smelled different. Old. Reassuring. Still, I wished we could stay outside in the light and air. Not between walls.

Bettina's mother had the same last name, Boscolo! That was the connection. I was relieved that my brain finally got there, then immediately, I wanted to run from it. As if my battered body could run from anything. I would tell Elliott. Or would I? Whatever Colonel Marra and Elisa wanted from me had to do with the forgeries in the States and the Voice. Or not. "How common is the name Boscolo?" I asked.

They both shrugged and *mmm*'d. It was neither usual nor unusual.

"The works were moved here and stored in thirty fireproof cases," Colonel Marra explained.

"Here?" I asked.

"Sì," said Colonel Marra. "Are you afraid of heights?" He smiled slyly.

"I'm fine." I just forgot to keep walking after I realized where I heard that name.

"He's teasing," Elisa reassured me. "We're not going up into the dome. We're going to one of the storage rooms in the Basilica's roof."

We took a passenger elevator and then a freight elevator, finally ending up at a cavernous space with wood floors and carpentry tools lined up against the walls. A factory-made wall, almost a room divider, which didn't reach the high ceiling, divided the room lengthwise. A uniformed officer from the gendarmerie defended the door to that section. He slowly hoisted himself up from his folding chair when he saw us.

After a few more steps, we stopped because Colonel Marra had to take a phone call. He listened to someone, raised his eyebrows, and turned around and stared at me. Keeping his eyes level, he said something in wily, smug Italian. I understood only two words: *Emma Kelly.* He hung up and grinned. "No, I have not seen Emma Kelly. I have no idea where she is. Vatican City is a very big place," he said, translating for me. He looked at Elisa and addressed her. "It seems our friend here has not one but two branches of the Italian police who want to speak with her."

"It's about my stolen rental car."

"That's the interest of the local police, not the carabinieri." That was the branch of the Italian national police responsible for combating terrorism. "They have a different concern."

"Elliott told me the car used for the bombing at the Pantheon may have been the one I rented." He hadn't used the word *may,* but whatever.

Colonel Marra sneered. "Where were you this morning?"

"Exactly what are you asking?" He waved his hands like windshield wipers to apologize or at least walk back his implication. "Sleeping. When I went to the parking garage at the Hotel Della Conciliazione this morning, the car was gone." He nodded at the name of the hotel like he was making a mental note of it. "I can hardly believe it, still." The thought of my photo being on international news froze my blood, but every word of that was true.

He nodded. "Sì. Stay here inside Vatican City for now. It would be best." He repeated the nod. That subject was dealt with, forgotten. Fini? Not for me.

"Are you saying I'll be arrested if I go outside the city-state?" I asked.

"I'm saying let's not test that. We have extraterritorial status similar to a foreign embassy. For now, no one knows you are here, and it will be best if we leave it that way. The storage room is over here."

The officer on guard was of an age that made me think the Vatican didn't believe in mandatory retirement. He unlocked the door with a key from a chain attached to his belt. It was flimsy and swung open with a tap, then the man stood back for us to enter.

Wooden cabinets stretched down one side of the room and the back wall. Elisa had a ring of keys in her cardigan pocket. She found the one she wanted and inserted it in the lock of the first container, then, leaving the key in, she lined up numbers on a combination lock. To keep myself from peeking at the dial, I counted the crates. There were thirty. The door popped open, and she motioned with a wave of her arm for me to look inside. It was empty. There was no shock or hand wringing from either of them. They knew there wouldn't be anything in there to see.

"They are all empty like this," she said sadly.

"These once held Boscolo's donated works?" I asked, just to clarify. "You have a senior citizen guarding empty boxes?"

"Supposedly and yes," Elisa said.

I pointed at the crate. "Does that mean you never saw the artwork in there?"

"I was at his home as they were cataloged and crated," she said. "Yes, they were in the containers when they were loaded onto the trucks."

"Now you see why that art moratorium was such good news for us," Colonel Marra said.

"Isn't art theft a job for your Swiss Guards or the Italian police? I don't know how I can help." Then, I answered my own question. "You don't want anyone to know the works are missing." They both nodded. "Because you don't know if Boscolo misrepresented them or not and if the paperwork was forged, like before?" More nodding. "Ahh," I said. Finally, I was getting it. "You have followed the news from the U.S. about Bettina Vogt. You know her mother is Vanessa-Maria Boscolo?"

"Yes," Colonel Marra said. "His sister."

"She misled me about her daughter."

"Don't be too hard on her. I doubt she knew her very well," Colonel Marra said. "Now, she never will."

"Why are we in here? You could have told me the containers were empty back in your office, Elisa."

"We needed to be sure we weren't overheard," she said. "Now, we need you to share information with us."

"Of course," I said. Never.

"Are the people who are responsible for last year's campaign for the destruction of art—I believe they called themselves the Messengers of Mary—also behind the epidemic of forgeries we are seeing now?"

I nodded. "But last year, we were looking for an organization. At the time, it was one person who was bankrolling the people he controlled." It was time to confront what it meant that the Voice thought he was a Medici. Truth didn't care if I was ready to hear it or not. Or how far-fetched it sounded to me. "This person who was behind the vandalism and destruction last year and is behind the current forgeries is the same. He uses people. First, he finds their desire, like Bettina Vogt's ambition to be a famous artist. Then he uses it. Now, he claims—"

"We know what he claims. About his family. The Medici." Marra was perspiring. No, he was sweating. He moved around like an angry bull, and I pulled back. He saw the effect he had and took a deep breath. Maybe the way they teach in anger management classes. "I apologize."

I nodded. We were good. "You told me this morning that you suspected the Medici were trying to overthrow—"

He interrupted me. "We don't suspect. We know."

"What happened? How do you know?" I asked. I thought it was a reasonable question.

"You do not need to be involved in that. Just the art. In the Renaissance *amici degli amici* was powerful," Marra said, pressing his fingertips together like he had eaten something delicious. "Do you know that phrase?"

CHAPTER THIRTY-NINE

"No," Elisa and I said at the same time.

"She doesn't," she said. "Emma, it's like friends of friends. A network of people who will do anything to stay in your inner circle. The Medici were masters at that."

"So, the person who calls me took this out of the Medici playbook," I said.

"He calls you?" Marra was obviously shocked.

"Yes, but his voice is disguised, and the calls are not traceable."

He whistled. "I had no idea."

"I need *you* to be honest with me. There's so much you know that I don't. Start by telling me who he is."

"We don't know," Marra said. He was back in control of himself. He stuffed his hands into his pockets and walked the length of the row of crates. He was back to pacing.

"Then tell me how exactly this worked. At a boozy family reunion, did Grandpa say, "Let's take over a country?" Then somebody sober said, "We should start with a small one. I know, the Vatican City State."

When he got to the end of the storeroom, he turned and said, "They plan to use our own art to overthrow us."

"Whatever was in these crates wasn't part of the Vatican Museum collection," I reminded him. "But I know he, or they, are using art to raise money."

"Sì," Elisa said. "But money will only get them so far. They plan to use this to discredit us. You saw what the media reported. And now, this. Can you imagine what the media would make of it?"

I nodded. "The Medici used art to cower their enemies or would-be enemies. To make such a display that those who would go up against them would think twice." Wasn't that how the Tyndales saw art? And religions used art for their own aims, to spread accounts from their Bible to the unlettered. "Please don't let them frighten you."

"Pope Leo X, Clement VII, Pius IV, and Leo XI were all Medici. It could happen again," Marra called across the room.

Elisa walked over and stood next to me. "For us, the stakes could not be higher. After the Holy City, they want to overthrow Italy."

"The Italian government is so chaotic, would anyone notice?" I looked at Colonel Marra's back. I wanted to see if he would laugh at my joke. He wasn't listening; he was on his phone. I shook my head. What was more important than *this* conversation? "Bettina Vogt's mother, Vanessa-Maria Boscolo, said Italians hate people from other regions. Wouldn't that make overthrowing the government easier?"

"She said that?" Elisa asked. "What we say and what we do are two different things. We complain about one another because we like to talk. There's a north–south divide, but that doesn't begin to compare to all we have in common. It's not true, but it could be if enough bad information is put out there."

"Like a self-fulfilling prophecy?" I asked.

"Yes, I didn't know the expression in English," she said.

"Is she a Medici?" I asked.

Elisa's eyes widened. "Do you think she is?"

"She told me someone promised to protect her daughter," I said. Left. Right. I thought she was referring to the Voice. She didn't know that he betrayed her by killing Bettina, at least not then. I remembered how tightly she clasped that cross.

"Yes, yes, go on," Marra prompted me. He walked back to us as he spoke.

No, I wouldn't go on. Who did she think would protect her daughter? The Vatican? "Are you in contact with her?"

"No, I believe she lives in the States," Elisa said.

I looked at Colonel Marra for his answer. He threw his hands up. *I don't know.* Liar. Her daughter was dead. Was he who had promised to protect Bettina? He was a disappointment.

I looked around this spartan space tucked in a corner of the roof of St. Peter's Basilica. There were alliances in this very room. Some would stand, and some would fall. Some were as old as history, and some were to come. Some were minor matters that would escape the world's notice, like my friendship with Elisa once she learned my secret. Would my search for the Raphael justify this life to her? Some would change the zeitgeist of an era. Would the formidable Colonel Marra and perhaps his boss stand strong with me to defeat the Medici if the day came when they had to choose between art and religion?

I wanted off. Maybe I would walk away with that older gentleman, just doing his job on guard, outside the door. "I don't understand how I can help. This sounds like the responsibility for law enforcement." I was bluffing. I would stay.

Elisa put her hand on my injured shoulder. It hurt, but she didn't know about that. "Emma, I know you, and you do not want seventy questionable works of art to go out into the market." She was a good person. Could the touch of a good person heal? "We would like you to look for this art."

"You want me to recover seventy pieces of art for you?" I stared in disbelief.

Colonel Marra said, "If you hurry, the cache may still be together. If you are slow, they may be scattered to the winds. And we do not necessarily want the works back."

"You mean, if they are inauthentic?" I asked.

"Yes," he answered. "We do not want them going into the market or making their way into the Vatican Museum. Where, after a reasonable amount of time, they will be discovered and labeled as forgeries that we acquired." It wasn't inconceivable. In their seventy thousand works of art, twenty thousand were on display at any given time. Some of Boscolo's collection could enter their storage, as Sabine's *The Annunciation* had.

"I gave you my pledge that we would check any item before it went on display," Elisa said. "My employees will begin receiving special training immediately or as soon as Emma agrees to work for us." Now she looked at me. "It could make a name for you in art recovery." She thought that was an incentive. That kind of recognition could bring my world down. "In exchange, we will give you access to records in our archives about the Ratline." That was an offering of dubious value to me. It was unlikely *Portrait of a Young Man* had anything to do with it.

Colonel Marra gave her the side-eye. She had gone off script. Still, he hadn't walked the proposal back.

Time to negotiate. I had no intention of taking on an impossible job. "I don't see any way to stop them from being sold without making their disappearance public. How would collectors, or dealers or curators know not to buy them?" My first step would be to list them on the Art Loss Register database.

He nodded. "As long as the Vatican is not mentioned. It must be in your name."

"Of course," I said. After all, *anonymous was a woman.* "If I agree to do this, it's for the Vatican Museums, not for the Vatican." Neither of them responded to that.

"I have something you should see, Emma." He held his phone out to me. "You too, Elisa. This was leaked to CNN."

I tapped the arrow on his screen to play the video from CNN Headline News. The young man being interviewed looked familiar. His linen suit. His good looks. "That guy works at the Hotel Della Conciliazione. What's he saying?"

"A picture is worth a thousand words. Keep watching."

Next up was a clip of my little rental car pulling up to the exit of the parking garage. The driver didn't stop. He crashed through the bar, and it snapped off at the hinge. This was all shown again, but this time from a camera in front of the car. Elisa and I both swayed back as the car drove toward us and then laughed at ourselves. The video was paused seconds after it crashed through the gate. The camera zoomed in on the driver. A large man, laughing, almost manic.

"A tronie," I whispered. Not a terrorist. He was Sheldon's partner until he turned into his attacker. My last image of them was of Sheldon grabbing my car keys and this guy chasing him out of the room.

Elisa lowered her glasses from her head. "He was killed by the bombs he himself planted."

I smiled. "Oh, karma."

"This says he was also responsible for the fire in the Cologne Cathedral," she went on.

I leaned down for a closer look. He was the man in the leather jacket yelling that the door was locked, though it wasn't. Someone else who had done the Voice's sinning for him.

"The police no longer need to question you," Marra said. "This is proof that your car was indeed stolen, and with this time stamp, the police know when it was taken and by whom."

"Who gave CNN this video? The hotel?" I asked.

"That handsome young man," he said, pointing at his phone with a proud smile.

"I should thank him," I said.

"I will do that for you. He's my nephew. You will not be questioned by any of Italy's police agencies," Colonel Marra said.

"Not even on the other side of the wall?"

He shook his head. "So that you can concentrate on this, you will be referred to by the media as an American tourist. That is all."

Chapter Forty

I was on my way home. Today, that was Bath, England, but I was going to London for a funeral.

The call I knew I would eventually receive came as I waited in my first-class seat. Not as pleasant as my call with the Met's human resources department when I told them I would work as a consultant any time they needed me. No retainer needed. Only confidentiality.

"Emma, you have made a deal with the devil to go to war against the devil. Do you realize that?" I hadn't heard that Voice from the Void since Tuesday. Almost a week ago.

"Hell help me," I said and hung up.

A Note from the Author

Dear Reader:

I would like to repeat the request I made in The Collector. *If you have any information that might help with the return of* Portrait of a Young Man, *please contact CLAE, the Commission for Looted Art in Europe, at info@lootedartcommission.com.*

Thank you,

Lane Stone

Acknowledgements

The safety of much of our beloved art found in museums is thanks to a combination of the design of the building, technology, and people. I am honored to have museum security professionals generously spend time answering my questions and sharing their thoughts and experiences. They and their staff protect the irreplaceable, yet they still found time to talk to me so I could give you, dear readers, the best experience. Shout out to a few of them: Mark, Tim, Mario, Bill, and my matchmaker, CJ. I am such a lucky writer.

As always, errors of fact, judgment, taste, and arithmetic are mine.

About the Author

Lane Stone, is the author of the Big Picture Trilogy art thrillers, starting with *The Collector*, followed by *The Canvas*. Her other series were cozies.

When not writing she's enjoying characteristic baby boomer pursuits: traveling and volunteering for good causes, like the Delaware River & Bay Lighthouse Foundation and the American Association of University Women (AAUW), and she serves on several boards.

She has a post-graduate certificate in Antiquities Theft and Art Crime.

She is represented by Dawn Dowdle, Blue Ridge Literary Agency, and is a member of SinC, MWA, and ITW. She blogs with Miss Demeanors. She loves to hear from readers at www.LaneStoneBooks.com.

SOCIAL MEDIA HANDLES:
  https://www.facebook.com/LaneStoneBooks
  https://twitter.com/themenopausedog
  @AuthorLaneStone (Instagram)
  AuthorLaneStone (Thread)

AUTHOR WEBSITE:

https://lanestonebooks.com

Also by Lane Stone

Tiara Investigations Mysteries:
   CURRENT AFFAIRS, A TIARA INVESTIGATIONS MYSTERY, Mainly Murder Press, 2011, cozy.
   DOMESTIC AFFAIRS, Cozy Cat Press, 2013, cozy.
   FOREIGN AFFAIRS, Cozy Cat Press, 2017, novelette in anthology, cozy.

MALTIPOOS ARE MURDER, co-written as Jacqui Lane, Entangled, 2014

Pet Palace Mysteries:
   STAY CALM AND COLLIE ON, Lyrical, 2017
   SUPPORT YOUR LOCAL PUG, Lyrical, 2018
   CHANGING OF THE GUARD DOG, Lyrical, 2019

The Big Picture Trilogy
   THE COLLECTOR, Level Best Books, 2022

As Cordy Abbott:
   DEAD MEN DON'T DECORATE, Crooked Lane Books, 2022

www.ingramcontent.com/pod-product-compliance
Lightning Source LLC
Chambersburg PA
CBHW030424120726
47903CB00003B/798